The Simple Li

LAUREN WELLS was brought up in Kent and, having travelled extensively in Europe, the Far East and America, has opted to return to her roots for a simple life of apple tree maintenance and trying to forget that she was ever a Civil Servant.

The Simple Life

LAUREN WELLS

HarperCollins*Publishers*

This novel is entirely a work of fiction. The names, characters and
incidents portrayed in it are the work of the author's imagination.
Any resemblance to actual persons, living or dead,
events or localities is entirely coincidental.

HarperCollins*Publishers*
77–85 Fulham Palace Road,
Hammersmith, London w6 8jb

A Paperback Original 1997
1 3 5 7 9 8 6 4 2

Copyright © Lauren Wells 1997

The Author asserts the moral right to
be identified as the author of this work

A catalogue record for this book
is available from the British Library

ISBN 0 00 649966 X

Set in Plantin Light with Photina display by
Rowland Phototypesetting Ltd, Bury St Edmunds, Suffolk

Printed in Great Britain by
Caledonian International Book Manufacturing Ltd, Glasgow

All rights reserved. No part of this publication may be
reproduced, stored in a retrieval system, or transmitted,
in any form or by any means, electronic, mechanical,
photocopying, recording or otherwise, without the prior
permission of the publishers.

This book is sold subject to the condition that it shall not,
by way of trade or otherwise, be lent, re-sold, hired out or
otherwise circulated without the publisher's prior consent
in any form of binding or cover other than that in which it
is published and without a similar condition including this
condition being imposed on the subsequent purchaser.

For Jon, David and Richard,
with love,
and with grateful thanks for their help,
both witting and unwitting

PART ONE

Autumn

CHAPTER ONE

Lawrence Langland wondered how on earth he'd come to do something so unbelievably stupid.

Driving along empty roads in the pre-dawn darkness, he relived – for about the hundredth time – the awful moment. Felt yet again the hot flush of horrified shame. In a subconscious effort to escape, he put his foot down, and the BMW shot up to 85 ... 90 ... 100.

Brighton, the scene of his humiliation, was now miles behind him, but it made no difference: he could still see the company vice-president's face, the stiff smile eloquently expressive of his disapproval; still hear his boss hissing: 'For Christ's sake, you bloody idiot, what the hell d'you think you're playing at?'

'What the hell d'you think you're playing at?' Lawrence repeated, slowing down to 70 as a concession to driving through a small sleeping village. 'A very good question, sir. I have absolutely no idea.'

The conference had gone well – very well. Lawrence's boss had been quite determined that it should. It hadn't been your run-of-the-mill annual sales conference; this had been the biggie, the biennial Whole Company Conference, when the entire kit and caboodle of UK divisions played host to a senior man from the American parent company, and everyone got together in some expensive location for three days of serious talks, interspersed with equally serious games of golf, saunas, sailing, or whatever else the location had to offer. Not to mention the working breakfasts, lunches and dinners.

The UK divisions took turns to host the Whole Company Conference. This October, it had been Lawrence's boss's turn. Benjamin Fishwick had gone about it, as Lawrence's friend, colleague and ally Olive Hogan had pointed out, like a naïve twenty-two-year-old preparing for her wedding. Even down to a cake with the company logo emblazoned on the icing, a logo which also appeared on the paper napkins for the finger buffet and the ubiquitous books of matches. For the best part of eighteen months, Barclay Dawson Products (UK Division, South East) had not been allowed to obliterate the words Whole Company Conference from their minds for much longer than half a day at a time.

Lawrence had found his enthusiasm for work beginning to wane. The conference put a great burden of extra stress on the accounts department, in which he worked, and Fishwick was becoming increasingly tiresome and officious. Maybe Lawrence would feel happier when the conference itself was underway – fired up with corporate zeal. But somehow, thinking of that ghastly logoed cake, he had doubted it.

And the conference had gone extremely well, there was no doubt of that. The American company vice-president – whose name was John Keir Franklin Willard, but who liked to be called JKF – had been positively effusive in his praise for Benjamin Fishwick's arrangements. For the comfort of the luxury Brighton hotel – although he had found his room 'a li'l on the *small* side, Fishwick, no room to swing a cat, ha, ha, ha!'; for the food – dished up at regular intervals in vast quantities – and for the efficiency and affability of the Barclay Dawson Products (UK Division, South East) staff.

The last day had been entirely devoted to organised

4

leisure – referred to as R & R – and JKF had been whirled through a hedonistic programme, beginning with a celebration breakfast on the glassed-in verandah overlooking the sea, then progressing to a specially arranged guided tour of the Pavilion, lunch at the Metropole, an afternoon of golf, then cocktails with a select band of favourite customers, before they all adjourned to take their seats at the final dinner.

Benjamin Fishwick didn't care much for public speaking. He was quite happy addressing – even haranguing – his own divisional staff, no problem. But a banqueting hall full of mixed staff and important guests, plus senior members of the Board and, most importantly, a visiting vice-president was a different matter. 'I am perfectly capable of it,' he'd said to Lawrence, who'd known it was a lie, 'but I feel I should give you the chance to experience speaking at such a prestige occasion.'

'Thank you very much, sir,' Lawrence had replied, knowing that Benjamin Fishwick's entire day, if not his entire conference, would have been ruined by nervous anticipation of having to give the summing-up speech at the final dinner. 'I'll do my best.'

'Know you will, Langland, know you will.' Fishwick had slapped him on the back and given him a cigar. Lawrence, who didn't smoke, put it away to give to Olive Hogan, who did. 'No need for anything very lengthy –'

No, Lawrence thought, you won't want me stealing the limelight for more than five minutes at the most.

'– just the usual stuff. Thank him for his speech, say how much it means to us all that he's been with us. Blah, blah, blah.'

I'm to say that? Lawrence wondered, trying not to smile.

'Finish up with something mildly amusing, hm? End on a light note.'

How I wish he'd never said that, Lawrence now thought

5

miserably as he overtook a milk float on the outskirts of Lewes. How I wish he'd said, don't whatever you do even *think* about cracking a funny.

It was JKF who had inspired the disaster, good ol' JKF, with the cliché-ridden speech pattern and the slow delivery. Somewhere in his interminable address, JKF had said something about the Winds of Change blowing through the industry, especially through companies such as theirs, who supplied both paper and board to the bulk packaging market, and plastic packaging to the food industry; Barclay Dawson Products was as affected as the next guy. As a cliché, the Winds of Change was one of JKF's favourites: he'd repeated it several times and it had stuck in Lawrence's mind.

So that, when he was making his reply, he kept thinking about the Winds of Change. And, when he'd said all the right things, got out all the statutory platitudes and the bum-licking compliments, something – devilment perhaps, to cancel out the toadying, or was it some deeper impulse, not yet fully explored? – drove him to add a little impromptu piece of his own.

'Talking about Winds of Change,' he'd said, 'reminds me of an occasion when Princess Margaret came to visit my university and was entertained to lunch in the campus refectory.'

He caught Olive Hogan's eye. He'd thought her slightly apprehensive expression was because he was going on too long; it was only afterwards, when it was too late, that she'd told him she was trying to warn him. To remind him that JKF, in his enthusiastic appreciation of all things English, was a fan of the Royal Family. A very great one, giving them the sort of mindless adoration only found nowadays among foreigners.

'Someone took a very nice photo of the Princess shaking hands with the university catering manager,' Lawrence had plunged on, smiling in happy expectation of an ecstatic response to his little story. 'He was handing her a specially printed, embossed menu. The following edition of the student newspaper reproduced this photo on the front cover, with a bubble coming out of Princess Margaret's mouth saying, "Oh dear! Navarin of lamb makes me fart."'

The punchline was greeted by a couple of blokeish hoots from the back and then absolute silence.

Lawrence glanced at Olive. She had buried her face in her hands. He didn't dare to look at Benjamin Fishwick.

He said, the words falling over each other, 'Well, that's about it. Thanks very much,' then sat down in his chair, wishing, more fervently than he'd ever wished anything in his entire life, that he was on top of a pantomime trapdoor which would miraculously open and remove him from the scene.

But of course he wasn't. And he had to sit there while Fishwick made his brief acknowledgement and rounded up the dinner. Had to make polite conversation afterwards, before everybody repaired to bed or to some serious drinking in the bar, dragging up things to say to his colleagues and noticing the expression in their eyes. Sympathy from the nicer ones. Glee from the more laddish reps who, he was sure, would dine out on the story for weeks. Disdain from his fellow senior managers. And that was hardest to bear.

And through it all he'd kept hearing again his own voice telling that stupid, fatuous, seriously unfunny story. Oh God, he thought, trying to respond to a bespectacled sales manager with bad breath wanting to discuss his promotional programme, it was a real double whammy. Not only did I take the piss out of JKF's clichés – OK, he deserved that, but it's not the point – but I also offended him by poking fun at a member of his beloved Royal Family, even if it was a not terribly popular one.

Over the sales manager's shoulder he could see JKF, in earnest conversation with Benjamin Fishwick and two other divisional chief executives. As if they sensed Lawrence's eyes on them, as one man they all turned to glare at him.

Lawrence had gone up to his room as soon as he could get away. Stuffed his papers in his briefcase, put his dinner jacket back in its zip-up bag, found the stray sock under the bed, wrapped the presents he'd bought for Isobel and the children and put them in his holdall. Then he'd tried to go to sleep.

It had proved impossible. Whatever subconscious prompting had made him tell that anecdote, it had been a daft thing to do. He knew, with frightening certainty, that there were going to be repercussions. At 3.30 a.m. he'd given up, gone downstairs with his luggage and, to prove that even if he was an idiot he was an honest one, settled his mini-bar bill with the night clerk in reception. I should probably stick around to make sure everything works smoothly in the morning, he thought as he threw his holdall into the BMW's boot. But I'm not going to. Sod it. Olive can see to all that. *Someone* can. Some other employee of my precious company.

Driving away through the deserted Brighton streets, he dared to face the fear that Barclay Dawson Products might not *be* his company for much longer.

I can't go straight home, Lawrence thought suddenly, still driving fast. Izzy'll think something awful's happened. She'll be worried.

Ignoring the insistent voice in his head that was saying something awful *had* happened, he slowed down, and, seeing a turning off the main road to some place he'd never heard of, took it.

The road was narrow and winding, and led through a copse of trees whose leaves were just beginning to turn rusty-brown. Bloody autumn, he thought morosely. Slowing down still more, he realised he had a headache, and opened the window to get some fresh air.

The countryside smelt good. Despite his anxiety over the ghastliness of the previous evening, he appreciated it, could even convince himself it was taking his headache away. It smells clean out here in this quiet lane, he thought. Nobody's smoking big cigars, nobody's doused himself in aftershave.

The lane turned a corner, and suddenly in front of him was a great black mass of hillside; he was driving along the foot of the South Downs.

Ahead and slightly to his right there was a perceptible lightening of the sky: dawn was coming.

Hardly knowing what he was doing, obeying some impulse he didn't understand, he parked the car in a gateway and, climbing a stile, walked quickly up the springy turf of the hillside, the leather soles of his smart town shoes slipping slightly on the damp grass. Hurrying, as if he were fearful of being late for an important engagement, he reached the top of the Down, panting, the pain of a stitch stabbing in his side.

The thin orange band of sky in the east was growing thicker by the second. He stood entranced as splotches of red and yellow spread outwards, thinning the blackness. Day was coming, light was returning to the earth. When the first tiny arc of the sun appeared, he wanted to cheer.

He was filled with awe, moved almost to tears. Why? he wondered. This is just a sunrise. It happens every day.

But I've never seen it before. This performance is put on every morning, and most of us – I, certainly – never bother to watch. How ungrateful we are.

Slowly, with great solemnity, he began to applaud.

He stood up on his hilltop until the sun had risen several degrees in the pale morning sky. Then, to the exuberant sound of the morning chorus, the birdsong almost too loud in contrast to the previous silence, he made his way back down to his car.

This is beautiful, he thought as he went slowly on through the lanes. It smells sweet, it smells . . . *good*. He couldn't think of a more accurate word. Out here, people aren't concerned with my world. They don't care about the packaging industry, they're not bothered that I've insulted a visiting vice-president, badly blotted my company copybook. They didn't see the way Fishwick looked at me, and even if they did, they'd probably say, 'So what?'

Wouldn't it be perfect if I could say 'So what?' too? If I could call in on Monday morning and say, I'm not coming in. I'm leaving. Had enough of Barclay Dawson Products, every last one of them. Had enough of conferences, accounts, finances, sales figures, productivity bonuses, canteen food, having to wear a suit every day, spending hours – days – on end in my car driving to see people I don't want to see. Had enough of *you*, Benjamin Fishwick. Enough to last a lifetime, and beyond.

Wouldn't it be perfect?

But I can't, of course I can't. I *have* to work for Barclay Dawson Products, or for some company like them. My background is accountancy, and now I'm a financial manager. And Barclay Dawson have looked after me well these fifteen years. I've been promoted several times, so that now I use the posh washroom. They give me this large, fast car to drive around in, and pay me so well that I can afford a four-bedroom house, with a name – Cedar Holt – not a number, in a very pleasant area of suburban Surrey, where my children go to private school and my wife, in between browsing through glossy magazines for novelty foreign recipes and places she can take me for our next holiday, has made a career out of shopping.

Fondly he thought of Isobel's gold-plated keyring, which bore the words *Born to Shop*. Never, he reflected, did a keyring say a truer word.

I wonder what Izzy would say if I arrived home this morning and said, darling, pack your bags and call the estate agent, we're leaving Ewell, moving to the country. I'm sick of Barclay Dawson Products, I'm resigning. No need to tell her it's highly possible my name has gone straight onto the eject-at-the-earliest-opportunity list. And I could be wrong – in fact I'm sure I am. It's far more likely that Fishwick has been charitable and put my behaviour down to boyish high spirits. Isn't it?

Izzy, my love, I'll say, I'm going to be a smallholder, whatever that is. An apple-grower. A hippy. Be a hippy with me! Grow your hair, make yourself a flowing caftan, and we'll plant cannabis in the greenhouse and smile all the time.

The vision was proving difficult; he was having trouble seeing Izzy in flat sandals and any garment costing less than £100.

Isobel, he thought, who has extensions on her nails, streaks in her hair. Who always, every moment of every single bloody day, looks like an illustration in a fashion magazine. Who buys her vegetables pre-washed, pre-peeled, pre-chopped up, in sealed plastic bags from the supermarket. Dear God, the kids probably think vegetables come out of the ground like that.

Isobel, who, despite the luxury lifestyle, often looked strained, though he only noticed in retrospect and never remembered to ask why. Who often – he didn't like to think how often – said she was too tired to make love.

He drove past a clutch of houses nestling beside a pub and a church, and noticed an area of allotments. Many had their own small shed, most of which were dilapidated and homely-looking.

He thought of his grandfather, who'd had an allotment. Lawrence had suspected he kept it as much as an escape from his wife as from any great delight in vegetable growing: Lawrence's grandmother had been a formidable woman. I loved Granddaddy's allotment, Lawrence thought, lost in reminiscence. I loved the earthy smell of the shed, loved being allowed to stretch out on Granddaddy's old camp bed and snooze in the sun on summer afternoons. Loved the sharp smell of freshly pulled spring onions, the hot sensation in your mouth when you bit into that firm, crisp white globe. Loved the kindness of Granddaddy, who would smile as he wiped away the onion-induced tears. Whose big hands were skilled at anything to do with the garden – with the earth – and equally skilled at making toy garages for small grandsons, and putting on bandages when they fell over and cut their knees.

I'd like an allotment. I'd like the time to make toy garages for my own son. To wipe the tears from my daughter's eyes when she discovers for the first time what a freshly pulled spring onion tastes like.

I can't. Can't have either an allotment or the leisure for quiet times with my children. Because I have to work, hard. Constantly. I'm on a treadmill, where, because of my modest talents, I've been promoted to a level where I bring in a very high salary. And, because the company pays me so much, I have to go on working like the devil to show I'm worth it.

There's no way off my treadmill. Is there?

'Oh, damn and blast,' he burst out suddenly. 'There has to be! This isn't all there is to life, it *can't* be! I want more! No, not more – I want *different*.'

In his mind's eye he saw the sunrise on the Downs. Saw the allotments. Remembered how he'd imagined saying to Isobel, I'm going to be a smallholder.

Why not? Why shouldn't we change our lives? People

do. There's so much redundancy around today that it's becoming rare for a man to do the same job all his working life. We could sell the house – it must be worth close on three hundred thousand – and move out to a cheaper neighbourhood. Get the kids into state schools. Izzy could . . .

Izzy. Yes, what about Izzy? What could *she* do?

The plan was stillborn, abandoned almost before he'd conceived it. The thought of Isobel calmly agreeing to sell up and move to the sticks would have made him laugh if he'd been in a laughing mood. Izzy in a muddy field with a Labrador? Izzy wearing sensible walking shoes? Izzy going on a *bus*, for heaven's sake? Ha! Not bloody likely!

He had travelled a long way from the Downs, and his dream image had been left as far behind as that wonderful sunrise. The roads were busy now, and he had to concentrate; there was no more room for fantasy.

There were roadworks on the M25. It was a relief finally to get to his exit.

He stopped in the high street to buy Isobel some flowers. Getting back into the car to drive the last half-mile to home, he thought, I'll mention it to her. I know she'll dismiss the whole thing, have a good laugh at my expense and probably think I've gone off my trolley.

But I'll still mention it.

It can't do any harm.

CHAPTER TWO

Isobel's paranoia had grown to a level where she imagined even the assistants in Marks and Spencer's food hall were sniggering and whispering about her behind their hands. 'That's that Mrs Langland,' they'd say. 'You know, *that* Mrs Langland!'

They're not, she reasoned with herself. Of course they're not. They can't be. How could they possibly know?

Although she lived on the edge of a conurbation of several hundred thousand inhabitants, her own little section of society was relatively small; her particular dinner party circuit probably numbered no more than fifty people. But if you multiplied those fifty by the fifty other people on each of *their* circuits, you got two thousand five hundred. And if you did the same for them, you were up to a hundred and twenty-five thousand. And it was necessary for *just one* gossip on Isobel's circuit to tell someone on another circuit, and for them to pass the juicy story on, and before you knew it somebody would have slipped the word to one of the women in M. and S.

I can't show my face in there! We're all going to starve!

It was Saturday morning. She was still in bed, feeling depressed, trying to decide what to do with the day. Lawrence was due home later. Could he go shopping when he'd unpacked? No, he's bound to be late. They'll probably take that loud-mouthed American company chap off to play yet another game of golf before he catches his plane home to Denver, or Delaware, or Dixie, wherever it is he lives.

Isobel remembered she had come across John Keir Franklin Willard at a company ball a few years ago – it wasn't the sort of name you forgot. He'd asked her to dance, then slid a hand like a piece of haddock under the thin strap of her evening dress and told her a little breathlessly that he just did love English roses, there was something about a gal with a creamy complexion and blonde hair that did things to his equilibrium (he had pronounced it 'ee-*kwai*-librium', as in the Burmese river).

Carefully removing his hand, she had told him frostily that actually her hair was mouse, her complexion was courtesy of Clinique, and hadn't he better put her down so that he could go hunting for the genuine article?

There had been a suspenseful moment during which John Keir Franklin Willard had made up his mind whether he was going to be amused or not. Then he had let out a great guffaw, hugged Isobel even closer to his rotund belly and said she had a sense of humour, and didn't that just beat all?

'Oh,' she had said lamely. She'd been driven to fake a sprained ankle to get away from him, which was a pity as it meant she couldn't really dance with anyone else – at least not while he was in the ballroom.

Lawrence won't want to go shopping at six in the evening, she thought. He'll probably be worn out anyway, and in no fit state to shop sensibly. I shall have to go.

She reached for her dressing gown and got out of bed, sending the load of Saturday papers and magazines, which the paper boy had earlier delivered, sliding with a thump to the floor. One of them knocked over her half-empty teacup, which spilt its tepid contents on the cream bedside rug.

'Bugger,' Isobel said quietly.

Then, feeling that already the day was proving too much for her, she went to fetch a wet cloth from the en suite bathroom.

The door was locked. When she rattled the handle, the voice of her daughter floated out: 'Go away!'

'Dory, this is *my* bathroom,' Isobel said, holding on to her temper. 'Would you please come out?'

'No.'

'Yes. You can use yours, it's –'

'I *can't*! Jacob's in there, he's been in there *hours* and he's got his boats in the bath.'

Isobel could hear her son downstairs. He was eight years old, and on Saturday mornings liked to sit glued to the TV watching cartoons. Isobel didn't interfere: it made up a little, she felt, for his being sent away to school as a weekly boarder. It had seemed a good idea; the school had an excellent reputation, and she and Lawrence could certainly afford it. But she knew how much he hated it; she hated him hating it, and didn't know whether taking him out of that school and sending him somewhere else would be giving in to him or being wise and far-sighted.

'Jacob's watching telly,' she said through the keyhole to Dory.

'Cartoons, I expect.' Dory's tone was full of fourteen-year-old disdain.

'Yes, but that's hardly relevant. If he's watching telly, then he's not in your bathroom, so you can go into it and I can have mine.' She thought, God, give me patience!

Dory muttered something.

'What did you say?'

'I said, he'll have left it in a state. He always does.'

Isobel went along the landing to the children's bathroom. Jacob's dirty socks and pants were on the floor and there was a grubby tidemark, which she wiped away. Other than that, it wasn't too bad. She fetched a new block of carnation soap from the top shelf in the airing cupboard: it was Dory's favourite.

'Please, Dory,' she said, returning to the keyhole. 'I've put out some new carnation soap for you. You can unwrap it.'

'Is it Roger and Gallet, in pleated paper?'

'Naturally.'

There was a pause. Then, reluctantly: 'All right, then. I'm coming out.' This is like a gangster movie, Isobel thought. 'But you're to promise on your honour that you won't look!'

There was a sound of splashing. 'I promise,' Isobel said, wondering yet again what it was about her daughter's body that Dory had to keep so carefully hidden. Sometimes, she thought, I wouldn't be in the least surprised to discover it's horns and a forked tail.

'I've borrowed these,' Dory said nonchalantly, emerging suddenly swathed in two of Isobel's clean towels, one round her head, the bigger one – it was actually a bath sheet – clutched to her chin and covering her as comprehensively as a mummy's wrappings.

Isobel watched as she tottered off down the landing, only her small feet and ankles showing. Her ankles, Isobel noticed dispassionately, were quite beautiful, the long, slim Achilles tendons edged by hollows on either side. Dancer's legs. She smiled: her mother had always claimed to have dancer's legs, making the remark in a hushed tone that suggested the Royal Ballet rather than the Huddersfield Hippodrome. Good old Ma, Isobel thought. It had been her suggestion that Isobel and Lawrence should call their baby daughter Isadora: 'Isadora Duncan was the greatest dancer the world has ever seen,' Mollie Adair had said, with her usual flair for overstatement and blinkered vision. 'Such freedom of movement!'

Mollie and Dory made a terrific team, virtually

unstoppable when they were both working towards the same goal. Thank God, Isobel reflected, I don't often have to face the pair of them together.

By the time Isobel had tidied up after Dory, fetched clean towels, run herself a bath with what was left of the hot water and soaked in it for fifteen minutes, the tea stain on the bedroom carpet was beyond the aid of simple measures like a damp cloth. Isobel, who had forgotten all about it, resigned herself to having to go out shopping, if only for carpet shampoo.

She sat in front of her dressing table, staring into the mirror at the dismal prospect of her own face. She lifted a lock of well-cut, subtly highlighted hair. God only knows, she thought, how much this one bit of hair cost at the last bout with the hairdresser. And what good does it do? I can have the most expensive haircut in Ewell – possibly I have – but when it sits up there on top of a face like five miles of bad road, I might as well nail a cloth cap to my head and be done with it.

She reached for moisturiser and foundation, and began the ritual task of putting on her make-up. The end result was passable. This is meant to cheer me up, she thought, frowning. It says so in the agony columns. Depressed? Feeling down? Made an absolute prat of yourself and wish you could be beamed up to some orbiting spacecraft? Don't despair! Try a new beauty product, treat yourself to matching bag and shoes, and you can face the world with confidence!

Except I can't. I've lost my confidence, every last iota of it.

She got up, striding over to the huge wardrobe that lined one wall of the bedroom. Extracting new black jeans and a black jersey tunic, she put them on. Yes, she thought, I know the colour consultants veto black, tell us it kills any spark of vitality in our faces. But black is how I feel.

She made a desultory attempt to tidy the tumbled bed, then went downstairs. There was no sign of Dory; Isobel guessed she was up in her room. There was the muted sound of distant music, a steady thump, thump, thump like a faraway heartbeat.

Jacob had obviously had his breakfast. The Shreddies packet stood open on the worktop, beside it the sugar bowl. Both were half empty. The remains of a pint of milk stood right on the edge of the sink. A little trail of Shreddies crumbs and spilt sugar led out of the kitchen; Isobel followed it along the hall and into the living room, where Jacob was curled up under a blanket, empty cereal bowl beside him on the sofa, eyes glued to *Bugs Bunny*.

'What's up, Doc?' Isobel greeted him.

He looked up. 'Oh. Hi, Mum.'

As a welcome, it was hardly hearty. 'Are you cold, darling?' she asked brightly. The October morning was sunny, and besides, the boiler must be pumping out thousands of calories of heat. 'Do you really want the blanket?'

'Yes!' He turned huge blue eyes up to her, looking as threatened as if she'd proposed to stop feeding him.

'But –' She stopped. He'd always liked snuggling down under a blanket; she'd wondered if it was his way of escaping when the frequent rows between herself and Dory had raged above his head. Maybe he still needs his security, she thought. Maybe he needs it more than ever, now that a belligerent elder sister and a short-fused mother have been replaced by a school full of young thugs out to make his life a misery.

She sat down beside him. 'How was your week?'

He shrugged. 'Okay.'

'Did anything nice happen?'

He looked at her with an expression far too mature for

19

his eight-year-old face. 'No.' Of *course* not, came the mute supplement.

'How's work going?' Surely that was a more hopeful opening. He was a bright boy and had always shone at nature study and science, which were his favourite subjects.

'I don't like the teachers.'

Her heart was going out to him. She wished she had the power to make his life better right there and then. But, even given that she could decide on some improving course of action, it'd take ages to implement, even longer to have an effect on this sad son of hers.

In desperation, she said, 'Would you like to go swimming today? We could –'

'*No!*'

She hadn't expected such vehemence. 'Jacob? Is anything the matter?'

He had clutched the blanket more tightly round him, right up around his ears, as if he wanted to block her out. 'Sorry, Mum.'

He had turned back to *Bugs Bunny*. Everything about him was silently shouting *leave me alone*. So she did.

Isobel was sitting at the kitchen table trying to compose a shopping list when the phone rang.

'Isobel? Is that you?'

It was a loud voice, quite unmistakable. 'Hello, Kristen.'

Kristen Hughes had started life as Christine, but had decided the name no longer kept pace with her image. Isobel and Lawrence were due to go to dinner with Kristen and Paul that evening.

'Isobel, quite devastating news. Paul's aunt has had a fall and broken her arm!'

'Oh dear.' Isobel got the distinct feeling her reaction wasn't up to the mark, but it was difficult to do better when she'd never met Paul's aunt. 'I'm so sorry,' she added, trying to sound sincere.

'The thing is, darling, Auntie's got into a panic and wants him there, so I'm going to be on my own this evening.'

'Well, should we –'

Isobel had been about to suggest they postpone the dinner arrangement, but Kristen overrode her interruption. 'I'm changing dinner for ten to a small supper for three, and –'

'That'll be lovely! Nicer, in a way, we can –'

'– just me and the Pope-Coopers, darling. *Do* hope you're not devastated!' There was a carefully musical, theatrical laugh.

Devastated? Isobel wanted to say. Of course I'm not! I didn't want to come to your blasted dinner party anyway. 'No, no, I quite understand,' she said, despising herself for the placatory note in her voice. 'I do hope Paul's aunt gets better soon.'

'Thank you, darling. Love to Lawrence. Byee!'

Isobel sat staring at the replaced receiver. Kristen hadn't suggested another date for the dinner party. Why hadn't she?

Because she knows. She's heard all about it, had a jolly good laugh, and has made up her mind I'm no longer the sort of person she wants sitting at her dinner table. *That's* why.

'Bloody woman!' she hissed. How dare she make judgements? She doesn't understand, none of them does. I've been accused, put on trial and sentenced, without the chance to defend myself. Not one of them has asked me for my account of events!

Slowly the anger abated. And in its wake came the realisation that her own account of what had happened would not exonerate her: she had been an absolute fool whichever way you looked at it. I don't *have* a defence, she thought

21

miserably. Temporary insanity, I suppose. But to be considered insane, even temporarily, would surely be almost as bad.

Her shopping list – 'carpet shampoo' – lay on the table. Picking up her pencil, she added, 'Red Ferrari. Harrison Ford. Smaller knees. Something to take five years off my face.' After reflection, she crossed out 'five' and put in 'ten'.

There was a crash from upstairs, which from long experience she recognised as the slamming of Dory's bedroom door. It was followed by the pounding of feet coming down the stairs, then Dory flounced into the kitchen.

'Mum, may I have my pocket money?' she said.

'What happened to please?' Isobel responded.

'*Please.*' Dory cast her eyes heavenwards as if having to deal with an imbecile.

Isobel reached for her purse. 'Dory, I don't like to interfere, but –'

'Am I really going out dressed like this? Yes I am!'

She was wearing a skirt in a shiny black fabric that looked like satin but was probably polyester. It was extremely short, but since she wore very thick black tights underneath, that scarcely seemed to matter. She had laced on her Doc Martens, and was now zipping up a cerise bomber jacket with fake fur round the collar. Whether by accident or design, she had happened on a perfect colour for her complexion and her smooth dark hair.

'Actually I wasn't going to say that,' Isobel remarked mildly. 'I think you look very nice.'

'You don't!' Dory said scornfully. Then, when Isobel didn't respond: 'Do you?'

'Yes. And your hair's lovely, really glossy.'

For a silly moment, Isobel almost believed her daughter was going to smile. But then Dory thought better of it. She said, 'You were saying you don't like to interfere but you're obviously going to. Well? What is it?'

Isobel didn't have the energy. 'Skip it.'

'What?' Dory repeated.

'I was just going to ask if you had any homework.' Why, she wondered, do I sound so apologetic? It's Dory's future, it'll be she who suffers if she fails every single GCSE and ends up on the dole with no job, no prospects and no life.

'Done it,' Dory sang out as she made a leap towards the back door. 'And anyway, look at Churchill!'

As the echoes of another slammed door faded and died, Isobel pondered upon Dory's parting shot. Why should I want to look at Churchill? *Winston* Churchill, I assume?

She was just working out that Dory had probably cited Churchill as someone renowned for not doing his homework when she heard a car in the drive.

She stood up and went over to the window; Lawrence's BMW was coming to a halt on the gravel.

She hurried outside. 'Lawrence? Is anything wrong?'

He was bending over the open boot, getting out his luggage. He turned to grin at her. 'I knew you'd say that! No.' He turned back to the bags. 'I thought it might be,' came his muffled voice, 'but it may after all be a good thing.'

She stared at him, puzzled. 'I'm none the wiser.'

'Come inside –' she took the proffered dinner jacket from him – 'and I'll explain. No, I won't,' he hastily corrected himself, 'I'll tell you what I've been thinking. Some of it.'

She was beginning to feel slightly anxious. Following him into the house, she laid his dinner jacket down in the hall beside his briefcase and holdall. 'Like a coffee?' she said.

'Love one. Let's sit at the kitchen table and have a talk.' He was staring at her intently while she started on the coffee. 'A *real* talk.'

'Oh God,' she said involuntarily. Then, grinning nervously: 'Sorry. I'm not sure I like it when people propose a *real* talk.'

To her surprise, he came over to her, took the kettle out

23

of her hands and put his arms round her. 'It's all right,' he said. 'Nothing to worry about.'

He was solid, warm. It had been a long time since he'd made her feel comforted and secure like this. Her troubles suddenly rose up and engulfed her: she leaned against him and started to cry.

'Izzy? Oh, Izzy, don't! What is it?'

'Dory's been Dory all morning, and I made a stain on the bedroom carpet,' she snuffled, putting the minor worries first. 'And Jacob – oh, Lawrence, what are we going to do about poor little Jacob?' She was crying harder, didn't seem to be able to stop.

Lawrence reached out and gently closed the kitchen door. 'Is he watching telly?' She nodded. 'That's okay, then, he won't have heard. Izzy, why is he poor little Jacob? Has something happened?'

She shook her head. 'No. Except that he hates that bloody new school. We've got to help him, Lawrence, we're all he's got, we –'

'What do you want to do?' Lawrence asked. His voice was calm, and he was gently stroking her hair. It felt soothing.

She paused. 'I suppose what I really want to do is put him in another school. But that'd look as if we thought he couldn't cope, and if he went to another school around here, it might be like running away, and . . .' She trailed off.

'Isobel, I'm going to say something, and I want you to promise not to dismiss it out of hand. Okay?' He held her away from him so that he could look into her eyes.

He called me Isobel, she thought. This must be serious. 'Okay.'

He took a deep breath. 'I've just endured yet another conference,' he began, 'and, quite honestly, I'm sick of it. Sick of the life, sick of the work.'

24

'Lawrence!' she exclaimed. 'What –'

'Let me finish.' He grinned, as if to apologise for appearing to issue orders. 'I just thought, just wondered, if there was any possible chance you might feel that life in suburban Surrey is beginning to pale, and that you might consider an alternative.'

'What sort of alternative?' she asked guardedly.

'Move to the country,' he said. 'Sell the house, buy something smaller, send the kids to state schools. Buy a smallholding.'

'What's a smallholding?'

'I was afraid you'd want to know more.' He sounded as if he thought her question was unreasonable. 'Actually I'm not quite sure, but it involves making a living from a small bit of land. Or I could grow apples. Something like that.'

She stared up at him. It was possible he was hung over, and therefore talking total rubbish that he'd forget all about in a few hours' time, after he'd had a long recuperative sleep. On the other hand, he'd just driven home from Brighton, and she knew he wouldn't have done so if he'd been *that* hung over.

The other possibility was that he really meant it.

She thought about it. Imagined telling Jacob he didn't have to be a weekly boarder any more. Imagined packing up the house, closing the pantechnicon doors, driving away from this ghastly town and all the malicious, tongue-wagging gossips. She ignored the small voice of reason that told her it was a perfectly pleasant town, full of perfectly ordinary people going about their business, just as they had always done. Imagined starting life anew in some place where nobody knew her, where no one had made unfair assumptions about her purely on the basis of one slip-up. Okay, a bad slip-up. But still, only one.

She opened her mouth to speak. To her faint surprise

she heard herself say, 'I think it's a good idea. Certainly one worth thinking about.'

Lawrence's jaw had dropped about a foot. Recovering, he said, 'Crikey. I mean, yes, of course we have to think about it.' He frowned, in a responsible-husband-and-parent sort of way. 'There are a great many considerations. A *great* many,' he repeated, as if she'd been suggesting they upped sticks and set off without further ado. Then, timidly: 'You really think it's a good idea?'

'Yes.'

'What about all our friends?' Then, with obvious reluctance, as if he were loath to remind her of a possible barrier to his plans, 'What about the shops?'

She thought, bugger the shops, but didn't say so, instead remarking mildly, 'I expect there are shops in the country. Within easy reach, anyway.'

Lawrence sat down suddenly. He stared up at her, looking quite pale. He said, 'I think I could do with that coffee now.'

CHAPTER THREE

Jacob sat in the back of the car, squashed into the corner because Dory had insisted on bringing a bag the size of a baby elephant, full of things she just had to have for a day out. He couldn't for the life of him think why she needed a full change of clothes, a cushion, and make-up, although he could understand the old copy of *Just Seventeen* with the Blur feature and her souvenir Tottenham programme. She had crushes on Ian Walker and Teddy Sheringham. And on Kula Shaker.

They were going down into the country to look at properties. That was what Dad called it. Jacob didn't quite understand: did he mean like when they went to a place called Hever Castle, where Mum had got a bit weepy over a woman who'd married a king who'd cut her head off? Jacob hadn't listened to the bossy guide – he'd had his eye on the adventure playground, which had been great. They'd had lunch in a pub garden, and Dad had asked Mum to drive home because the beer had been specially nice and he'd had one too many. One over the eight, he'd said, but it wasn't eight, it was four. Jacob had been counting, to see if Dad would drink as many pints as that king had had wives. One over four was five, so he hadn't.

Jacob didn't really think today's outing was to look at that sort of property. He had a pretty good idea they were going to look for a new place to live. Out in the country. Which was such a wonderful prospect that he didn't dare think about it much in case he'd got it wrong and that wasn't what was happening. Or in case Mum changed her mind and said she didn't want to move after all. In case Dory got her way and *made* Mum change her mind.

He glanced across at his sister. She had her Walkman on, and he could hear the sss-sss-ch-ch-sss noises you always heard when someone near you was listening to headphones. Her eyes were shut and her face was set in one of her worst scowls. Granddad had told her the wind would change and she'd be stuck like that. Dory rarely smiled, and Jacob was beginning to think Granddad might have been right.

He had some sympathy for her, because he knew she loathed trips into the country. But not much sympathy, because she was a bit of a pig. Always wanting her own way, refusing to accept that Jacob might sometimes want his own way, too. Making him do what she said because she was bigger than him. Another of the things Granddad told her was that might wasn't right. Dory can't have been listening when he said that.

Granddad was Dad's father. His name was Douglas, which Jacob thought was a very grandfatherly name. Nobody got called Douglas nowadays, or at least nobody at Jacob's school was. He didn't think so, anyway, but everyone had to be called by his surname, so it was a bit difficult to say for certain.

Jacob didn't want to think about his school. It made him unhappy. He'd gone there in September, and they'd said it'd get better once he wasn't a new boy any more. It hadn't. Perhaps he was still a new boy. They hadn't said when it stopped.

He made himself think about Granddad instead. It was funny how Dory specially liked Mum's mum, and he specially liked Dad's dad. It made things even, somehow. Each of them, him and Dory, had their special grandparent, each grandparent had their special grandchild. Not that they saw as much of Grandma as they did of Granddad, because Grandma had gone to live in Belgium with her friend Audrey Jolly and Audrey's daughter, Harriet, who was always called Harry. Harry did some job in Brussels to do with European law, and they all lived in a huge flat. You could see Heysel Stadium from the little balcony – Jacob knew that because Grandma had sent him a photo. Someone called Fran shared the flat. Fran was Harry's friend.

Harry. Jacob said the name in his mind. It was a funny name for a woman. Actually she was quite a funny woman; Jacob, Mum, Dad and Dory had gone to see them all off at Gatwick, and Harry had been wearing what looked like a man's suit. She had very short hair. Dad had whispered to Mum, 'That one's a dyke or I'm a Dutchman,' and Mum had gone 'Sssh!' and looked quickly at Mrs Jolly, who was close enough to have heard – Dad wasn't very good at whispering. But Mrs Jolly had been busy with her cases – she had an awful lot of them – and didn't hear. Jacob had amused himself thinking how, if Grandma and Mrs Jolly swapped surnames, Grandma would be Mollie Jolly.

Grandma was a widow. Mum's dad had died when Mum was being an air hostess, before she'd married Dad. He had died of a stroke. Jacob didn't really know what that was, any more than he knew what dyke meant. Granddad, too, was – what was it when it was a man? – a widower. Jacob could just remember Granddad's granny. He had been taken to see her in hospital, and she'd been in a very high bed and hadn't stopped complaining the whole time they were there. Jacob had felt sorry for her, but even more so for Granddad, who had looked so miserable. When Granny had died, soon after that, lots of grown-ups had said it was a blessed relief for her to be out of her misery.

Jacob had thought it must be a relief for Granddad to be out of her misery as well.

'Grandma, Granny,' Jacob muttered. 'Grandfather. Granddad.'

Dory leant across and punched him. 'Shut up, I'm trying to listen.'

Jacob pulled away even further into his corner. They were on a motorway – he thought it was the M25. They had gone past a services place called Clacketts Lane. That was a good name. Clackett. There was a boy at school called Clack, and the other boys used to call him Cack. 'Ha, ha, ha, Clack's cacked his pants! Cack, cack, cack!' they said. But Clack had pushed one of them down some stairs and punched another one, and they'd stopped. There was a lot of punching at Jacob's school. A lot of pushing boys down stairs. A lot of dragging boys into dark corners of deserted changing rooms and twisting their arms behind their backs. A lot of making boys give bigger boys their pocket money, or else the bigger boys put your head down the stinky lavatory and pulled the chain. That was horrid, because you had to tell the teacher why you had wet hair, and you couldn't tell them the truth or the bigger boys would do it again.

Don't think about school, Jacob told himself sternly.

They were on a smaller road now, and Dad was going slowly because Mum had said she wanted to look at the countryside. Jacob looked too. There were trees with bronzy leaves, and other trees with no leaves at all. 'Deciduous,' he whispered. In a field he saw two big horses, and in another there were sheep. There were a few houses, but they were set further apart than in the street at home. Most of them had big gardens. Would Mum and Dad choose a house with a big garden?

Mum pointed to something. 'Look, Lawrence, that house has its own pool.'

Dad said that building an outdoor pool in England represented a triumph of optimism over experience.

Jacob wondered if they would have a house with a pool. He liked swimming. Sometimes Mum or Dad took him to the town pool on Saturday mornings. Mum had offered to, that awful Saturday morning two weeks ago when he'd felt so bad about Wainwright. Wainwright had been up to his usual game of lurking in the changing rooms after games on Friday afternoon, and pouncing on the slowcoaches when the games master had got tired of waiting and gone back to Big School. Jacob hadn't got the hang of untying wet, muddy rugby boot laces with fingers like slivers of ice; it hadn't been the first time Wainwright had caught him. Wainwright had demanded money. Or chocolate. Or sweets. Wainwright wasn't fussy, he'd take whatever you had in your pockets. Jacob pretended he hadn't got anything, and Wainwright lifted him up by the collar of his rugby jersey and slammed him against the wall. One of the pegs where you hung your clothes was driven into Jacob's shoulder; it hurt so much he felt dizzy. While he was lying on the floor, Wainwright went through his pockets and found the pound coin that Granddad had given him to buy sweets; Jacob had been saving it to spend it on the way home, if Mum would stop at the shop.

Listening to Wainwright's heavy footsteps as he marched triumphantly out of the changing rooms, Jacob wept for his hurt shoulder – and for the total failure of his feeble attempt to stand up to the bullying.

Then on the Saturday morning Mum had suggested going swimming. She'd have seen the bruise – everyone in the pool would have seen it, it was gynormous – and she'd have wanted to know how he'd got it. Jacob was still feeling shaky about it, and he wasn't sure if he could tell a convincing lie; more likely he'd have blubbed again. And then Mum would have gone on about it, then she'd have demanded to see Mr Beach and everything would have been a million times worse.

The car was slowing down; pulling off the road; stopping in a gateway.

'What do you think?' Dad was saying. He and Mum were staring out through the windscreen. Beyond the gate – which looked a bit rickety – was an open space. Beyond that was a track winding up into woodlands. There was a big board which said 'FOR SALE' in big red letters. Mum and Dad seemed to be reading the smaller writing beneath it; Jacob did the same.

> OXLEAT WOOD. A useful parcel of commercial woodland in a rural location on the Kent/East Sussex border. Comprising chestnut coppicing with standards and underwood. Crossed by stream, access to main road. In total about 45 acres.

Mum said, 'Chestnut coppicing.'

Dad said, 'Yes. Chestnut's a good cash crop, everyone wants chestnut.' Dad had sent for a booklet called *Coppicing: Traditional Woodland Management*. He had left it by the loo, and Jacob had had a glance at it. It didn't look very interesting. Recently, other books with diagrams and charts in them had appeared. They weren't interesting either.

Mum said, 'Mm.'

A stream, Jacob thought. A stream running through a wood. He craned past Dory to get a better look, and she stuck her elbow in his ribs. He moved out of the way. Why were they looking at woodlands?

Mum and Dad didn't say anything for ages. They just sat there, staring out at the woods and the sign.

Eventually Dad said, 'It's the right sort of size. Big enough to make something out of it, not so big that I'd need to employ lots of people.'

'There's no accommodation,' Mum said.

Dad laughed. 'Accommodation! No, doesn't look like it. Wouldn't it be nice to have a house down in that dip? I expect that's where the stream runs.'

'It'd be damp,' Mum said.

'I expect you're right. There may be houses for sale nearby. Shall we see?'

Houses? For sale? It sounded as if they really meant it. Jacob couldn't bear the suspense any longer. 'Dad, are we really going to live down here?' he burst out.

Dad turned round, reached out his hand and ruffled Jacob's hair. 'Would you like to, son?'

Jacob nodded. *Like* to? Of course he'd like to!

Dad looked at Mum. 'Well, we're seriously thinking about it. A move out of town might do us all good. Get away from the traffic, urban civilisation, working all the hours God sends.'

Jacob wasn't listening. 'Would we come here?' he asked. 'Right here? To these woods?'

'We might, darling,' Mum said. 'We'd have to get details, and perhaps look at some other possibilities. Then we'd have to decide which one was best. We'd have to think about what Dad would do to earn money, we'd have to find a house to live in, and see about schools for you and Dory. When we'd considered all those things, we'd make our decision.'

He said, hardly daring to believe it, 'You mean I'd go to a different school?'

'Yes, darling.'

Why? he wondered. I'm a weekly boarder, Mum could take me to school on Sunday evenings from here just like she does from home, it's not all that much further. He opened his mouth to say so, then abruptly shut it again.

If Mum and Dad thought that moving to the country meant he'd no longer have to go to his hateful school, then he certainly wasn't going to be the one to query it.

He was aware of Dory beside him, removing her Walkman and very deliberately winding up the leads to her headphones.

She said expressionlessly, 'If you lot move to the country, I shall leave home.'

Mum looked at her. 'Don't be silly, Dory. You're far too young.'

Dory leant forward. 'Then I'll run away!' she spat out. 'Go to London, sit in Piccadilly till someone picks me up and puts me on the game! That'll teach you!'

'No you won't, darling,' Mum said calmly. 'You have no idea what you're talking about.'

Dad muttered something about anyone unwise enough to pick up Dory soon putting her down again.

'Yes I have!' Dory screeched. 'I've seen films, I know what goes on! There'll be heaps of people mainlining heroin and dying of AIDS all around me, and I'll pick up bad habits!'

Dad burst out laughing, but Mum shushed him. 'Dory, we haven't decided anything yet,' she said. 'You know we've been thinking about moving, I told you so the other week. And Dad explained how he won't necessarily go on working for Barclay Dawson, but that he'll –'

'You said he'll have to give the car back!' Dory wailed. 'You *can't*, Dad!' She clutched on to her door handle as if the car were going to be magicked away that very second.

'A BMW won't be much use if I'm going to be a woodsman,' Dad observed.

'I expect you'll buy a *van*,' Dory said scathingly.

'Now that's not a bad idea,' Dad said. 'What do you think, Izzy? A nice beaten-up old Transit? A Ford Escort with closed sides and "Ramsbottom and Son, Plumbers" inadequately painted over?'

'Don't tease her, Lawrence,' Mum said quietly. She turned back to Dory, and tried to take her hand. Dory

34

snatched it away. 'Darling, we have to think what's best for all of us, and –'

'Don't patronise me!' Dory yelled. Then she wrenched open the car door and leapt out, clambering over the rickety gate and running off up the track through the woods.

For some moments Jacob and his parents sat staring after her. Then Dad said, 'Now that's not a bad idea, you know. We really should have a look round.' He got out of the car. 'The ground's dry. Anyone coming with me?'

'I'll stay here,' Mum said. 'A wood's a wood as far as I'm concerned. It's you who needs to have a look.'

'Jacob?'

Jacob was already halfway out. He slammed his door and ran round the back of the car to join his father, who took hold of his hand. Together they climbed the gate and set off up the track.

Dory had found the stream. She had in fact put her right foot in it; she'd trodden on a patch of green stuff that looked like very bright grass but was actually water with some horrible sort of weedy things on top. Shaking out her open-toed shoe, feeling the cold water seeping between her toes, she decided that this only went to confirm her belief that the countryside was gross.

Why do they want to move? What's wrong with where we are now? The house is all right, Mum likes being near the town so she can go shopping a lot and have lunch with her friends. I expect they talk about hot flushes all the time and HRT.

She had to admit to herself she didn't actually know what HRT was, but she thought it was something to do with the Royal Family.

She took off her shoe and wriggled her toes around to dry them. She was wearing tights, which ought to dry quite quickly. She suppressed the thought that her mother had been right to suggest Dory wore trainers or boots, since they might be doing some walking in fields and on rough paths; Dory had only worn her sandals to make a point. 'You can't tell me what to wear!' she'd insisted. She wished now she'd listened and worn her Doc Martens.

I'll have to change schools too! she wailed silently. Go to some gross school with *farmers'* daughters and girls who wear sad clothes because they can't get to decent shops. And whatever will I do on Saturdays? No precinct to hang around, no group of school friends to cruise with, no one to dare to go into Boots and try out the perfume testers, no one to choose eyeliners with.

No best friend to discuss boys with.

Damn parents! *Damn* them!

She balled both hands into fists and swung a couple of punches. Left, right. This new thing – this let's-move-to-the-country, won't-it-be-lovely? – was just typical. Impotent with fury, she felt the frustration of months batting about in her head, searching for an outlet. Mum and Dad seemed to have gone blind. They just couldn't see that she wasn't a kid any more, she was a *person*, entitled to consideration, entitled to being consulted about things!

In her distress, Dory wasn't quite sure what the things were that she ought to be consulted about, but what she sensed was a deliberate shutting-out, a feeling that her parents were concerned with matters – vaguely worrying matters – that they ought to be discussing with her, but from which they were deliberately excluding her.

Why won't they share things with me? It's my life too. Haven't I a right to be involved?

Take this trip today, she thought. Mum and Dad just *announced* we were going out for the day, never mind asking me if it was convenient! And it's Saturday! Supposing I'd arranged to meet Daisy and Catherine? *They* weren't to know Daisy's mother's taking her to buy new shoes and Catherine's got a cold!

I might have seen Rupert Smythe again. He sort of said he'd be in town this afternoon. And Catherine says her brother says he thought he saw my name written on Rupert's English rough notes book.

And now, because of my blasted parents and their silly ideas, even if it *was* my name, and even if Rupert *does* go into town, it's no good!

I *hate* my parents! They *spoil* everything!

Why do they want to uproot us when we're totally happy, and dump us down here in this rotten place? I bet Dad's got the sack, that's what! He's been made redundant, and we've got to move somewhere cheaper!

She leaned back against the branch of a tree, eyes wide with astonished realisation.

Why didn't I think of it before? Dad's been sacked, like Caroline Stacey's dad, and we'll have to sell the house and move into a semi, like they did! Oh God, and I'll have to go to a *state* school!

'No!' she shouted. 'I *won't*!'

From close at hand came the sound of cracking twigs. Her father appeared at the top of a slight rise.

'Oh, there you are, Dory.' He slithered down the bank and came to lean against her tree. 'Jacob's up there climbing an oak tree. They're called standards, according to my booklet. They leave a few big trees while the little chestnut saplings are growing, to give them shelter. At least, I think that's why.' He grinned suddenly, and Dory thought it made him look younger. 'I'll have so much to learn. *If* we go ahead with this, that is.'

She said after a moment, 'Do we have to?'

'We don't exactly *have* to.'

She looked up at him. 'You haven't been made redundant, have you?' she asked in a small voice.

37

He shrugged. Benjamin Fishwick had been frosty and supercilious since the conference. 'I – maybe. I haven't been made redundant yet, but it may come to that. But that's not really it. I want – I feel that . . . Dory, it isn't easy to explain. I'm sick of being what I am, and I'd like a change. Can you understand that?'

'What about us?' she shouted. 'Mum hates the country, so do I! What will *we* do while you're busy having a change?'

'You have a point,' he conceded. 'I'd imagined Mum would hit the roof when I suggested moving into the country, but actually she seems quite keen. And I wondered if you would like a pony?'

He was looking at her with a silly great smile, as if he'd been saving up a treat and had at last given it to her.

She said, 'A *pony?*'

'Yes.' He put his arm around her. 'I know how much you've always wanted one, how we had to say no because keeping a pony in the suburbs would have been ruinously expensive. But you can have one now. We'll find some bit of land, maybe have a little stable built, and you can . . .'

He was rambling on, going into ecstasies describing tack rooms and hay barns, and finding some lovable and friendly-natured grey – or bay – which she could trot around the lanes and through the woods on. 'And we'll get you one of those special hats, maybe some boots too, and . . .'

Hadn't he noticed? Had he had his eyes closed all these months since this time last year, when she'd had her last lesson and said she didn't want to ride any more, because doing up buckles on the tack broke her nails and she always came home smelling of horse sweat?

Was he blind, or just stupid?

'. . . some nice new jodhpurs, some of those tight cream ones and –'

'You're too late!' she yelled across his happy daydreaming. 'I wanted a pony *then*, but I don't any more!'

He looked hurt, as if she'd thrown a present back at him. 'All right, Dory, all right. You don't want a pony.' He paused, as if he were wondering whether or not to go on. Then he said tentatively, 'What *do* you want?'

He must have already known the answer. But, just in case he was in any doubt, she gave it to him anyway. At the top of her voice – which was gratifyingly high – she shouted, '*I don't want to move to the bloody country!*'

CHAPTER FOUR

Lawrence was feeling marginally better about Dory by the time they got home.

They'd had lunch in a village pub half a mile from the woods. Dory had refused to eat at first, but when the landlord's wife brought Jacob a huge plate of sausage and mash, covered in rich, fragrant, onion gravy, she changed her mind and said she wanted that, too.

Lawrence and Isobel shared a ploughman's, which had come with a big wedge of Stilton. Isobel, surprisingly, ordered a large gin and tonic. She never drank at lunch time; Lawrence wondered if she had found the morning particularly stressful.

He had a pint of beer from the local brewery. It was superb. He felt comforted, optimistic, and, now that he had seen the wood, his enthusiasm was growing. He hoped his family could all be persuaded to move down there.

After lunch they wandered round the village. It didn't take long. There were no houses for sale, but a somewhat dilapidated cottage facing the green had a 'To Let' sign outside. Without saying a word, Isobel got out her little notebook and wrote down the agent's phone number.

They drove home via the nearest town, which looked a lively sort of place. There was a pedestrianised area in the centre, and groups of young people had congregated at one end. Dory was looking out of the window; a boy whistled at her, and for the first time that day her face broke into a smile.

'Looks an interesting sort of a place,' Lawrence ventured as they stopped for a red light. He was watching his daughter's expression in the rear-view mirror; she was still wearing the remains of her smile.

They got back in the middle of the late Saturday afternoon crush of home-going shoppers. Crawling along in heavy traffic, suddenly Isobel gave a gasp. Lawrence glanced across at her.

'Are you all right?'

She had slid right down in her seat, and had her hands up over her face. 'Go *on*!' she hissed.

'I wish I could, Izzy, but as you may or may not have observed, there's a queue of cars in front of us, and – oh.'

At that moment the congestion eased, and he shot away.

'What's –' he began.

'Nothing. I'm perfectly all right.'

She had turned away. Risking another quick glance as once again they had to slow to a stop, he noticed that her shoulders were tight with tension.

In bed that night she turned to him, without a word wrapping her arms round his neck and pressing her body against his.

He was about to respond – eagerly; it was ages since she'd invited intimacy – when he realised she was weeping.

He held her, waiting to see if she would explain.

She didn't.

'Is there anything I can do?' he asked after a while. It seemed inadequate, in the face of her distress.

She shook her head. 'Nothing.'

He went on holding her close. Soon she stopped crying and reached under her pillow for a tissue. She wiped her eyes, blew her nose in a determined way, and lobbed the tissue in the direction of the waste-paper basket.

'Missed,' he observed.

She rolled over, turning her back to him and settling down.

Some time later, her voice came out of the darkness. 'Lawrence?'

'Mm?'

'Are you asleep?'

'Not yet.'

'Can we leave soon?'

He wondered why she should ask that. Was she secretly dreading it, and wanting them to go quickly before she lost her courage? Did this house – this life – mean so much to her that she would mourn the loss of it, even if – when – its loss became inevitable?

He didn't know. It seemed likely, but she would say, wouldn't she? Or maybe not. He dare not ask and risk upsetting her again.

'We can go as soon as we've settled on a place to live and sold this house,' he said. 'Before we sell the house, I suppose, if we decide to rent somewhere to begin with.'

'I'll get the details of the cottage in that village tomorrow.' She sounded happier.

'Okay.'

When he was almost asleep, she said, 'Thank you.'

He wondered what she was thanking him for.

Isobel lay listening to Lawrence's steady breathing. She wished, in a way, that he was as tense as she was. Then he'd be awake and she could have gone on talking to him, told him –

Told him what?

Not *that*. He didn't know – at least, she fervently hoped he didn't. And wouldn't he have given some sign if he'd found out? If some well-meaning soul had had a quiet whisper in his ear? He was his usual self – a bit unobservant, with a tendency to forget things and then pretend he hadn't,

42

but he was always kind and affectionate, ready to see the funny side.

Would he see the funny side of what I did?

No. She couldn't convince herself that he would.

Deliberately she turned her thoughts away from that; it made her feel guilty, and guilt was uncomfortable. Painful. She thought instead of today's trip, of the village, the woodland, and this nerve-racking prospect of moving to the country. Oh, but it wouldn't be that bad, would it? Surely she could cope. She *must*! She had been handed the unexpected lifeline of Lawrence's suggestion that they move away at the very time when, for her, living in Ewell was threatening to become impossible. Her life could be blown apart at any moment. Why, just this afternoon, driving home, hadn't she nearly –

Don't think about that!

Recalling her shame made her hot with embarrassment. The sensation faded, and then she suddenly felt cold. Lawrence had his back to her, and she moved across the bed towards him, curling her body round him. He grunted, but didn't wake up; with a faint sigh, she settled down to try to get to sleep.

Lawrence was on the point of handing in his notice when Benjamin Fishwick summoned him and informed him he was being made redundant.

'Just like that?' It was abrupt, to say the least. Even though he had been about to resign, he felt he should register some sort of a protest. 'Why?'

Benjamin Fishwick looked slightly discomfited. 'Well, as you know, Lawrence, we are now working much more closely with Southern Division, and to some extent – I could almost say to a large extent – certain posts are being duplicated where duplication is not, in fact, proving necessary, which of course is not an economically sound state of affairs, nor one which Barclay Dawson Products feels it can go on supporting, and – '

'So Colin Leigh of Southern Division is going to assume responsibility for both our jobs and I'm getting the push?'

'Er – yes.'

'Why?' Lawrence asked again.

'Er – '

'Is it because I upset the Big White Chief at the Whole Company Conference?' Fishwick began to look distinctly embarrassed. Lawrence pushed on. 'It is, isn't it?'

Sometime early on in his life, Fishwick must have been told that the best form of defence was attack. Fishwick had never felt comfortable with Lawrence Langland, who was far cleverer than him, and not afraid to disagree. But here Langland had lain himself wide open to attack. 'Well, Lawrence, you did make a bit of a bloody fool of yourself, didn't you?'

'I thought it was quite funny.' Somehow, he didn't care any more.

'That's as may be. But let me give you a piece of advice, Lawrence.' Benjamin Fishwick leaned forwards across his Wembley-sized desk, pointing his Parker at Lawrence. 'Next time a smutty schoolboy anecdote like that occurs to you, save it for the rugger club changing rooms.'

'I'll try to remember that.' Lawrence fought to keep his expression serious. 'Actually I don't play rugby any more. I gave it up in favour of squash. But I could tell my smutty anecdotes in the squash club changing room, couldn't I, sir?' he added earnestly.

Fishwick looked as if he were about to be irritated. But, glancing down at Lawrence's file, open on his desk, he seemed to think better of it. 'You'll have to hand in the company car, of course,' he muttered. The gravity of what he was doing apparently affected him.

44

Perhaps, Lawrence thought, it's only hitting home now that he's informing me I'm losing the car.

'You'd better read this.' Fishwick pushed a large envelope across the desk. 'It'll tell you all you need to know. Any questions, ring Parsons in Personnel. Now I must wish you good day.'

'Righto, sir.' Lawrence realised his jaunty tone wasn't appropriate. He added glumly, 'Not such a good day for me, is it, sir?' then left the office before the laughter broke out of him.

Going down in the lift, back to his own office, he tore open his envelope. Parsons in Personnel had written him a carefully phrased letter, which he didn't bother to read. He was far more interested in the form stapled to it, on which was written the sum that Barclay Dawson Products were proposing to pay him to compensate for being made so abruptly redundant.

Jacob was at long last beginning to believe it was really going to happen. There was a 'For Sale' sign outside the house, and Mum had spent all weekend making it look really tidy. She'd made him clear up the mess on his bed-room floor; it had taken him most of Saturday afternoon. She had written a letter to Mr Beach, too.

'I'm really going to leave school?' he asked her.

She smiled. 'Leave this school, yes. You'll have to go to another one, though. But only for the next ten years, so it's not too bad.'

'Will the new one be like this one?'

She studied him, as if trying to work out what he meant. 'You won't be a boarder, if that's what you're asking.' He wasn't sure if it was; the boarding in itself wasn't the bad bit. It was the boys he had to board with. 'You'll go to a local primary school,' Mum was saying. 'There's one on the village side of that big town we went through, remember?'

'Will there be rugby?'

'Rugby? Oh no, I don't think so. I think I read somewhere they play football. Well, the boys do. The girls play netball.' She was rummaging through a sheaf of papers. 'I've got their little booklet here somewhere . . .'

Football. He didn't care about little booklets. He was going to play *football*!

He thought of something. 'Mum?'

'Yes, darling?'

'Will the boys at school know I'm leaving?'

'I shouldn't think so, not unless you tell them. Why?'

He didn't want to say that it was because when McDonnell had suddenly left – he was going to live in Kenya – they'd nailed his locker closed and hidden half of his stuff, to serve him right for bragging about it. Jacob didn't want that happening to him. 'Oh, no reason.'

'Mm,' Mum said absently. She was still hunting for her little booklet, and he slipped away.

Football! He thought he'd better find his boots and ball, and go and get some goal-kicking practice.

The next day, Granddad came over for lunch. There was a lot of talk around the table about things Jacob didn't quite understand, things to do with Dad leaving his job and being a woodsman instead. Jacob liked the sound of woodsman. It really looked as if Dad was taking it seriously; he had sent off for heaps more booklets, and he was talking about doing a course at an agricultural college. Mum told Jacob Dad had been working late into the night on some graphs and lists of figures, and he spent most of the weekend reading books and things, and some magazines that had started arriving.

'So you don't approve, Pa?' Dad said to Granddad.

'I do and I don't,' Granddad replied. 'Some of it I heartily approve of.' He shot a look at Jacob. 'Sending this young

46

man and his sister to state schools, now, *that* I approve of and no mistake. I don't hold with private education, never have done. But giving up a well-paid position to grow trees – I'm not so sure about that.'

'It's not exactly growing trees,' Dad said. 'More of a sound financial scheme than that. I'm expecting to sell what I grow, you know. There's money in it, I assure you. I've gone into it very thoroughly, and I'm sure – pretty sure – I can make a go of it. It'll be fine.'

Granddad wiped his moustache and put down his napkin. 'Well, you're the qualified accountant, you ought to know where there's money, I suppose.' He glanced again at Jacob. 'Anyway, *pas devant*, eh?' He leaned towards Dad and whispered, 'Mustn't put worries into young heads.'

Jacob knew *pas devant* meant 'not before'. He was still trying to work out why Granddad had said it, and why it should put worries into people's heads, when Granddad got up. 'Delicious meal, Isobel,' he said.

Mum smiled at him. 'I'm glad you enjoyed it, Douglas.'

'Now, unless you want any help with the dishes –' Mum shook her head, just as she always did – 'then I think there's an hour or so before it gets dark for this young man and me to hone our football skills.'

'I'll get the ball.' Jacob was out of his seat before anyone could change their mind.

On the way to the park, Granddad said, 'Will you be sorry to leave your school?'

'No!' Jacob said fervently before he could stop himself. 'I mean . . .' He couldn't think of any way he could make it sound as if he wasn't quite so desperate. Still, did it matter any more? 'Don't tell Mum or Dad,' he confided, 'but actually I don't like it there.'

'Aah.' Granddad nodded sagely. 'Rather what I suspected. I don't hold with private education.'

Jacob still didn't know why it was called private. There was hardly any privacy in his school – even the lavatory doors stopped about eighteen inches short, top and bottom. And you had to have a shower with everyone else. 'I don't hold with it, either,' he said.

Granddad chuckled. Then he said, 'You haven't been very happy there, have you?'

Jacob felt a lump rise in his throat. He tried to cough it away. 'It's all right.'

'Hm. I doubt it.'

There was silence between them for some time. Then, just as they got to the park, Granddad said, 'Know what I'd do if there was some lout of a big boy making my life miserable?'

'No, what?' Jacob asked eagerly.

Granddad eyed him. 'We're talking hypothetically now, you know.' Jacob didn't know what hypothetically meant; Granddad seemed to realise. 'That means we're talking about a pretend situation. Saying what we'd do if it was real.'

'Oh. Yes, I see. What would you do, Granddad?'

Granddad had a twinkle in his eyes. 'If someone had been bullying me, this is what I'd do.' He leaned down and whispered in Jacob's ear for quite a long time; Jacob had to ask him to repeat a bit of it.

'Have you got that?' Granddad asked. 'Just in case you're ever in that situation?'

Jacob grinned. He couldn't stop grinning. 'I've got it.'

Jacob's very last day as a weekly boarder at his horrid school was a Friday: games day.

On the way down to breakfast he slowed down, deliberately letting Wainwright catch him up. Wainwright dropped a hand like a clamp onto Jacob's shoulder, twisting him round and pinning him against the wall.

'Got any money, scumbag?'

'No, Wainwright. I'm sorry, I spent it.'

The fist tightened. 'What on?' Although Wainwright was four years older, he'd apparently forgotten you didn't end a sentence with a preposition.

Jacob hesitated. Wainwright shook him. 'All right!' he yelled. 'I spent it on chocolate!'

Wainwright smiled nastily. 'And just where is this chocolate? Not in your locker, I bet. It wouldn't be safe there, would it?'

Jacob tried to hold out a bit longer, but Wainwright's fingers were hurting. 'It's in my pocket,' he gasped.

Wainwright stuck a big, heavy hand inside Jacob's blazer. He was triumphantly holding up the block of chocolate when they both heard footsteps.

'Wainwright! Langland! What are you boys doing?'

'Nothing, sir,' Jacob said. Wainwright mumbled something; his mouth was full of chocolate.

The master eyed them suspiciously. 'Well, whatever you're doing, stop it and hurry down to breakfast.'

'Yes, sir,' said Jacob.

'Mms, mr,' Wainwright added.

Jacob twisted out of Wainwright's reach and ran down to the refectory.

The school Under Twelves were playing in a match that afternoon, and the rest of the school were to watch. Wainwright played in the front row: the big red number on his back said 3.

Jacob stood hugging himself as he watched the two teams run out onto the field. The opposition wore red and black hooped shirts and black shorts; the school's jerseys were navy blue and their shorts were white.

Play was fairly uneventful for some time, as the two teams sized up each other's strengths and weaknesses. Then the referee blew his whistle and signalled for a scrum; Jacob could see several members of the pack start to smile. They were very good at scrumming, and had scored a pushover try in their last match.

Wainwright was grinning even more widely than the others.

Wainwright was a bully because he was bigger than most of the others. Not taller – he wasn't all that much taller than Jacob – just bigger. He ate a lot, and he usually ate very quickly, swallowing great mouthfuls at a time. And he had dreadful wind; it was rumoured he could fart for well over a minute without stopping. A favourite trick of his was to save up a fart till the scrum went down, then let it out in the faces of the boys behind him.

From the look on his face, that was just what he was about to do now.

Jacob watched, hands clenched in anxiety.

The scrum went down. Wainwright's fart was audible from the touchline – it was a goodie. Several boys sniggered, and the opposition's games master, who was running the line, pretended he hadn't heard.

Directly behind Wainwright, the Number 5 was straightening up out of the scrum, an expression of extreme disgust distorting his features. Into a moment of silence, rare on the playing field, he shouted, 'Sir, ugh, sir! Wainwright's crapped himself!'

Both packs were dispersing now, some holding their noses and making exaggerated retching noises. His head hanging in shame, Wainwright stood alone. The back of his white shorts was marked with a spreading brown stain.

By the time Jacob went to collect his bag, the story had spread throughout the school. Wainwright had a new nickname: Shitty Wainwright. It wasn't very original, but then the boys hadn't had very long to think about it. The boy who played at Number 5, who was even bigger than Wainwright, had punched him in the showers for ruining an afternoon's rugby, 'and if you ever fart in my face again, I'll kill you,' he'd said, according to enthralled listeners.

Jacob's joy at the success of his plot was tempered by a sneaking sympathy. Not only had Wainwright disgraced himself in front of all those people, he'd got his head punched into the bargain.

Back home, Jacob's mum asked him for his blazer, which she was going to sell at the school second-hand shop. Going through the pockets, she pulled out the packet of chocolate which Jacob had collected from the back of his desk.

'Whatever's this?' she exclaimed, holding it up. 'Laxative chocolate! Oh, darling, you shouldn't eat this, it'll – well, never mind. I expect you bought it by mistake. I'd better throw it away. I'll get you some ordinary Dairy Milk when I go shopping.'

Mum, that *is* ordinary Dairy Milk, he wanted to say. It's wrapped in the laxative chocolate wrapper because its proper wrapper was round the laxative chocolate.

The remains of which was probably even then working its way through Wainwright's lower bowel.

CHAPTER FIVE

Isobel stood in her bedroom wondering whether she would have any possible use for her Manolo Blahnik mules in her new existence. Of course she wouldn't.

She threw them in the large cardboard box in which she was putting aside good used clothes for the Oxfam shop. It was the second box; the first one was in the boot of the car on its way into town. Lawrence was going to make the most of the car this weekend, because it was to be collected on Monday morning. The day after tomorrow.

'Will someone come for it?' she'd asked. It seemed horribly final.

'I was meant to drive it back myself,' he'd answered cheerfully, 'only I said I wouldn't. Told them if they want it, they can come and get it. I've a good mind to leave it parked on a double yellow line, and hope it gets clamped *and* issued with a thumping great parking fine.'

She'd managed to dissuade him from that. She didn't want anything to happen that might draw attention to them – any more attention than would be attracted by the two removals vans due to pull up outside the house first thing on Monday morning.

Tomorrow she and Lawrence were going down to the country to complete the purchase of a third-hand VW van. It had three seats across the front, and, in the otherwise bare van section, one seat which was set sideways, its back to the side of the van. The rear compartment had a sliding door. Lawrence had raved about it, said it would be ideal for carrying all manner of things – he hadn't specified what – and assured her that VW engines were marvellous, they gave you thousands and thousands of miles of trouble-free motoring. Isobel wasn't at all sure that reliability and versatility were going to compensate for the whispering, leather-scented luxury of the BMW. But there was little point in saying so.

They were also going to look again at the cottage. They'd only had time for a brief glance so far. They'd signed the tenancy agreement and were meant to be moving in on Monday. The agent had said they could drop the signed agreement in at his office on their way to the cottage, together with their deposit.

Isobel wasn't convinced of the wisdom of having one more look at their future home. On the one hand it was sensible, because it wasn't too late to change their minds and say it wasn't suitable after all.

On the other hand, where else were they to go on Monday with two pantechnicons full of furniture? Wasn't it better to keep what few illusions she had managed to retain and *not* have this one final look?

Well, it was academic anyway, because they were going. Isobel's sister, Maude, had been bribed to come over to Cedar Holt and look after Jacob and Dory, and Lawrence was going to drive Isobel down to the village. He was being quite vindictive about the BMW; he intended to find lots of lanes coated with cow muck, horse muck, any old muck, and drive repeatedly backwards and forwards through the places where the shit lay deepest.

Isobel stood gazing at a row of strappy, elegant dresses, picking out a Nicole Farhi number that had knocked a considerable hole in her budget. Next to the dresses were skirts, jackets and a couple of suits; she liked Jaeger and Ralph Lauren for their lines. Everything was in the same style, the sort of minimalist look she'd always favoured, which showed her size 10 figure to the best advantage. She had quite strong shoulders, which were better dressed in tailored, very well-cut garments than in frills and lace. When she'd first met Lawrence she'd been an air steward-ess, smart in a navy suit and a neat bowler hat, her hair swept up in a chignon which it had taken her a whole weekend to get reliably perfect.

Lawrence, who'd been flying the Atlantic to attend a course at Barclay Dawson headquarters in Chicago, had chatted her up – successfully. Against her better judgement, she'd heard herself agree to meet him for dinner when they were both back in London. She said, 'Give me your number, I'll call you.'

'Why can't I call you?'

'Because . . .' Because I never give out my private number to passengers, would have been the honest answer. You never knew, it was better to play safe. But Lawrence had such a nice face, such earnestness in his brown eyes, that it had seemed unnecessarily unkind to act suspicious and reply with the brutal truth. 'Because I don't know when I'll be at home,' she said instead, 'and my flatmates aren't very good at saving messages.'

He seemed content with that. He gave her his business card, writing his home number on the back. During the Chicago stopover, she found she kept thinking about him. He stayed in Chicago for a week; by the time he was home, she was in Hong Kong.

She phoned him the evening she got back.

They went out to dinner, and she liked him as much as she thought she was going to. At twenty-two, she had sev-eral relationships behind her, and all had foundered on the rocks of her job, with what one former boyfriend had called its 'bloody inconvenient hours'. None of her previous men had been quite like Lawrence. None had *looked* like him, for a start; he had thick, unruly dark hair and round brown eyes, which combined to give him the youthful air of someone who hadn't long got out of the confines of the sixth form. But, as she very soon discovered, this was deceptive: he had a quick mind and a lively sense of humour, and he rarely acted without having first made a thorough assessment of the pros and cons. This was, she decided, probably as a result of his accountancy training. A girlfriend had jeered at her for going out with an accountant, resurrecting the tired old joke about accountants being boring; Isobel, remembering how, on their second date, Lawrence had hired a convertible Rolls and swept her off to Glyndebourne, to picnic on the grass and poke fun at the aggressively modern programme – they'd slipped away after an hour and found a cheery little pub in a nearby village – had merely smiled and said, 'Quite.'

They were married six months later; she gave up flying when she got pregnant with Dory. She didn't miss her job; sometimes she reflected that the only residual effects left by those years of flying were an intimate knowledge of most of the world's major airports and a predilection for navy suits.

She reached into the cupboard for her favourite black dress – Louis Féraud, deceptively simple, a perfect fit. No way am I not taking this, she thought, holding it fondly against her. But what about all the rest?

I'm taking them, she decided suddenly, every last item. I can always dispose of them later if I find I no longer wear them. I might even be able to sell some of them – I might be glad of the money, in a few months' time. The thought gave her a small cold feeling in the pit of her stomach. I'll work on my mother's law – she hurried away from the uneasy subject of money – under which you reassess the necessity of any item regularly, and chuck it out if it's been a year since you used it.

She fetched a suitcase from the attic, and carefully folded and packed her entire 'smart' wardrobe.

Then, not sure why she suddenly felt so miserable, she went downstairs to get lunch ready.

Maude arrived early the next morning; Isobel and Lawrence were still having breakfast, and the children hadn't yet surfaced.

'You look nice, darling,' Maude said, bending to give Isobel a kiss, then going round the table to do the same to Lawrence. She brought with her a pleasant waft of perfume. It was a new one, Lawrence didn't recognise it. 'I like the shirt. And the sweater – cashmere?'

'Yes.'

'The pigs and the peasants will appreciate it.' Maude sat down and helped herself to coffee. 'How are you, Piers?'

'Fine, thank you,' said Lawrence. Maude always called him Piers. When Isobel had first taken him home to meet the family, Maude had asked him if he was descended from the bloke who wrote *Piers Plowman*, and it had been ages before he'd actually looked up the reference. He'd never got round to reading the book; he didn't think an allegorical poem written in the late fourteenth century looked like his cup of tea. He wasn't sure it looked like anybody's cup of tea.

Maude was probably the exception. She had taken her degree at Girton, and gone on to do a PhD in some obscure study into the effect of Norse legend on Early English writing. Or something – he'd never really listened when she talked about her work. It amused him to watch Izzy nodding sagely, as if she followed every word.

As sisters, they didn't seem to have much in common. But, he had to admit, they'd never let it make any difference to their closeness. They supported each other, always had done, apparently. Sometimes he suspected they'd acquired the habit because they'd had to present a united front when facing their mother: Mollie Adair was a strong-minded woman.

Mollie had called her daughters after medieval English queens; possibly in the hope that they would live up to their regal forebears and become strong-minded too.

'So, you've got this place on the market?' Maude asked, mouth full of toast and marmalade.

'Yes,' Isobel said.

'Any interest?'

'Quite a lot, actually,' Lawrence said. 'Izzy's shown heaps of people round, and one couple came back for a second look. We haven't heard anything from them yet, although the chap had a tape measure.'

'Which you rightly assumed to be an indicator of serious interest.' Maude nodded, frowning in concentration. Lawrence reflected that she'd be high-powered stuff as a lecturer.

'We did,' he agreed. 'We're hoping they'll make an offer.'

'Good properties are rare just now,' Maude said knowledgeably. 'People with attractive, expensive houses like this one are having no trouble. It's the poor hapless ones who are up against it, those with middle-range houses and small flats in unsmart areas. Not to mention all those with negative equity.'

'Quite.' Lawrence felt obscurely guilty.

'It was all very well in the eighties,' Maude went on. 'Building societies practically made you take out big mortgages, and all those people on a roll took them up without imagining anything could ever go wrong. But of course it did, and now –'

'Maude, Lawrence and I have to be going,' Isobel interrupted. Lawrence was glad she had done: he wouldn't have dared stop Maude at full throttle. Isobel got up. 'The stuff for lunch is in the fridge. There's heaps of everything.

57

Basically, the kids'll help themselves to whatever they want.

'Good, they can feed me while they're at it,' Maude said equably. She didn't seem to resent Isobel interrupting her.

Lawrence got up too, jingling the car keys in his pocket. 'Come on, then, Izzy.'

'Cheerio, darling.' Maude kissed Isobel again. 'Bye, Piers.'

As they left the house, they heard her turn on the kitchen radio and retune it from Classic FM to Radio 3.

Lawrence wanted to have another look at the woodland, but Isobel said they ought to do the house first as it had priority.

'But it'll be too dark later for walking through the woods,' he protested. 'Whereas we can put the lights on in the house.'

'*Please*.' There was a note of desperation in her voice.

'Okay, okay!' he said hurriedly.

They parked on the village green, and walked up the path to the cottage. The 'To Let' sign had been taken down, which he thought showed a nice sense of faith on the agent's part, considering they hadn't actually delivered the signed contract yet. Not to mention paid the deposit. Isobel took the front door key out of her bag, unlocked the door and opened it. It caught on a flagstone. Lawrence put his shoulder to it and pushed gently. Then he pushed harder, and abruptly the door gave and he fell into the house.

'Won't you come in?' he said, turning to smile at her.

She looked apprehensive. 'It smells a bit damp.'

'It's because it's been standing empty. We'll open all the windows, let some fresh air blow through. That'll make all the difference.'

He led the way along the dark passage to a door at the end, which turned out to be the kitchen. It had an old stone sink. There was a white Rayburn against the interior wall.

The back door opened on to an overgrown garden, where there was a shabby-looking outhouse.

Retracing their steps, they went into the living room. This had a wide chimney in which sat a squat wood-burning stove. Beside the fireplace was a huge log basket, half full. The stove shared a chimney with the Rayburn.

'We should be nice and warm,' Lawrence said encouragingly. 'We'll get a load of wood, and whatever fuel the Rayburn takes. We'll get Jacob to be i/c wood supply, and –'

'I/c?'

'In charge of. We'll offer to give him a fiver a week if we never run out of wood in the basket.'

'Better make it seven pounds fifty.'

'Okay,' he laughed. 'I don't suppose it'll be any good offering Dory a similar deal.'

'Dory,' Isobel murmured. 'Oh, Dory.'

He knew what she meant. But it didn't seem the moment to start being anxious about Dory, and how she was going to settle. Or not settle, which seemed far more likely.

'Let's have a look upstairs,' he suggested. 'The stairs were by the front door – here.' He found a light switch, and clicked it down. Nothing happened. 'Well, I expect we can manage. I'll lead the way.'

He went up the narrow stairs and opened the first door he came to. The room was almost as dark as the hall; old tattered curtains were drawn across the window, which was overgrown with some sort of creeper. 'This is quite a decent-sized room,' he called out to Isobel. 'Just a bit dark, that's all. Let's try the others.'

All three bedrooms were dark, depressing and smelt predominantly of damp, mixed with fusty, sweaty old clothes and boiled cabbage. Lawrence tried drawing back the curtains in the main room – the material felt unpleasantly crusty to the touch – and the grudging daylight filtering through the ubiquitous creeper displayed a saggy double bed with a stained mattress. 'We'll get the agent to take that away,' he said. It was becoming quite difficult to go on sounding cheerful.

'Where's the bathroom?' Isobel said dully.

He went back onto the landing. 'Here?' He tried the last door. The bathroom, surprisingly, looked good: newish fittings, big bath, clean white paint, lovely view out over woodland and fields.

Isobel came to stand beside him. 'Well, at least we're finishing on a high,' she said.

He'd always loved her courage. 'Come on,' he said, taking her hand. 'It's okay, isn't it? I mean, we can make it okay. Let's go to the pub and have another of those Stilton ploughman's. Then I'll take you to the woods.'

She smiled faintly at his feeble joke. Then they went downstairs, locked the door and walked across to the pub.

Isobel wished she could have a large gin and tonic, but she would have to drive the car home while Lawrence took the van. She wondered how she would get through the rest of the day without an anaesthetic.

The house was horrible. *Horrible*, she repeated to herself as Lawrence queued at the bar to order the food. Smelly, damp, dirty, overgrown, fusty. It'll have to be cleaned thoroughly before we put any of our stuff in. And where are we going to *put* everything? I hadn't realised how small it is – we'll have to leave some of our things in store, or even sell them. God only knows what I shall do if it's wet tomorrow – *tomorrow*! Dear Christ, we're moving tomorrow! – and all the walls, floors and insides of cupboards I wash stay wet.

Oh God, I don't want to go. Don't want this to happen.

The sun came out, sending a cheery ray of brilliance across the bar. Someone said, 'Nice to see a bit of sun.' Someone else laughed. Isobel turned to look out of the window. The cottage in the sunlight looked different; almost attractive.

Lawrence came back with their beers. 'Get your laughing gear round that,' he said. 'Food won't be long. I was telling the landlord we're moving into the cottage tomorrow, and he says he'll ask the woman who cleans for him to come over and give us a hand. We'll have to pay her, of course.'

'That was kind,' she said. It was heartening to know that people here *did* clean, that they didn't all live like the last occupant of the cottage.

'He says it'll be good to have people living there again,' Lawrence went on. 'He says to drop in tomorrow evening, when he's quiet, and he'll tell us a few things, like what time the buses run, where to get the best bread, that sort of stuff.'

'Oh. That'll be useful.'

'Friendly bunch, aren't they?' He waved his pint towards the assembled crowd at the bar. There was a pleasant hub-bub of conversation.

'They seem so,' she agreed cautiously.

'We'll soon settle in.' He had taken hold of her hand not holding the glass, and was squeezing it. 'You'll see. I know it won't be easy, but we've done it now. The die is cast.'

'Please don't talk about dying,' she said, only half in fun.

'I wasn't! It's die, the singular of dice, not die as in dying.'

'Is it?'

'Mm. Maude told me.'

'Oh.'

He wished he hadn't said it, even if it wasn't that sort of die. It had made Isobel look sad.

After lunch they went to the woods. Lawrence got a pair of wellingtons out of the back of the car; they were still in their plastic bag.

'I bought you a pressie,' he said, taking them round to

61

Isobel in the front passenger seat. 'Look! Size five's right, isn't it?'

'Spot on.' She unlaced her smart brown shoes and slipped her feet into the boots. 'But you might have got me green ones.' She grinned up at him, and he realised she was joking. 'I'll have to buy a Barbour to go with them.'

'And a headscarf with horseshoes on it,' he said. He was glad she was happy again. She seemed to be, anyway. He wasn't sure he was brave enough to look at her apparent cheerfulness in any depth. It still seemed a minor miracle that she'd agreed to the move, and, in the rare moments when he took a break from the thrill and excitement of his own plans to look at how country life was going to be for her, he could scarcely believe she *had* agreed.

He had a nasty feeling he was being cowardly. That, given an opening, she would break down, remind him of all the things they were giving up.

Forgoing suburban life was fine by him. He had already gone over everything, and he knew, as well as anyone could know, that what they were doing was right for him. But would the same apply to Izzy?

All things considered, it was, he resolved, better not to go into that. Having her *seem* happy was going to have to do.

He locked the car and they set off up the track. It was good, he reflected, that, this time, armed with all he had recently been learning from all the bumph, he knew far more about woodlands than he had done the last time they were there. Knew, for instance, that large sections of the chestnut were ripe for coppicing, and how much, roughly, he could reckon on getting for his crop. He explained to Isobel that the alder growing on the lower ground, down towards the stream, was useless for anything except pulping, but that he could make a bit by selling it for that purpose. The birch trees growing among the chestnuts, though, were weeds in this context; birch was an opportunist tree, an early coloniser of cleared spaces.

Isobel nodded.

Lawrence went on to explain that the cut bases left behind when the chestnut had gone were called stools, and that the chestnut was planted in areas known as cants, which were equal in number to the coppice rotation period, which was from five to twenty years.

He got out his notebook and pencil, his mind now in working mode, and began to make notes.

Isobel wandered away. She followed the track up to the top of the rise, then turned right and went down a narrower path towards the stream.

It was very quiet in the woods. There was no wind, and now and then shafts of late sun illuminated the bare trees. The stream running swiftly in its bed was the only noise.

She walked on down to the water. The stream bed lay in the middle of a flat area, with the woodlands rising on either side. It would have been pretty in spring, with wild flowers growing. Now it looked dead. Sad.

She could hear Lawrence up among the chestnuts, his progress marked by the cracking of twigs. He's happy, she thought. He's going to make something of this. Make a life for himself. For all of us.

This is where we're going to live. That cottage will be our home, at least for the time being. My executive, BMW-driving husband is going to turn into a woodsman, my children will leave their private schools and be thrown into the state system, because, even if there were suitable private schools with places for them, Lawrence and I could no longer afford the fees.

And me. What am I going to do?

The reality of the future was hitting her. Hard. Like a blow to the stomach, making her feel sick and breathless.

I'm a townie! Restaurants, shops, theatres, other people's smart houses, shopping trips and gossipy wine-bar lunches with Maude, that's my world. That's where I belong! Not in a rented cottage with a saggy bed and a stained mattress! I wear high fashion, not a waxed jacket and wellies.

I should *never* have agreed to this absurd move. I should have persuaded Lawrence that once a financial manager, always a financial manager, made him find another job in another Barclay Dawson Products. We could have kept our lovely house, our comfortable life.

I let a misjudgement cloud my common sense. I got myself into a situation that made me feel ashamed, humiliated. More importantly, that threatened my marriage. And I got my fingers burnt. Badly. I'm terrified of it becoming – already *being* – common knowledge, and the prospect of people knowing – God, I feel sick even at the thought of telling Maude! – makes me want to run away and hide.

She stared around her at the still, bare woods.

But do I really want to hide *here*?

So I made a fool of myself, so they're all gossiping about me, pointing the finger! So what? It'll be someone else's turn in a while, the spotlight will soon have moved on from me.

But it's too late to go back. Cedar Holt is on the market, we're probably about to get an offer. The children's schools have been notified, and they're enrolled down here. State education, from now on, for both of them.

I can't undo all that just because I think I've changed my mind.

Can I?

From above, she could hear Lawrence singing.

Can I go up to him, right this instant, and say, 'Lawrence, I'm sorry but I don't think this is really me after all'? When, since the first moment he mentioned this idiotic plan, I've given every appearance of going along with it?

No. I can't.

I can't talk to him any more, not about deep-down things.

Her feet felt very cold. Looking down, she saw she was up to the ankles in icy water.

Silently, she started to cry.

PART TWO

Winter

CHAPTER SIX

Lawrence backed the van off the hardstanding in front of the cottage and made his way jerkily down the road that led across the green. The van was cold, with attractive swirly patterns of frost across its snub-nosed front. He knew there was no point in putting the heater on, since the engine would scarcely be any warmer by the time he reached the woods, but he did it anyway. It was a gesture.

He had bought himself khaki woollen fingerless gloves, which went some way to keeping the circulation going in his hands. It was, he reflected, a shame that his first forays into being a woodsman should coincide with the bitterest November in years.

Not that he was really being a woodsman yet. He hadn't done much except walk around his land looking at things, familiarising himself with his acres, trying to reconcile the things he was reading about in his huge stack of papers and books with what he was actually looking at on the ground.

It wasn't easy. In fact it was dauntingly difficult. He'd done his homework, learned the theory and could make the figures add up, but now he had to turn to the practical, cultivate these trees. He'd never grown anything in his life before. Now he was here, he realised just how essential the course at the agricultural college was going to be. Otherwise, it was likely that, out of sheer ignorance, he would do some stupid thing that would cost him a small fortune

69

to put right. He had already spent quite enough of a small fortune on buying Oxleat Woods; there wasn't enough left in the kitty for remedying silly mistakes. Not on a large scale, anyway.

He spent many waking hours mentally going over and over the finances. Everything added up, and he knew it did, but the reality of what he had done had a nasty habit of sneaking up and clobbering him over the head when he wasn't expecting it. Barclay Dawson's redundancy cheque, added to what they'd got for Cedar Holt, amounted to a pleasingly large sum; they'd paid off the mortgage on the house two years ago, when a policy he'd taken out for Izzy with the money her father left her had matured, so the full amount was theirs.

They had paid £40,000 for Oxleat Woods, and he was keeping twenty thousand in an instant access savings account for the things he was going to have to buy: second-hand tractor, trailer, that sort of thing. He felt a surge of excitement every time he thought about buying a tractor. Until such time as they found a house to buy – and nothing seemed to be coming on to the market at present – the remainder of their capital could be invested to provide them with a reasonable income – nothing like what they were used to, of course, but it should be enough. If they were careful. And, soon, he'd be making money on the woodlands.

He didn't allow any doubt about that to enter his mind. Any doubt *whatsoever*.

He parked the van and went to lean on the gate, staring in at the trees. The air was very cold, but there wasn't a breath of wind; the bare branches were quite still. He climbed the stile and went a few yards up the track. On either side the chestnut stools flung out their shoots of straight, clean wood. Is it ready for cutting? he wondered. It looks ready. He felt the gulf between the theory and the practice. It was so important to get everything right.

He had the sudden feeling someone was watching him. Turning round, he saw a short, square-built man leaning on the gate. He was dark, dressed in a faded bib and brace and a donkey jacket.

'Good morning,' Lawrence called.

'Morning.' Then: 'You've bought the woods.'

'Yes,' Lawrence acknowledged.

'Aah.'

The man went on leaning on the gate. Lawrence went back down the track to join him.

'You going to work it?'

'Yes, I thought I would.' Lawrence tried to sound cool and confident. 'There's some good wood in there.' He hoped he was right.

'Aah,' the man said again. 'Ready for cutting, that over there.' He pointed a hand holding the vestiges of a thin roll-up cigarette in the direction of the wood to the left of the track.

'Yes, that's what –' That's what I thought, Lawrence had been about to say. But it might have betrayed his uncertainty. 'That's what I'm planning right now.'

The man grinned. 'Going to carry it out in your van?'

'Of course not! I'm going to get a tractor and trailer.'

'Aah. Up the auction?'

'Yes.' Auction? He'd have to find out when and where it was.

'Best get your tractor in there while the ground's good and hard,' the man said, confirming the accuracy of Lawrence's assumption. 'Be a bugger trailering once it gets sodden.'

'Mm,' Lawrence agreed sagely.

There was a contemplative silence while they both went on leaning on the gate and staring up into the trees. Then Lawrence said, 'I don't suppose, Mr –'

'Badger.'

'– Mr Badger, that –'

The man chuckled. 'Not Mr. It ain't my surname.'

'Oh. Well, er, Badger –' surely it's not his Christian name, Lawrence thought, it must be a nickname – 'I was wondering if you're – well, if you're looking for work?'

'I might be and I might not be.'

His answer seemed to leave room for manoeuvre. 'The fact is, I'm new to this sort of thing,' Lawrence said in a burst of confidence. 'Woodland management, I mean.' He glanced at Badger, who was still gazing impassively up along the track. 'Well, actually I'm new to everything in the country. My only experience of growing things is cutting my lawn, ha, ha.' A fleeting smile crossed Badger's deeply tanned face. 'I was just wondering if you'd care to give me a hand. I mean, work for me. That is, *if* in fact you happened to be looking for work.'

Badger was silent for so long that Lawrence wondered if he'd actually heard. Have I offended him? he thought wildly. God, perhaps it's the worst sort of insult down here, to assume anyone who stops to pass the time of day must automatically be out of work and hoping you're going to take pity on them and offer them a job, and even now he's working out how best to retaliate, whether to use his rather large fist or cut me down to size with some devastating remark, and –

Badger said calmly, 'I might just do that.' Then, turning away, he said, 'Morning' again, and strolled off up the road in the direction of the village.

Lawrence watched as the stout figure rounded the bend and disappeared from view. Then he got out his notebook and hurried once more up the track. Feeling elated suddenly, he thought what fun it'd be to go home at lunchtime and tell Isobel he was going to an auction to buy a tractor.

*   *   *

Isobel sat by the Rayburn, reluctant to leave the kitchen and go upstairs to make the beds. The kitchen was a haven of warmth, the only comfortable spot in the house until Lawrence lit the stove in the living room, and he didn't usually do that till evening. 'It'll be fine once I'm bringing wood home,' he'd said when she complained about not being able to use the living room all day. 'There's masses of dead stuff lying all over the wood floor. We'll have so many logs we'll be able to keep both stoves going all the time. But while we've got to buy coal to supplement, let's economise, shall we?'

It made good sense, and actually she rather liked the kitchen. It was just that it seemed a bit poverty-stricken to huddle there all day; it made her feel like a downtrodden scullery maid, or some long-suffering woman in a nine-teenth-century novel.

'I'm neither downtrodden nor long-suffering,' she said aloud. 'I shall finish my tea, then brave the Siberia of upstairs and just hope there's not too much tidying up to do.'

The children's rooms, predictably, dashed her hopes. She made their beds, collected what was obviously dirty washing from each floor, drew back Dory's curtains – Jacob slept with his open because he was teaching himself about stars from a book from the school library – then went to do the bathroom. Lawrence had been last in; she noticed with gratitude that he'd left it reasonable.

She went downstairs again, and through the kitchen to the little scullery where they'd plumbed in the washing machine. The machine was almost new, a state-of-the-art job that pinged when you pressed in the buttons, pinged again to tell you when it was finished, and helpfully indi-cated what it was doing at any given moment on a digital display. She'd been in awe of it for the first couple of weeks, but now treated it like a friend and confidant. It spun clothes so fast that anything other than cotton came out almost

73

dry, which was just as well as they hadn't managed to squeeze in the tumble dryer. The only place it could have gone was Dory's bedroom – she had bagged the bigger of the two bedrooms that weren't the master one, on the grounds that she was suffering more than Jacob from this move to the blasted country – and she had put her foot down.

'I am not having a tumble dryer in my bedroom,' she'd said. 'I totally refuse to have Jacob's dirty underwear flopping around in my own personal space.'

Isobel had forborne to point out that it would be Dory's underwear too, and anyway it wouldn't be dirty as it would just have been through the wash. It was useless to argue with Dory at any time, but especially when she was banging on about her own personal space.

Anyway, Isobel had reasoned, we don't need a tumble dryer, we've got a Rayburn. They'd found a drying rack in the outhouse. The rack's frame was made of four long struts held together by metal supports that held the struts in a curve; it had ropes attached, and a simple pulley. She and Lawrence had giggled over it, suggesting various unlikely uses; Lawrence said it was a sledge for people with very thin bottoms. Then they'd noticed the hooks in the ceiling either side of the kitchen stove; when they held up the rack, a procedure which, according to Lawrence, was called 'offering up', it had fitted perfectly. The ropes and the pulley enabled you to lower it to load it with drying washing, then raise it again so that the clothes hung above the heat. Lawrence remarked that they'd have to be careful not to air clothes when anything smelly was being cooked, and Jacob had chimed in that there was a boy in his class called Toffee who smelt of curry, did they think his clothes were aired over the cooker?

Isobel had said yes, probably. Dory had sniffed in a superior manner and said *nobody* was called Toffee.

Dory, Isobel thought, putting her feet up on the Rayburn's fender and wiggling her toes in the warmth. Poor Dory, displaced and miserable. She had an idea Dory was suffering at her new school; they'd got her into the grammar school in the town, which Dory thought was frightfully infra dig. She'd said 'infer' for 'infra', which Isobel found touching; funny, she reflected, how you can feel furious with your child for being so impossible, yet have your heart ache for them at the same time. Anyway – she made herself move on from the dangerous ground of feeling sorry for Dory – it was partly Dory's own fault: she wasn't even *trying* to fit in.

Since the move, Dory had altered the way she spoke, so that now she sounded like a cross between the Princess of Wales and Celia Johnson. She had also started speaking very deliberately, drawing out some of her 'a' sounds; Isobel had to admit, it sounded dreadful. If, as seemed likely, Dory was making a point, telling all those grammar school girls that *she* wasn't one of them, she was a natural private school student who had happened to have been sent to their school through no fault of her own, then it was scarcely the way to make friends and start enjoying herself.

'Oh, Dory,' Isobel whispered, 'give them a chance. Give this a chance, this new life. You've got to, because we can't go back to the old one.'

They had sold the Ewell house to the couple with the tape measure, who had made an offer a few days after their second visit. The offer was a few thousands below the asking price; Lawrence said it wasn't acceptable in view of how short a time the house had been on the market, whereupon the tape measure couple had said they'd pay the asking price, on condition the Langlands completed as soon as possible.

'Damn, we should have asked more!' Lawrence said, banging down the phone.

'If we had, we might not have sold it,' she had replied, amazed at her own coolness.

They'll be living in our house now, she reflected, Mr and Mrs Tape Measure. Watkins, their name was. They'll be busy putting up curtains and gloss-painting, stamping their new territory. Cedar Holt is theirs, now. There really is no going back.

Do I want to?

She frowned. Her instant reaction was no, but she didn't entirely trust it. I'm going to reserve judgement, she decided. Some things are turning out well – Jacob's over the moon, I've never seen him so happy, and the cottage is proving not to be as bad as it looked – which admittedly would have been difficult. But it's watertight, now that Lawrence has fixed the loose slates, and these old stoves do chuck out some heat. Lawrence is enjoying himself, or he will be when he stops looking anxious. He has, on his own admission, a lot to learn. But he'll get there.

She thought about Lawrence being happy. If someone had asked me six months ago if it would make *me* happy to see him so chirpy, she reflected, I'd have said I didn't give a damn either way, and anyway how would I know as I so rarely saw him?

What a life it was. What a stupid way for us to live – for *anyone* to live. You marry because you love each other, then you buy a great big house and have a couple of children, saddle yourself with expenses and responsibilities so that one of you has to work all the hours God sends to earn enough to cope. Then the prime purpose of having got married – because you loved each other and wanted to be together – is no longer fulfilled. So you each develop your own interests, and before you can say Jack Robinson, you no longer have anything in common. So you fall out of love, get divorced, and chuck away something that was once very precious.

76

She sat staring at the friendly white shape of the Rayburn, squatting solidly in the chimney.

Has that happened to Lawrence and me? Has this move come too late?

She didn't know. Suddenly she remembered how they'd laughed over the clothes rack.

How long is it since we had that sort of fun together? Years. Maybe there is still a chance. Impatient suddenly, she got up, stretching, thinking: anyway, if there is, we stand a better chance of capitalising on it down here than we did in Ewell. There, I would have –

Deliberately she arrested the thought. It was too soon: the wound was still too raw for her to think about what she might have done.

She fetched a basket of dry laundry from the scullery and plugged in the iron. I must get someone to look at the wiring in here, she thought. I'll ask around.

The villagers had been welcoming; the man in the pub, whose name was Pete, had provided a lot of help over small matters such as who to phone to get coal delivered, and the theory behind septic tank drainage. Isobel had seen a card in the post office offering cleaning services; she'd phoned the number, and a woman called Judith Hearst had answered, and agreed to come and help Isobel get the cottage straight. Isobel had thought the rate she charged very cheap compared to the agency-employed cleaner she'd had at Cedar Holt, but then presumably Isobel would be paying cash, which would no doubt go straight in Judith Hearst's pocket. That, Isobel decided, was Mrs Hearst's business; probably it was the way it was done in the country.

Judith Hearst was due that morning. Glancing up at the clock – their electric wall clock was very modern and looked incongruous on a cottage wall – Isobel saw it was ten. Punctual to the minute, Mrs Hearst knocked on the door.

'Come in,' Isobel said, opening the back door.

77

Mrs Hearst came quickly inside and shut the door behind her. 'Don't want that lot coming in with me,' she remarked, nodding behind her.

'What – oh, the cold!' Isobel had thought at first that Mrs Hearst had a collection of animals with her, pushing to get into the house. On second thoughts, though, she didn't look like a woman who would be accompanied by sundry undisciplined pets. On the contrary: she looked neat and efficient, in a worn but clean skirt and jersey, both of which were loose enough to work in comfortably. She stood eyeing the kitchen, as if sizing up the job. She seemed, to Isobel, more remote than the chatty Mrs Herbert who had cleaned for her in Ewell.

'Cup of coffee before we start?' Isobel offered.

'Tea'd be nice. Milk, no sugar.'

'Sit down, do.' Isobel took a pile of Dory's garments off the chair. 'I'm just doing the ironing.' Why on earth did I say that? It's pretty obvious. 'Do you have children, Mrs Hearst?'

'One son, Sam. And my name's Judith.'

'Oh, right. I'm Isobel.' They exchanged a slightly uneasy smile. 'And how old is Sam?' Hell, I sound as if I'm interviewing her.

'Fifteen. Sixteen in a couple of months.'

'And he's at school locally?'

'The boys' grammar.'

'Ah.' She felt she should volunteer some information in exchange. 'My daughter's at the girls' grammar. Her name's Isadora – it's pretty dreadful, but it seemed a nice idea at the time, and my mother was keen. And actually we call her Dory. She's fourteen.'

Mrs Hearst – Judith – was nodding. 'I've heard tell of your Dory.'

It was an ambiguous comment. 'Oh. Oh, and there's my son, Jacob – he's eight, and he's at Banner Primary.'

78

'Good school, Banner Primary.' Isobel was glad Mrs Hearst approved of something. 'Sam went there. They did right by him.'

'Mm.'

There was a silence as Judith stirred her tea, then drank it. Finishing, she got up, put the mug in the sink and rinsed it, then said, 'What do you want me to do?'

Although it was only fleeting, Isobel got the distinct impression that Judith resented having to ask that. Resented having to be there at all, cleaning for someone else. But then a fairly stiff smile spread over the lower part of her face, and Isobel decided she had imagined it.

'I thought today we'd make a start upstairs,' she said. 'I've been doing day-to-day stuff, and I went through the bedrooms as well as I could when we got here, but there wasn't time to do a proper job before we had to move the furniture in. I thought we could clear the bedrooms in turn, then start from scratch.'

'Got any carpet shampoo?'

'Yes. Actually I've got a machine thingy.' Isobel fetched it from the scullery. 'It's pretty good.' Judith was eyeing it as if she considered no such high-tech device could possibly replace the good old-fashioned method of hanging your carpets over the fence and banging them with a beater till they cried for mercy. She's probably a closet Luddite, Isobel thought. She smothered a grin and saved that up to tell Lawrence.

Judith took a firm grip on the shampooer's handle. 'You come and help me shift furniture,' she said, 'and I'll get started.'

'Oh. Right, okay.' Isobel led the way up the stairs. 'In here first – this is Jacob's room. It'll take less clearing than Dory's.'

'You could be getting on with that,' Judith pointed out. 'Then it'll be ready when I've finished in here.'

Isobel, who had conjured up a picture of the two of them working side by side, cosily discussing a wide range of interesting topics, realised her picture had been seen through rose-coloured spectacles; Judith Hearst, clearly, was a woman not given to cosiness and, moreover, one who liked to work on her own.

'Right,' she said again. She backed towards the door. 'I'll be across the landing if you want my help.'

'I'll remember that,' Judith said drily.

As Isobel faced up to the challenge of Dory's bedroom, she reflected that there was about as much chance of Judith Hearst seeking her help as there was of Dory's scattered possessions flying Mary Poppins-like back to their rightful places. With a faint sigh, she pushed up her sleeves and began.

CHAPTER SEVEN

The short winter days closed in early; Isobel, listening out for sounds of her returning family, would draw the curtains, stoke the Rayburn and prepare herself for the various joys and troubles that invariably came home with them. She had done the equivalent at Cedar Holt – although there, since Lawrence came home so much later, she would have been more likely to pour him a stiff gin than to make him a cup of tea. But somehow then it had been different; she had never felt as involved as she did now.

Dismissing any more profound explanations – she was wary of discovering aspects of the new life to be surprisingly good, in case later this proved not to be the case and she was left with the inevitable disappointment – she put her increased involvement down to the fact that the house was so small that there was nowhere to hide.

Lawrence had engaged some chap called Badger to show him the ropes. The first thing Badger had done was to take Lawrence off to an auction of farm machinery and encourage him to buy a tractor and a trailer. Then he'd told him he could get grants from the government towards the cost of planting trees, whereupon Lawrence had got into a right stew in case he missed something he should be claiming. He'd gone off to see some chap in the NFU office – he was now a fully paid-up member of the National Farmers' Union, and had a car sticker on the van to prove it – and then had spent hours on the phone to the Ministry of Agriculture, Fisheries and Food, resulting in the arrival of another stack of pamphlets, explanatory leaflets and forms. He'd made a desk out of the old playroom table, using Jacob's Playskool boot house as a pending tray. The desk was in the corner of the living room; the reduction in available space was compensated for, on days when he was working at home, by Lawrence having the stove going all day.

It felt strange, having him at home. Isobel was seeing much more of him than she had done for years, more, perhaps, than she had ever done. She found she quite liked it.

He was still in a fever of anxiety over his claims and his grants. Isobel, all too aware that business in government offices was likely to grind to a halt till the New Year, was wondering how she'd cope with his tension over Christmas.

Dory was acting as if the prospect of the end of term was the only thing keeping her going. She was claiming to be off her food, although Isobel could detect little sign of it. But unfortunately Dory – like far too many children of the nineties, Isobel reflected – knew every last detail about both anorexia nervosa and bulimia, even down to the conditions likely to spark either – or both – off, and the best way to deal with sufferers.

'Rejection of food is a way of claiming control of your life,' she said grandly over supper one night. 'You won't let me control one single rotten aspect of my life, so I'm resorting to the one thing I have left.' She shot a vicious glance at her mother. 'You can't *make* me eat!'

She made it sound like a challenge. Isobel, cross at seeing a plateful of lovingly prepared shepherd's pie with broccoli and carrots pushed aside as if it were a dead rat, was about to make a crushing reply. But Lawrence, whom she'd supposed to be too immersed in his forms and his brochures to have noticed the exchange, spoke first.

'Eat what you want, Dory, and leave the rest,' he said calmly.

She said peevishly, 'I don't want *any* of it. I *hate* shepherd's pie, it's poor people's food!'

'No it isn't, not with lamb the price it is.' Lawrence was quite unflustered. 'Give me your plate, I'll have it.'

He reached for Dory's plate, but she grabbed it and held on tight. 'I'll try and eat a bit,' she muttered.

He looked disappointed. 'Must you?'

There was the very faint suggestion of a smile on Dory's face. Then, bending her head so her hair fell concealingly forward, she ate her supper.

Isobel thought how different life might have been had Lawrence been home for meals when Dory was in the formative years of her infancy.

Jacob, too, was tense, but for a different reason: he was to be Joseph in the Banner Primary School nativity play.

Isobel wondered if he'd been given an important role to help him feel welcome in his new school. If so, it was a kind gesture on his teacher's behalf. She was the sort of woman of whom you'd expect kind gestures; she was about fifty-five, calm, grey-haired, large in a motherly way, and her name was Mrs Lovatt. When Isobel had gone to see about getting Jacob admitted to the school, Mrs Lovatt had had as beneficial an effect on Isobel's jangled nerves as a long soak in a bath scented with jasmine essence.

'How has he been doing at school?' Mrs Lovatt had asked.

'Fine, academically.' Isobel proffered Jacob's latest report.

'And socially?'

It's not a moment for dissimulation, Isobel thought. 'He's hated it.'

'Ah. I think you'll find he won't hate it here.'

He hadn't. Being Joseph was the cherry on the cake. Jacob was also in the football team – well, almost: he was substitute at the moment and had played one game, when the left back had unexpectedly gone home with a tummy upset – and he'd got an A for his mini-project on What Birds Do in Winter.

His role in the nativity play necessitated the learning of quite a lot of lines. During the precious forty-five minutes between Jacob's return from school and Dory's, Isobel sat in the warm kitchen with him, cups of tea and a plate of biscuits before them on the table, while Jacob went through his stuff.

'Don't worry, Mary, there's one more inn at the end of the street,' he said earnestly, face screwed up with the effort of concentration. 'I'm sure we'll be lucky, this time.'

He got up from his chair, strode determinedly across the kitchen and rapped smartly on an imaginary door. Isobel, looking down at his copy of the play, saw that the next person to speak was the innkeeper. 'Shall I do the next bit?' she whispered. Jacob, his attention still fixed on the inn door, nodded.

'Who's there?' she demanded. 'Who's that, knocking loud enough to wake the dead and disturbing my sleep?'

Jacob giggled. 'You're much better than Toby Wilson,' he said.

'Thank you,' she replied. Then, assuming the voice of an angry innkeeper, 'What do you want?'

'My wife and I are in dire need of a night's lodging,' Jacob said. Isobel wondered in passing if speaking grammatically correct prose for the nativity play would get Jacob and the other children out of bad habits such as, 'Me and Billy are going to his house for tea.'

'Mum!' Jacob hissed.

'Oh – sorry.' She consulted the script. 'No chance!' she said firmly – the innkeeper was obviously *au fait* with late-twentieth-century idiom. 'We're full to bursting. It's this census, you see.'

'We only need a little room,' Jacob said winningly. 'A corner somewhere would do. You see –' he dropped his voice confidingly – 'my wife, Mary, is about to have a baby.'

She tried to obey the stage direction: *Innkeeper scratches head and looks thoughtful.* 'There's my stable,' she said. 'I'm afraid there's no bed, but it's warm and dry, and the straw is clean.'

Jacob's face lit up with joy. 'Thank you,' he said, beaming, 'you're a very kind man.'

He went on staring at her, still smiling, and, responding, she smiled back. Then, through clenched teeth, he said, 'I can't remember what happens next.'

'Oh – just a minute.' She'd been too carried away with the drama to turn the page. '*The innkeeper leads the way to the stable, and Joseph follows, leading Mary on the donkey.* How are you doing the donkey?'

'Michael Frazer bends down and holds on to Billy Morris's waist, and Katie Shaw – she's Mary – sits on him.'

'I see.' It sounded fraught with potential mishaps. She glanced back at the script. 'There's a carol here – "Away in a Manger" – then the next scene is Mary holding the baby and you ushering in shepherds and kings.'

'I know that bit,' he said confidently. 'We went through it heaps of times at school because there's such a lot of kings and shepherds and they all have to stand in the right place.'

'Only three kings, surely?'

'Of *course*, but they all have an attendant to carry the gift and someone to hold their train, and they have to stand in front of the shepherds and the angels and the oxes and the asses.'

'Oxen,' she corrected automatically. She had forgotten the overriding rule of primary school productions: that you had to have as many walk-on parts as there were children in the class.

There was the sound of clumping footsteps up the path, and the back door opened as if yielding to a battering ram.

'Dory's home,' Jacob said unnecessarily. He gathered up his script.

'Shall we go through it again tomorrow?' Isobel suggested.

'Yes, please. I need to do the bit where I thank them all for coming and we sing "O Come all ye Faithful".'

Dory burst into the kitchen. 'I've got chemistry homework and Mrs Nugent gave me a D for my history test, I *hate* her and I'm not doing the retest!'

Taking a deep breath, Isobel said, 'Oh dear. Come and sit by the Rayburn and I'll make you a cup of tea.'

Christmas was fast approaching. Isobel was becoming unpleasantly aware that for the family to spend the days of the holiday cooped up within four constricting walls wasn't going to be much fun; inevitably there would be comparisons with Christmases Past. Dory was bound to mourn the parties she used to go to; they hadn't been much, just a handful of giggling girls having a sort of movable feast, at one parental home one evening, somewhere else the next, with duplicate cans of Coke, crisps and little sandwiches, the same terrible music, wherever they were. But, this year, the parties would go on without her.

Isobel had noticed, her heart sore with compassion, Dory's reaction to the Christmas cards that had arrived for her from her Ewell friends, eagerly opening them as if hoping – praying – that one or two might include invitations. They hadn't. It seemed to be a case of out of sight, out of mind; probably even the cards would stop next year.

Would Lawrence miss the drinks cupboard groaning

with alcohol? It had been his contribution to Christmas shopping to back the BMW up to the door of the off-licence and fill the boot with anything that caught his eye. One year she'd found herself drinking a glass of tequila and vermouth as she tried to focus on the Queen's speech.

He wouldn't be doing that this year.

Jacob won't brood, she thought. As long as he can sit down in front of a television, he'll be happy.

What about me?

Round about now I'd be in the midst of *my* shopping, and I wouldn't be going to the off-licence. Maude and I would meet up in Kingston, each with our list, and steadily work our way through till either our feet gave out or the credit cards melted under the friction of repeatedly being slid through the reader. And, when we'd finished with the presents, I'd make sure there was time to find the perfect little number for the Christmas Eve party with the friends and neighbours.

Dreamily, she conjured up a few male faces that she might have kissed under the mistletoe.

Abruptly she stopped.

No! Dangerous territory. Keep out.

Christmas, this year, was going to be in a piddling little cottage in a country village, and they were all just going to have to make the best of it.

Isobel was brooding over what to do to improve matters while she waited for Judith Hearst to present herself for work the next morning. It was so hampering, not to be able to solve the problem by lavish spending; she and Lawrence had gone through his income and expenditure book together, and agreed to a ceiling of thirty pounds for each of the children. They could only run to that because they were giving each other just a token present.

She thought she'd buy him a pair of thick socks. She

wondered what he would get her. She didn't hold out much hope of it being something she'd be truly delighted about, since she was incapable of thinking of anything costing under a fiver that she could conceivably want. Still, she reassured herself, it's not as if we're really short of money, it's just that Lawrence says we have to be a bit careful till he's made certain of an income.

For a dangerous moment the risks involved in what they were doing – what they'd already done – threatened to throw her into a panic. 'Don't panic, Captain Mainwaring,' she muttered under her breath.

It'd be okay. It'd *have* to be.

Judith let herself in, calling out, 'Morning.'

'In here,' Isobel called back. 'Tea's on the table.'

'I won't say no,' Judith said, coming in and unbuttoning her coat. 'Bitter out there. We've got a burst pipe in the loft.'

'Oh, no! Is there much damage?'

Judith shrugged. 'Hard to tell what's leaking pipe and what's damp seeping down the walls.'

'But –' Isobel had been going to say, but you shouldn't have to live like that! However, since nobody would *choose* to have water running down the walls, then clearly it wasn't from choice. She was beginning to understand what it was like to have to do without the comforting knowledge that, whatever the domestic problem, there was some trained specialist available, at a price, to come and put it right for you. And – remembering the pride she'd detected in Judith – maybe it wasn't something she wanted to talk about. 'Can you get it mended? Do you want to go back home and wait for a plumber, or something?'

Judith snorted. It could have been laughter, or it could have been scorn. 'Can't get a plumber. They can charge their own prices just now. No, Mike's fixing it.'

'Oh.' There didn't seem anything else to say.

They sat in silence, drinking their tea. Obscurely, Isobel felt guilty, as if Judith's revelation about the pipe had somehow put her at an unfair disadvantage. Wanting to make a corresponding revelation of her own, she said, 'My daughter's an awful worry at the moment. She hates the new school.'

Judith nodded. 'So I gather.'

Isobel's head shot up. 'You do? Why? How, I mean?'

Judith met her eyes. 'She was mouthing off at the bus stop. Telling some of her classmates how much better they did things in her old school.'

'Oh, hell.' It would have been nice to say, she's not normally as bad as that, only it would have been a barefaced lie. 'How do you know?'

'Sam told me.' There was a quirk of a smile on Judith's face. 'He said he quite admired her for standing her ground when the other girls were having a go at her.'

Having a go at her. Oh, poor Dory.

Judith was still looking at her. Apparently reading what was in her mind, she said, 'I wouldn't worry. Sam says he'd back your Dory against all comers.'

'He said that?'

Judith nodded. Suddenly things didn't seem quite so bad; Isobel felt herself start to smile.

'Better get to work.' Judith got up, returning the smile. Reaching in her carrier bag, she extracted her apron and tied it round her waist. 'You can't get those wraparound jobs nowadays,' she observed, 'the ones that covered your top half as well.'

'Was that what they called Mother Hubbards?' Isobel wondered aloud. 'There was a picture of Mother Hubbard in my nursery rhyme book wearing something like that.'

'Mother Hubbards? I never heard them called anything but aprons.'

'The missionaries used to issue them to South Sea

Islanders to cover up their naughty bits. Somerset Maugham mentions it.'

Judith stood looking down at her, humour in her eyes. 'Somerset Maugham, eh?'

'Yes. I've got his short stories, in four paperbacks.'

'Saw them on your bookshelf.' Isobel was about to offer to lend them when Judith said, 'There's a lot of things you don't hear about any more. Like pressure cookers.'

'And Hula-Hoops. I often wonder what happened to all the Hula-Hoops.'

'Little liver pills,' Judith supplied.

'The Dagenham Girl Pipers.'

Judith laughed suddenly, a warm, infectious sound nothing like the snort of derision she'd given earlier. 'The Dagenham Girl Pipers,' she repeated, chuckling. 'My goodness, I remember them. Can't stand pipe bands myself.'

Halfway out of the room, she turned. 'Don't worry too much about your Dory,' she said. 'She'll do.'

Rinsing out the teapot, Isobel wondered why she should find Judith's pronouncement so comforting.

In the middle of the afternoon she had a brainwave. She'd been upstairs, looking with pleasure at the bedrooms and the bathroom; before going home to confront her burst pipe, Judith had given everything polishable a thorough polish, and now the old woodwork shone. There was a smell of lemon from the bathroom, and the curtains, washed, ironed and freshly rehung, looked almost new.

The house looked so good that she wanted to show it off. On the heels of that thought came the brainwave: what was worrying her most about the coming Christmas holidays was the prospect of having her family shut in together for several days on end. So why not dilute them a bit? Why not invite a guest or two?

Running downstairs, she was thinking furiously. Who

would be likely to say yes to an invitation? People on their own, who won't be snowed under with family plans. People like Douglas.

Lawrence had come home just after lunch and was shut in the living room with his pamphlets and his paperwork. 'Lawrence?' she said, putting her head round the door.

'Hm?' He looked up, frowning.

'Sorry to disturb you, but what do you think about asking your dad for Christmas?'

'Fine by me.' He went back to his papers. 'Izzy, I'm sorry but I'm terribly busy. Do what you think best.'

She backed out of the room, quietly closing the door after her. Then she went to the phone and dialled Douglas's number.

'It's those hicks from the sticks!' he said cheerfully when she'd said hello. 'How are you, my dear? Are your doors and windows frozen shut and your extremities dropping off with frostbite?'

'No, and no,' she replied. 'At least, my extremities are fine, and nobody else has complained yet. Douglas, what are you doing for Christmas? Can you come to us?'

'To *you*?' He made it sound as if she were proposing he orbit Jupiter for the duration of the festive season. 'Well, I was going to pop down to the King's Head for a prelunch snifter, then go home to a duck and the Queen's speech, but I suppose . . .' There was a brief pause. 'Love to come, Isobel my sweet. Thank you for asking me.'

Don't thank me, she wanted to say. It's as much for my benefit as yours. More so, in fact. 'You can have the Queen,' she said. 'Promise.'

Douglas said, 'Better not tell the Duke of Edinburgh. Want me to bring my duck?'

'No, I'm getting a huge turkey. Just bring yourself.'

'Very well. Love to the children, and Lawrence.'

'Theirs to you. Bye.'

The receiver still in her hand, she phoned her sister.

'Maude? It's me. Look, there's so much tension in this house that if we're on our own for Christmas, one of us will end up murdered, so will you come down?'

'Isobel, I hate the country, especially when it's cold.'

'It's not cold in the house. The wood-burning stoves are roaring away like the Queen Mary's furnaces.'

'I was going to work till midnight on Christmas Eve – did I tell you about my article on the oral tradition on Lindisfarne? – and then I was going to have all of Christmas Day for self-indulgence.'

'Come here and indulge,' Isobel pleaded.

'You really need me?'

'I do, I do!'

'What about Piers? How does he feel about having his sister-in-law around?'

'Fine, honestly.'

'Well, all right. But I'm not joining in any hearty outings.'

'No need, and we'll let you win at Trivial Pursuit.'

'*Let* me win?'

'Okay, okay! Oh, Maude, thanks. Thanks so much. I can't tell you what a relief it is to know you're coming, I –'

'That's enough fawning,' her sister ordered. 'What shall I bring?'

'Nothing.'

'Presents?'

'Oh – well, presents, yes.'

'What do you want?'

'Something absolutely useless and totally frivolous.'

'Right. See you late on Christmas Eve.'

Standing in the hall, feeling absurdly pleased with herself, suddenly two things occurred to Isobel that took the edge off her delight.

The first was that, even if she could bribe Dory into sharing her room with either her brother or her aunt, they were still going to be awfully short on space.

The second – which was a lot more worrying – was that, in the heat of the moment, she had entirely forgotten that Douglas and Maude couldn't stand each other.

CHAPTER EIGHT

Jacob still felt heady from the applause. The nativity play had gone with hardly a hitch, and Mrs Lovatt had given him her special 'well done' smile at the end, when the cast were taking their bows and all the parents – including Mum – were clapping like mad.

There had been one very hairy moment when Michael Frazer had missed his footing and almost hurled Mary off the donkey's back and into the front row of the audience. But Jacob had instinctively flung his arms round her waist and saved her, and from somewhere had come the inspiration to make it look intentional: 'Hold on to me, darling,' he'd said, 'I'll look after you.'

He'd heard several *Aahs* from the mums. He hadn't been at all sure if it said anywhere in the Bible that Joseph had called his wife 'darling', but Dad called Mum it, so it couldn't have been all that wrong.

Mrs Lovatt said afterwards that Jacob was a real old pro, whatever that was, with the stage in his blood. And she ought to know, Jacob reflected as he carefully folded up his Joseph costume, she was in some drama club in the town where they put on lots of plays. She'd borrowed a wonderful donkey's head from her club, which Billy Morris had worn – she said it came from some play by Shakespeare and belonged to someone called Bottom. That had made them all snigger. Jacob couldn't believe she'd really said Bottom. It was rude.

94

He handed in his costume, then ran outside to find Isobel. She was standing talking to the headmaster, Mr Montgomery.

'Ah, here comes your young man,' Mr Montgomery said.

'Hello, Jacob,' Mum said. She smiled at him. One of the things he really loved about her was that she didn't embarrass him by hugging him in public, drooling all over him and calling him 'sweetheart' and 'my little love' like some of the other mothers did. 'I really enjoyed the play,' she added. 'It was jolly nice that we were allowed to join in some of the carols.'

'We thought you'd be all right on the well-known ones,' Jacob said. He heard Mr Montgomery laugh and glanced up. Had there been something funny about what he'd just said?

No, it was all right. 'Miss Everett is very fussy,' Mr Montgomery was saying to Mum. 'She refuses to have loud parental voices drowning out the children when they've worked so hard to get it just right. Sometimes the fathers sing the wrong words.'

'The wrong tunes as well, I dare say,' Mum said. 'I don't blame her. Anyway, carols like "Away in a Manger" are far better suited to children's voices.'

'Quite,' Mr Montgomery said. Then, looking down at Jacob: 'You made an excellent Joseph. Well done.'

'Thank you, s – Mr Montgomery.' It was difficult to remember not to call Mr Montgomery sir.

'It seems to me you've settled in well with us,' he went on. 'Do you think you have?'

Jacob nodded. 'Yes, thank you, sir.'

'That's the ticket. I'm expecting to see you in the school football team next term. Left back, isn't it?'

Encouraged by his friendly tone, Jacob said eagerly, 'Actually I only went on as left back because Simon

Horrocks had to go home with a tummy upset. Best of all I like to play in the forwards.'

'Well, I expect you'll be able to talk that over with Mr Hargreaves,' Mr Montgomery said. 'Now if you will excuse me, Mrs Langland, Jacob, I must just have a word with Katie Shaw's mother. Happy Christmas to you both.'

'Happy Christmas,' Jacob and Isobel chorused.

'He seems very nice,' Isobel said as they went out to the van. 'And I've had such a lovely time. I wish Dad could have come too, but he's seeing a chap from the NFU today about insurance.'

'Oh.' That didn't sound very exciting.

'He'd much rather have come to the play,' Mum went on. 'He says he's going to come and watch your first football match next term.'

'Does he?' That was great. 'But won't he be at work? Oh, no! I suppose not.' Getting used to Dad not being out of the house from first thing in the morning till after supper time was nearly as difficult as remembering to call Mr Montgomery by his name.

'I think,' Mum said cautiously, 'that we're going to have to be a bit careful over this. Over Dad's work, I mean.'

'Careful?' He tugged at the van's passenger door, which was inclined to stick.

'Yes. We must avoid making Dad think we think he doesn't have a proper job any more.'

'He hasn't though. Not like he had before.'

'No, I know. He's what's called self-employed now. Instead of working for Mr Fishwick and doing what he tells him to do, Dad works for himself.'

'Okay.' If it meant Dad not being away so much and having the time to come to school football matches, Jacob didn't care who he worked for.

96

'Self-employed,' Mum said again. 'Can you remember that?'

'Of course. Dad's self-employed.' He grinned across at his mother. 'Not out of work.'

'Quite,' Mum said. Then she started the van and pulled out into the traffic.

'There's Brian Dent!' Jacob shouted suddenly. 'He's waiting for the bus. Can we give him a lift?'

Isobel was already signalling, drawing in to the side of the road. 'Where does he live?'

'In the village. He lives in a caravan,' Jacob went on, awed all over again at the thought of someone living in a caravan.

'Does he? In *our* village? Where?'

'In that little lane that goes up behind the green.' Jacob was opening the window, beckoning to Brian Dent. 'Brian! *Brian!* D'you want a lift?'

Brian saw them, picked up his schoolbag and hurried along the pavement. 'Yeah, thanks,' he said, scrambling in beside Jacob.

'Hello, Brian,' Isobel said. 'Were you in the play?'

'Yeah.'

'It was very good. I really enjoyed it.'

'Yeah.'

'Brian was a camel,' Jacob said. He didn't think Brian wanted to talk to Mum.

She must have realised it, too, as she didn't say anything else till they got to the village. Then she said, 'Where shall I drop you, Brian?'

'Here'll do.' She stopped by the green. He got out. 'Thanks for the ride,' he said. Then he ran off up the worn bit of track that cut through the grass of the green.

'He doesn't talk much,' Jacob said, feeling the need to apologise for the friend he'd imposed on his mother.

'That's all right,' she replied. 'He thanked us for the lift. That's the main thing.'

97

Jacob felt vindicated. 'He can burp Archbishop of Canterbury,' he said.

'He can *what*?'

'He can say Archbishop of Canterbury in a burp. Well, quite a lot of burps. None of the rest of us get beyond Arch. Brian says we let too much air out on the first bit so we don't have anything left for the other words.'

'Good Lord.' Mum seemed really impressed.

'He says I can go and see his caravan. Can I?'

'Yes, if you like.'

'Great! Can I go tomorrow?'

'Yes, if it's all right with Mrs Dent.'

'There isn't a Mrs Dent. Brian's dad lives with his aunt. She's called Miss Hoylake, and she's really old.'

'Perhaps we should check with Miss Hoylake about you going to tea.'

'It won't be tea, it'll just be to look at the caravan. Anyway, Brian gets his own tea. His aunt's not there much.'

'Good Lord,' Mum said again. Jacob smiled to himself; she was really funny sometimes.

Then the smile turned to a smile of happiness. He'd been Joseph and it had been okay. Now he'd given Brian Dent a lift home, which might make Brian like him more than he did already, and that seemed to be quite a bit.

Brian Dent knew where there was a badger's sett. What Jacob was hoping was that, if Brian got to like him a lot, he'd show him where it was.

Dory came out of school fuming with undischarged anger. She'd had to play netball in the biting cold, and Mrs Nugent had ignored her protests about redoing the history test and made her do it in the lunch hour. I *hate* bloody Mrs Nugent, she thought. She's a real cow. Serve her right if I get a worse mark than last time. I just hope I do!

As if those two things weren't bad enough, that morning

she'd had a Christmas card from Daisy Marshall, who, with a total absence of tact that must surely have been deliberate, and therefore equated to bitchiness, had mentioned oh-so-casually that they were all going to Catherine's the evening before Christmas Eve. And – this was the killer – that Catherine's brother said Rupert Smythe might be there, because apparently Rupert fancied Catherine.

Dory ground her teeth in renewed anguish. Life back in Ewell was going on just as if she'd never left; her absence had left as much of a hole as you'd get in a bucket of water. They were all having such fun, and there she was, stuck in some rotten village like some political exile! Why didn't her parents have done with it and take them all to bloody Siberia? She wasn't sure where Siberia was, but you often heard it mentioned in the context of people being exiled.

Everything felt . . . weird, now. It was difficult to get used to Dad being around so much, difficult to get used to Mum sitting with her feet up on the Rayburn wearing a pair of Dad's old socks to keep her feet warm. Dory wished she could sort of *talk* to Mum, but she seemed to have put herself in a position where talking to your mother was like admitting defeat. Anyway, Mum was a bit weird, too. Weird with Dad, weird with everybody. She seemed to be thinking, much of the time. Unavailable for talking. To Dad, to Dory, to any of them.

She hefted her heavy bag higher onto her shoulder as the bus appeared round the corner.

She was near the front of the queue, and was heaved up the steps by momentum from the rear. Fumbling in her bag for her season ticket, she realised she'd left it in her desk.

She had some money. Hurrying, dropping a two-pence piece, she counted out the coins.

She was fourteen pence short.

'Come on, it's bleeding freezing out here!' someone yelled from the pavement.

'I haven't – I left my bus pass at school,' she hissed to the driver.'

'Another fourteen pence, love,' he said as if he hadn't heard.

'I haven't got it,' she whispered, feeling the hot blush creep up her face.

A big tanned hand wearing a silver ring dropped fourteen pence onto the little tray where you put your fare. 'Here,' a boy's voice said. 'Is that enough now?'

'Yup.' The bus driver pushed the handle on his machine, and Dory's ticket flew across the tray and into her hand.

'Thanks,' she said, turning to see a tall boy with fair hair, cropped short. He was wearing the uniform of the boys' grammar. 'You –'

Someone pushed into the boy, who was bumped against Dory. 'Sorry,' he said. 'Go on, find a seat.'

She hurried down the bus, finding an empty double seat halfway along. To her surprise – for he seemed to be with a bunch of his friends – the boy sat beside her.

'You're Dory, aren't you?' he said.

'Yes.'

He smiled at her. He had very white teeth, the sort that looked as if you never had to have a filling. 'I'm Sam Hearst.'

She recognised the name. Her mother had mentioned a boy called Sam, who was the son of Mrs Hearst who cleaned for them.

This was embarrassing. Dory didn't feel she could take money from her mother's cleaner's son, because if someone had to be a cleaner, it probably meant she was poor.

'It was very kind of you to lend me the fourteen pence,' Dory said rather stiffly. 'I'll repay it tomorrow, on the bus into school.'

'Okay,' he said easily. 'Or you can get your mum to give it to mine next time she's in cleaning for you.'

He said that easily, too. Dory, who couldn't have said such a thing at all, never mind easily, was very impressed. Sam obviously didn't mind about his mother being a cleaner. *How* couldn't he mind?

She couldn't think of anything to say. She half hoped Sam would go and sit at the back with his friends so she could stop feeling awkward about not saying anything. But he was really nice-looking, so she half hoped he would stay.

'How do you like village life?' he asked her presently.

'Not much,' she replied honestly. 'There's nothing to do.'

'Tell me about it,' he said. 'It's worst in the winter. The summer's okay. We all go up the Rec.'

She didn't know what a rec was. 'Ah,' she said.

He laughed softly. 'Recreation ground,' he said. 'It's on the road into the town, down that lane off to the right. You know?'

'Yes.' She took a breath to steady herself. 'What happens at the Rec?'

He shrugged. 'There's football, tennis courts. Some of them play hockey on the Astroturf. It's hard on your legs, though. Tears the flesh off.'

'Ugh!'

He laughed. 'You get great scars on your knees.'

'Do you play hockey?'

'No. We play football on the Astroturf when there's no hockey.'

'My little brother plays football. He's at Banner Primary.'

'I went there. It's all right. Who does he have for football, Mr Hargreaves?'

'I've no idea.' For the first time Dory wished she'd listened to Jacob when he went on and on about school. 'He's going to be in the school team,' she said, realising she sounded as if she were boasting about it. 'Well, he's only a substitute so far, but he played in one game.'

'That's pretty good, considering he hasn't been there long,' Sam said.

'Did you play in the school team?' she asked.

'Yeah. We won the cup in my last year. I had to switch to rugby when I got to the grammar, but that's okay too.'

'Oh.' Dory knew even less about rugby than she did about football.

Something hit Sam on the back of the head, and he put a hand up to rub the spot. He turned round and shouted, 'Pack it up, Dan!' But he was smiling.

Dory could feel the blush starting again. If Sam's friends were going to start throwing things at him because he was sitting next to her, she wished he'd go away. She felt sure he was looking at her, and leant forwards so that her fall of hair hid her face.

'I'd better go,' Sam said. 'Me and Dan are going to his house to do some stuff on his games console.'

'Okay,' she muttered. She was aware of him standing up, hauling his bag up off the floor.

'See you,' he said. She shot a glance upwards, and saw him go down the bus and push his way into the back seat.

She turned to stare out of the window at the dark countryside flashing past. Her anger, she realised, had gone, replaced by an excited sort of buzzing in her stomach.

Having to play netball and re-do her history test didn't seem so bad, now. Nor did the thought of all the fun they were having back in Ewell. And tomorrow morning she'd *have* to talk to Sam again, because she'd be giving him back his fourteen pence.

Lawrence spent over an hour with the man from the NFU, at the end of which he'd insured his new tractor and trailer. The chap had said he ought to take out third party insurance, now that he was a landowner, in case someone trespassing in Oxleat Woods got injured, and sued. He had also helped Lawrence do a contents policy for the house. Lawrence was quite astounded at how much less the sum of their contents was worth here than it had been in Cedar Holt; he hadn't realised they'd disposed of so much valuable stuff. Izzy had sold an antique dresser and a little velvet-covered nursing chair when they moved into the village, he recalled, plus some other oddments of furniture and two or three paintings neither of them liked much; she'd told him what she'd got for the items, but, since he'd suggested she keep the money for her own personal spending, he'd forgotten how much it was. Finally, the NFU chap had asked him how he was going to invest what was left of his redundancy cheque and the money from the house sale, remarking that it could earn him a fair old income.

I could have told *him* that, Lawrence thought as he stood by the Rayburn waiting for the kettle to boil. I could have said, actually, my dear chap, I'm a chartered accountant and I know more about finance than you'll ever learn, and my capital is already securely invested. But the man had been friendly and eager to help, so Lawrence had kept his mouth shut.

The cottage, the sleeping woodland waiting for spring to kiss it awake, the new tractor, the kindly chap from the NFU, all seemed worlds away from Ewell and Barclay Dawson Products. Lawrence shook his head, smiling. I don't believe it, he thought, I'm going to wake up from this happy dream and discover I'm late for a meeting with Benjamin Fishwick and on the carpet for wrecking some new deal.

He poured boiling water on the teabag in his mug and went to the fridge for milk. And sugar – he was taking sugar again now that his active lifestyle allowed a few extra calories.

Sitting down at the table, he reached for his notebook and pencil, and added a few details to the drawing he was making of his new vegetable garden. It was only small: there wasn't a lot of point in doing anything elaborate in the garden of a rented house, where their residence was only temporary. He shaded in a patch and wrote 'Brassicas'. Then, behind it, 'Sweet Peas'. Badger had told him it was good to mix flowers in with the vegetables, provided you chose varieties that attracted beneficial insects. 'Friends', Badger called them, as opposed to 'foes' like slugs – 'Don't have delphiniums, they're buggers for attracting slugs' – and cabbage white butterflies.

The cottage was too small for the four of them, Lawrence reflected. Isobel had got their name down with all the town estate agents, and had asked to be sent details of any suitable houses in the village that came on the market. So far, there had been nothing; the property market appeared to have stagnated. There weren't, in any case, many houses in the village. But I want to live here, Lawrence thought, right here, near to my woods. It may be ages before anything turns up.

He grinned. Perhaps he and Izzy could have a go at driving a few families out. I could keep pigs in the back garden, he thought, or Izzy could pretend to be a neurotic townie who drinks too much and embarrasses people by turning up for morning coffee reeling and smelling of gin.

Izzy. He pictured her getting ready for Jacob's nativity play, trying on several outfits till she was satisfied, polishing her tan Gucci loafers and brushing her fine suede gloves. She'd looked great. She'd put on a pound or two since they'd left Ewell, and it suited her. He thought so, anyway. He wasn't sure if she did.

She seemed happy. He heard her humming sometimes, and she was sleeping well. But she didn't really talk to him

– they only communicated at a basic day-to-day level, only a little better than it had been in Ewell.

We used to have such a laugh together, he mused. She always had such a quick sense of humour. I've never known another woman who made me laugh like Izzy did. But we lost all that when I got so involved with work. I stopped bothering, I suppose. Took her for granted. The most common female complaint against men, according to the agony aunts: 'He takes me for granted.'

He glanced up at the washing, airing on its rack above the Rayburn. Isobel had arranged it neatly, not wasting an inch of space, so that every garment from quite a big wash was exposed to the warm air rising from the stove. She arranges everything neatly, he thought, here in this fairly basic cottage just as she did in the huge Ewell house.

Does she *mind*? he wondered suddenly. Does she resent having to housekeep in this ridiculously spartan little place after what she's been used to, having to put on her wellies to go out to the freezer in the outhouse because the ground's so wet and claggy; having to drive around in a rattle-trap van when she was used to a BMW? Being on her own, when before she had a whole host of friends to visit and giggle with?

Something was wrong with that, though. Frowning, he thought back, and realised that Izzy hadn't gone out for lunch or on a shopping bender with one of her friends for weeks before the move.

Why?

He remembered how surprised he'd been when she didn't chuck out his tentative idea that they move out of town; when, far from laughing at him and scornfully saying she'd rather be dead than live in the country, she'd said she'd think about it. And then agreed.

Why?

She's been unhappy, he thought. Preoccupied, not wanting to make love. Uncommunicative.

But then I've been preoccupied and uncommunicative. Barclay Dawson saw to that.

His mind returned to the thought of making love. They had done, a few nights ago, and it had been wonderful. For him, anyway, although he thought that might have been because of its rarity value. It was only the second time since they'd arrived at the cottage, and the first had been pretty disastrous because Izzy had cried afterwards. Not because of anything he had done, though – or at least he didn't think so, because she'd done her crying held tight in his arms.

He'd thought perhaps it was just because she was still adjusting to the new life, reacting to the stress of the move.

Now, thinking further back, he wasn't so sure.

She had become – withdrawn, he thought described it best. In her own world, where, judging by her expression sometimes, she wasn't very happy. Was that why she'd agreed to move out of Ewell? Because she was unhappy, preoccupied with something she couldn't share with him, and didn't much care *where* they were?

Dear Christ, suppose she was ill?

He dismissed the thought. Made himself dismiss it; it was too frightening.

Anyway, she didn't *look* ill. She actually looked well – better now than in her brittle and rigidly dieting Ewell days.

We *can* recapture our closeness, he told himself. Then, ruefully, he reflected that, since they spent so much more time in each other's company, they were damn well going to have to.

Dear old Izzy, he thought, I wish I –

He heard the van draw up outside. Getting up to refill

the kettle, he turned his thoughts away from his wife and prepared some intelligent questions about the school nativity play.

CHAPTER NINE

At her wits' end – and angry with herself for letting a minor
domestic matter upset her equilibrium – Isobel finally asked
Judith's advice on how to cram four adults, a sulky teenager
and a child into a very small three-bedroomed house.

'Hm.' Judith frowned over her tea. 'Sofa's not big enough
for your Jacob to sleep on, not really. Anyway, it'd mean
he couldn't turn in till the rest of you had gone to bed.'

'I know,' Isobel agreed lugubriously. It had been so different at Cedar Holt. There was a totally pristine spare
room, for one thing, ready and waiting for the unexpected
visitor. And both children's rooms had contained an extra
bed, for when they had a friend to stay over. There was
no room for these beds in this house; they had gone into
store.

'Got a Put-u-up?'

'I haven't – no. Nothing like that.'

'We've got a camp bed and a sleeping bag. Well, they're
Sam's, but he wouldn't mind. You could borrow them.
There's that bit of space under the window in your room.'
Warming to the subject, she leaned forward. 'Jacob could
go there. We'll sell him the idea, tell him sleeping on a
camp bed's good practice for when he goes camping in the
summer.'

'I'm not sure he's going to go camping.'

'He will,' Judith said. 'They all do, the lads round here.
There's a meadow they use – have done for donkey's years

– hidden away in the woods behind the Rec. It's where they go for the rites of passage – you know, first beer, first fag.' She grinned briefly, an expression Isobel hadn't often seen on her face before. 'First girl, for all I know.'

'Oh,' Isobel said weakly.

'So Jacob's in with you, which leaves his little room for his granddad.'

'Jacob suggested he and his grandfather share his room.'

Judith shook her head. 'No, you don't want that. The young and the old don't mix when it comes to sleeping, not if my old dad's anything to go by. You can hear him snorting, farting and grinding his teeth from outside the door.'

'Right.' Isobel tried not to smile.

'Then this sister of yours –'

'Maude.'

'– Maude can share with Dory. It's a big bed.'

'I don't think Dory will like that. She's very fussy about her sleeping space. Even Teddy's had his marching orders.'

'Dory'll just have to lump it.'

Isobel wasn't at all sure that her daughter was actually very good at lumping it. She made up her mind to go into town and get one of the single futons she'd seen advertised in the local paper; Dory had been pleading for one for ages, and they were on special offer at the moment. Being granted her wish might make her more accommodating about sharing her room with her aunt. Well, it might . . .

'When are they coming?' Judith's voice broke into her thoughts.

'Maude's not coming till Christmas Eve – the afternoon. Douglas arrives tomorrow.'

'Right.' Judith got up. 'I'll give your room a good going-over, then we can shift your bed across a bit and I'll get Mike to drop off the camp bed and the sleeping bag later. It's clean, the bag – I washed it after Sam got back from CCF camp last summer, and it's not been used since.'

'Judith!' Isobel exclaimed softly.

'Hm? What?'

Isobel felt slightly awkward; what she wanted to say might well sound rather personal. But then she and Judith had tentatively been drawing closer; if they hadn't, Isobel wasn't sure she could have involved Judith in these absurdly time-consuming arrangements. Making up her mind, she said, 'We haven't known each other all that long, but I have the clear impression that you're the sort of person who would *never* put a sleeping bag away without first washing it.'

Judith stood looking down at her for a moment. Then a gentle smile spread over her face, making her look suddenly pretty. 'Thanks,' she said. Then she disappeared into the hall, and Isobel heard her steady tread going upstairs.

Douglas arrived on the midday train, and Isobel went with Lawrence to collect him from the station.

The station was a couple of hundred yards down the road from the pub, so they called in for a quick drink on the way. The bar was gaudy with paper chains and Christmas cards hanging on lengths of string; most of the cards seemed to feature boozy Santas, hiccuping reindeer and variations on the theme of overindulgence.

Isobel, remembering the touching earnestness of Jacob's school play, said, 'It's not really Christmas, is it?'

Lawrence, sitting down beside her with a pint and a half of best bitter in his hands and two packets of crisps clenched in his teeth, looked around the bar.

'No,' he said, depositing the crisps in her lap. 'Let's count.'

She was obscurely happy that he'd caught her meaning straight away.

'. . . twenty-five, twenty-six . . . thirty-two cards with drunken Father Christmases or pissed dads trying to carve turkeys and so on . . . twelve olde worlde scenes . . . seven robins . . . eleven floral thingies . . . two nativity scenes and three angels.' He turned to her, his face mournful. 'Oh dear.'

She said, expecting him to say no, 'Shall we go to Midnight Mass on Christmas Eve?'

He studied her for a moment. 'We never have.'

'We've never lived in a village before and had a church almost on our doorstep.'

'No.' Then: 'Okay. If you like.'

'You're sure?'

'Yes. Dad'll be with us – he certainly won't want to come, so he can stay home and babysit.'

'Don't let Dory hear you say that.'

'I won't, I don't want to be verbally scalped.'

'Maude will hoot with derision,' Isobel said.

Lawrence reached for her hand, squeezed it, then let go. 'We're used to Maude's derision.'

She felt suddenly very close to him.

They finished their beer in silent companionship, then went to meet Douglas's train.

Douglas was very pleased to find he had been allocated Jacob's bedroom, his pleasure based on the fact that it was too small for anyone to come and seek him out if he wanted to retire for an after-lunch snooze or simply a little privacy. Anyone except Jacob, that was, but Douglas never minded being sought out by Jacob. The important thing was that Isobel's daunting sister wouldn't follow him up there. He was slightly afraid of Maude; he didn't understand women like her, and he had tried to cope with her by adopting a hearty avuncular stance, slightly roguish, just stopping short of calling her a 'damn fine filly'.

Maude had been unimpressed. Regarding him steadily from intent blue eyes behind frighteningly intellectual-looking spectacles, she'd insisted on drawing him into a fierce discussion on immigration she was having with Lawrence – *why* did she always call Lawrence Piers? – then, when he'd reluctantly given his views – which he supposed were possibly a little right wing – called him a reactionary with his head firmly stuck in the sands of upper-class security and short-sightedness.

And this harridan was going to be under the same roof for all of Christmas. Unpacking his suitcase – it was solid leather, a twenty-first birthday present from his godmother, and weighed a ton even when empty – he sighed. Still, he consoled himself, I'll be with Lawrence. And Isobel, bless her. And little Jacob. He smiled a secret smile, delighted at the thought of Jacob opening the present he'd bought him. He'd be so pleased. Douglas couldn't wait to see his face.

Douglas had had to resort to the advice of his friend Mrs Achieson for Dory's present, since he had absolutely no idea what a teenage girl of the nineties would appreciate. He'd got it hopelessly wrong last year, buying her some doll thing from Woolworth's. Mrs Achieson had burst out laughing when he'd told her; that had been when she'd offered to help him this Christmas. They'd had a very satisfactory little outing to Eastbourne – their nearest town – and Mrs Achieson had led him into a very loud shop called In Gear, where the assistants wore tiny black skirts and matching vests, with great clumsy shoes like surgical boots. Dear me, Douglas had thought sadly, they don't look like girls did when I was a spry youth. An assistant with a dead-white face and what looked like pale blue lipstick had dealt with Douglas's purchase of a pink angora sweater with cap sleeves, which didn't look long enough to reach Dory's waist.

'Are you quite sure?' he whispered to Mrs Achieson as the sweater was casually folded and stuffed into a plastic bag.

'Absolutely,' Mrs Achieson whispered back. 'My granddaughter has one in mauve; she hardly takes it off. My daughter has to wash it while she's at school and hurry to get it dried, aired and back in Cybill's room by the time she comes home.'

Standing in the spare room of his son's house, Douglas took the sweater, now wrapped in navy-blue paper with gold stars – Mrs Achieson had advised him over that, too – out of his suitcase and prayed that Dory would like it as much as Mrs Achieson's Cybill liked hers. He was almost as wary of Dory as he was of Maude; it would certainly help the bonhomie of Christmas Day along if Dory liked her present.

He sat on the bed, thinking about Mrs Achieson. I wish she were here, he thought. But Mrs Achieson had gone to Canada to spend Christmas with her son. Then, when she came back, she was going to her daughter – Cybill's mother – and family for New Year. Dear, oh dear, it would be almost a fortnight before Douglas and Mrs Achieson could resume their little outings.

Douglas stood up, remonstrating with himself. I shouldn't grumble, he thought. I'm very lucky. I have my health, my wealth – a modest amount, anyway – and my daughter-in-law has invited me for Christmas. He went to look in the mirror on top of the chest of drawers, straightening his tie and smoothing down the bits in the middle of his eyebrows that always stuck up. Mrs Achieson had suggested he pluck them, but he'd drawn the line at that.

Mrs Achieson's name was Evadne. It was a lovely name. Just before she'd gone off to Canada, they'd had a nice little lunch in a cosy place they knew at Jevington, where they'd exchanged presents – he'd given her a cameo brooch and she'd given him a silk tie, the one he had just straightened. They'd also exchanged a chaste kiss under the mistletoe, and she had said softly, 'Douglas, why don't you start calling me Evadne?'

Now he smiled at himself. Sod the eyebrows, he thought, I'm doing all right.

Lawrence had the brilliant idea of setting supper in the kitchen, which meant he and Isobel could sit nattering to Douglas while Dory and Jacob went into the front room to watch telly. As he opened the Christmas bottle of port and poured out three glasses, he could hear Dory stridently insisting that they watch her choice of programme, on the slim grounds that what Jacob wanted to watch was 'gross'.

Only two more days, son, he said silently to Jacob. He and Isobel had added, to their thirty-pound limit for the children's presents, Jacob's gifts from Isobel's mother and Jacob's godfather – phoning round to ask, somewhat embarrassingly, if they could have anything that might be coming Jacob's way in money rather than in kind – and it came to just enough to buy Jacob his own small television; fortunately, one of the shops had a special pre-Christmas offer. Lawrence had rigged up an extension to the aerial lead, and he and Izzy had tried out the new telly. It worked beautifully. Lawrence had a sneaking feeling that arranging for Jacob to watch on his own was somehow giving in to Dory's domination of the remote control, and some stern part of him said he ought to enforce a fair and judicious system whereby the children took it in turns to select pro-grammes.

A wise and responsible parent would do that, he reflected, listening as Jacob's hopeless protests faded and died. But then this wise and responsible parent didn't have to live with Dory.

Over the port, Lawrence answered his father's questions about how the woodland was shaping up. There wasn't much to tell, really; Lawrence and Badger had done a lot of clumping around looking at things, and Lawrence could now drive a tractor and back a trailer without hitting anything. They were going to start cutting in the New Year; Lawrence had arranged a buyer for his wood, and the first load was due to be delivered at the end of January.

Douglas gazed round the kitchen, which was looking shiny and bright in the light of the candles on the table. 'And you, my dear,' he said, turning to Isobel, 'how are you adapting to country life?'

Lawrence watched her. It was a question he had longed to ask, but he was wary of what the answer would be.

Isobel returned Douglas's smile – it had always been a delight to Lawrence that they were so fond of each other – and said lightly, 'Pretty well. The house is a lot better now that we've got it straight – there's this lovely woman called Judith Hearst who's been helping me – and the children are okay. Jacob loves his new school, but Dory's taking a while to adapt.'

'Mm,' Douglas said. 'But how about *you*? Don't you miss life in Ewell? Your friends, the social whirl?'

Isobel's face seemed to close up. With a tight little smile, she got up and crossed to the stove. 'Not really. More coffee, anyone?'

Not for the first time, Lawrence wondered just what had happened in Ewell that Izzy hadn't told him about.

Dory lay in bed on Christmas morning, hands behind her head, reflecting how neat her new futon looked with its bottle-green sheet and its striped cover. It was very comfy, too. She'd insisted on Auntie Maude having the bed, not out of any consideration for Maude's comfort, merely because she was eager to try out the futon. Maude hadn't been fooled; regarding Dory steadily, she'd remarked, 'New, is it? Well, you of all people, Dory, aren't the magnanimous sort who'd allow someone else the pleasure of trying it out for the first time. Don't worry, kid, I'll have the bed.'

Dory had felt only slightly abashed. Auntie Maude was all right – oh heavens, she'd told her to drop the Auntie, said it made her feel about ninety. Maude was all right. You knew where you were with her.

Maude came back from the bathroom, wrapped in a huge white chenille robe, her head in a towel. There was a lovely smell – sort of flowery, and spicy as well.

'What's that?' Dory asked.

'What's what?' Maude was reaching into the cupboard, taking a slinky grey tunic and a pair of black leggings off hangers. 'Be more specific, child.'

'The smell.' Dory didn't even notice that she hadn't taken exception to being referred to as 'child'.

Maude paused, loosening the towel round her head and smiling a distant smile. Sort of soulful, Dory thought. 'Bath oil. A friend gave it to me – he brought it back from Paris.'

'It's lovely,' Dory said. Then: 'Maude! You didn't have a bath?'

'Yes. Why?'

They weren't meant to have baths. Dad said it was showers only unless given special permission. When Dory had protested, Dad had said he was perfectly willing for her to have a bath as long as she went outside and chopped the extra wood needed to fuel the Rayburn and reheat the hot-water tank. Suddenly a hot, deep bath had lost its appeal.

'Oh – nothing. It doesn't matter.'

Maude came and sat on Dory's bed, looking as if she understood. 'Wartime restrictions, huh?'

'What?'

'I expect your parents are threatening to do what people allegedly did in the war, which was to paint a line on the

116

bath at four-inch height, and behead anyone who filled the bath above it.'

'They didn't behead them!'

'Yes they did. Special bands went out in army lorries, and people used to grass up their neighbours. "'Er at the end's 'ad nearly a foot!" they'd say, whereupon 'er at the end would be carried away, kicking and screaming, locked in the Tower and beheaded at the earliest opportunity.'

'You're making it up,' Dory accused, delighted.

'Of course I am.' Maude extracted a travel hair dryer from her wonderful Italian leather bag and plugged it in. 'Don't believe the half of what they tell you about the war.'

'I won't,' Dory promised fervently.

'Go and have a shower, or whatever,' Maude ordered. 'Then I can get dressed in peace.'

'Okay.' Dory scrambled out of bed and put on her old dressing gown – how lovely it would be to have something as luxurious and enfolding as Maude's white robe – and hurried off to the bathroom before the smell of Maude's bath stuff faded. And before anyone else beat her to it.

'Is the old fart coming down for breakfast?' Maude asked her sister as they worked together in the kitchen, Maude laying the table and Isobel setting out cereal packets and making toast.

'Please don't call him that.' Isobel hated it when Maude was sharp. 'I know you think he's a stuffy old buffer, but he's Lawrence's father and I love him.'

'*Love* him?' Maude laughed. 'Isn't that a bit steep, even if it is Christmas?' She had been as derisive as Isobel had predicted over the Midnight Mass outing, and Isobel was still feeling a little sore.

'I love him all the time,' Isobel replied. 'Now get out of my way, Maude. I've got a sticky honey pot in my hand

and you'll bellyache all day if I get honey on that elegant tunic.'

'You seem to have left elegance behind in Ewell,' Maude observed, staring at Isobel's worn jeans and baggy sweater. 'Along with quite a lot of other essentials, such as that BMW, a lovely, roomy house, a decent social life and easy access to London.'

Isobel paused till her thumping heart slowed again, then said calmly, 'Not all those things are essential. And I'm not really dressed yet – I'm going to shower after breakfast and put on something nice.'

'Pressies after breakfast?' Maude asked winningly, as if she was aware of having trodden on delicate ground. 'And a long talk, in the near future,' she muttered.

'What?' Isobel hoped she'd misheard, but was very afraid she hadn't.

'Nothing. Where do you keep the cereal bowls?'

Late in the morning, they all assembled in the front room, where a small Christmas tree stood in the window surrounded by presents. Isobel had just taken a couple of paracetamol; the tension had got to her. Over breakfast, Maude and Douglas had eyed each other like the hunter and the hunted, and Isobel was wondering how long it would be before some sort of unpleasantness started.

There had already been some ominous silences. Isobel reflected that having people so obviously holding themselves in and *not* saying things was nearly as bad as having them let rip. It was Maude's fault, really. Over the late-night hot drink the previous evening – which Isobel had arranged to fortify both herself and Lawrence, going off to church, and Maude and Douglas retiring their separate ways to bed – Maude had started talking about the Queen's speech, saying it was a total anachronism nowadays, when so many social disasters had befallen the Royal Family.

Really, she *shouldn't* have been so provocative, Isobel thought. It's unnecessary, when she knows perfectly well Douglas is a royalist, and would go on being one even if the heir to the throne were guilty of deadlier sins than adultery. Douglas had stood up for the Queen's speech, *and* the Queen, in a touchingly old-fashioned defence that would have been absurd had Isobel not known he believed every word of what he was saying.

Maude had shot him down in flames, neatly defusing his every argument and making him look naïve and unworldly. It was easy for Maude; an elderly and not very quick-thinking man was no worthy adversary for someone of her calibre.

Isobel put a stop to it by collecting up the cocoa mugs and saying firmly that she wasn't going to entertain arguments under her roof when it was so very nearly Christmas Day. On the way to church, Lawrence had hugged her and said quietly, 'Blessed are the peacemakers.'

This morning, Maude kept eyeing Douglas with a quirk of a smile, as if she were just about to make some witty quip but managing to restrain herself. And Douglas, poor old boy, looked as if he'd rather be anywhere than the Langlands' small house, where you didn't stand a chance of escaping from an uncongenial fellow guest unless you went and hid in your room.

And, just to add to the general merriment, Dory had been bossing Jacob around since she'd descended from her room. Really, Isobel thought, can't she have a day off, just today?

Now it was gift-opening time: in her present mood, Isobel held out little hope of it improving the emotional temperature in the house.

But she was wrong.

She forgave Maude all her little peccadilloes when they opened her sister's presents. Maude had obviously given a great deal of thought to her Christmas shopping, buying a large and expensive book on growing vegetables for Lawrence, a Liberty scarf for Isobel, a Gameboy for Jacob, a pair of pigskin gloves for Douglas and – greeted with the greatest amount of delight – a silvery-grey chenille robe for Dory.

They were all suitably grateful, and Isobel was glad they'd got something decent for Maude; she'd decided to avoid the potential pitfalls of the surprise gift, and asked Maude what she wanted. Maude had mentioned two new publications, both of which she was going to buy anyway; Isobel had bought them both.

Maude could be relied upon to give good presents. The surprising thing was that Douglas had chosen almost as well; Jacob was nearly as pleased with his Swiss Army pen-knife as he was with his new telly, and when Dory opened her angora sweater – with an expression on her face that clearly said she was expecting another doll – she exclaimed, so spontaneously that it was obviously not just being polite, 'It's fantastic! Just what I've been saving for! Oh, Granddad, how did you know?'

Isobel, handing round the glasses of sparkling wine that Lawrence was pouring out, watched as Douglas lifted his glass to an invisible presence and muttered, 'Evadne Achieson, I love you.'

CHAPTER TEN

Throughout January, Lawrence was preoccupied with his woods. He had enrolled at a local agricultural college to do a National Vocational Qualification on tree and woodland management. For the next thirty weeks, every Tuesday was going to find him back in the classroom.

He was preparing to cut his first cants. Badger said cutting was best done when the sap was down, so they'd better get a shift on. Lawrence didn't know exactly when the sap started rising, although he'd read somewhere that this mystical-sounding process was delayed in a hard winter. A hard winter was, without a doubt, what they were having.

He'd imagined that Badger would know the practical details about the actual cutting, as he seemed to know about everything else. However, when they stood beside the first chestnut stool and Lawrence went to start up the chain saw, he noticed Badger frowning hard.

'Okay?'

'Hm.'

It wasn't a very satisfactory answer, considering the portentousness of the moment. 'Badger?'

'I'm wondering about this here,' Badger said.

'Which particular aspect?'

Badger gave a faint grin. 'This cutting. Now it comes to it, I'm remembering all the things that can go wrong.'

'Christ,' Lawrence muttered. Then, more loudly, 'So, do you think we should wait a bit? Get some advice? Wait till I've done cutting on my NVQ course?'

Apparently missing – or ignoring – the mild sarcasm, Badger stood deep in thought for some time, glowering out at the frosty scene before them. Eventually he said, 'Reckon you ought to get the fencing people to cut. They'll pay you less for your wood if they do all the work, stands to reason, but you'll get your stools treated right, and you won't go making no mistakes it'll be the devil's job rectifying next time.'

'Ah.' Lawrence's initial reaction was to think, bloody Badger, now's a fine time to tell me you don't know how to cut chestnut. He was relying on Badger at this early stage to provide the practical help; Badger was hands-on, he was theory. Then he recalled the letter from the fencing company who were buying this first precious load of wood, where they'd said they were willing either to take delivery of the cut lengths or come to do the job themselves.

The difference, financially, was considerable. But then, as Badger sagely pointed out, the job would get done properly, with none of the stools being damaged by slapdash cutting. And I can watch them like a hawk, Lawrence thought. Then that, plus what I'll learn on the course, will mean I'll know exactly what to do next time.

'Okay,' he said.

Badger glanced at him. Lawrence thought he looked relieved. 'Sorry,' he said.

'Don't mention it.' Lawrence reached in his jacket pocket for his notebook, where he'd written the fencing people's number, and for his mobile phone. It was about the only piece of Ewell technology that had survived the move to a simpler life, and he'd hung on to it because it made sense, if he were going to be working out of doors all the time, for people to be able to reach him and not trouble Izzy all day phoning the house and leaving messages. Besides, as Izzy had pointed out, it'd come in handy if he tripped over a tree root and severed his femoral artery on a bit of rusty old metal. Izzy always did have a flair for the dramatic.

He put through the call, and arranged for the fencing people to come over later in the morning to size up the job. The young man he spoke to said they'd probably get in there by the end of the week.

'That's good,' Lawrence said to Badger, putting the phone away. 'I was afraid they'd say they couldn't start for ages.' He grinned sheepishly. 'Call me a bit of a kid, but I can't wait to see the cutting begin.'

Badger grinned back. 'Me neither.'

While they waited for the fencing men, they strolled down into the valley where the stream ran. The banks were almost bare, except for the occasional brave stand of tough grass stems, dead and dry now and lightly frosted.

It was a pretty scene.

'There's a bloke in the village with a JCB,' Badger remarked.

'Oh yes?' Lawrence, used to Badger's suggestions coming out via the scenic route, waited.

Badger pointed along the valley. 'That's alder, see. You could grub them out, flog them for pulping, and clear a bit of ground.'

'Right.'

There was a long pause. Then Badger went on, 'You might keep chickens. Free-range, like. Plenty of stuff for them to scratch around in, though you'd have to supplement with some corn and that. You'd need someone to test the stream, too. Make sure it ain't got no nasties in it.'

'What about foxes?' Lawrence asked. There was no use even thinking about this promising idea if it meant snaring, shooting or otherwise disposing of foxes, since both Dory and Jacob would make his life hell if he so much as politely asked a fox to leave the premises. They couldn't have been listening properly when he and Izzy read them *The Tale of Jemima Puddle-duck*; the more antisocial aspects of fox behaviour seemed to have passed them by.

'You'd need henhouses,' Badger said. 'Lock your hens in at night, so old Foxy-Loxy can't get at them.'

'Would it cost a lot?'

Badger shrugged. 'Fair bit. Still, you'd be making money on the eggs. You could sell them to the pub, and to the teashops out the forest way. Ted in the post office'd probably carry a few, too. People'll always buy free-range eggs.' He thought for a moment. 'You could do a nice snap of your birds, pecking away in this here valley, display it over the egg boxes. Town folk'd probably pay twenty-five pence extra.' He grinned. 'Specially if you can catch one or two of the hens smiling.'

'I might just do that.' Maybe it was something Izzy could do, he was thinking. She could be i/c chickens, and the profit from egg sales could be her income.

He was brought up short at the idea of Isobel tending chickens. Izzy, in the Dior suit, with the hundred-pound hairdo and the perfect make-up!

But she wasn't that Izzy any more. Shaking his head, he realised he didn't really know *what* she was. He hadn't liked to ask about her clothes and things, which used to be so important to her. She might take it the wrong way; think criticism was implied.

'You could always dam the stream,' Badger said, deflecting Lawrence from his disturbing thoughts. 'Be nice for trout down there. You could stock it, then charge people to come and fish, so much per rod per day.'

'Would they pay for that?'

'You bet. They all want a slice of real country living, those toffs in their four-wheel-drive vehicles who spend all day choking in London. You could probably sell them fresh air, if you bottled it and put on a fancy label.'

'Trout,' Lawrence repeated. 'My own trout stream.'

'You need to make your acres work for you,' Badger said. 'This bit of land's lain fallow for years, just waiting for someone to come along and claim it. There's all sorts of earners you can do.'

Lawrence remembered something in his last lot of bumph from the Ministry, something about farmers making nature trails across interesting areas of countryside, which they then charged the public to walk through. You couldn't charge much, but every little helped.

And we could have a refreshment stall, he thought, sell cups of tea and soft drinks. Izzy could bake cakes with her hens' eggs. We could –

'Fencing lorry's here,' Badger said.

They walked up the track to meet it.

Isobel, coming back up the garden path with another load of logs, stopped for a moment to look at Lawrence's new vegetable plot. Not that there was much to see, yet; he'd started to dig one day the previous week when the weather was briefly warmer, but he had soon discovered that one mild morning didn't do a lot to thaw ground that had been frozen hard for weeks. Still, he'd marked out the plot and dug half a row, so it could honestly be said he'd made a start.

He was doing something called double digging. He'd explained it to her while she massaged his aching back. 'You dig trenches two spits deep, then –'

'What's a spit?'

'A spade depth. You go down two spades' depths, then you put the top spit from the second trench into the first one, so you end up with trenches one spade deep, but with well broken-up soil at the bottom.'

'I see. Then what?'

'Then you dig in lots of manure, then you're ready for the spring planting.'

He had, she thought, made it sound so easy. But, as yet, the careful plan he'd made for his vegetable garden was still just that: a plan. She supposed they'd just have to wait till the weather eased.

She went on into the house, removing her wellies on the boot-scraper. It was a novelty, living so close to nature; in Ewell when it got cold, she'd simply turned up the central heating. Here, when a hotter house meant more wood fetched in to feed into the Rayburn, you were far more aware of what was going on out of doors.

It was a novelty, too, to see how much they could manage without. In many ways it was just a matter of adapting to new habits; when you were in town doing the shopping, it was as quick to go to the library and choose a few books as it was to go to the bookshop and buy them. And it amazed her how well they got by without the fan of credit cards they'd both kept in their wallets – again, it had merely meant the adoption of a new routine. When she went to do the weekly big shop at Safeway, she drew cash from the bank's hole in the wall instead of putting the shopping on the card. When the van – horrid van! But it was far more economical than the BMW – needed filling up, she and Lawrence paid from their own cash in hand. It hit hard sometimes, which wasn't a bad thing as it made you think twice about using the van, but there was the reward of no longer having to pay out a huge cheque when the credit card statement arrived.

She heated milk on the top of the Rayburn and made herself real coffee with hot milk, sitting down in her chair in front of the stove and cradling the mug in her hands. Her nails, she noticed, needed filing. She wondered how long it was since she'd polished them. Now that she no longer bothered with extensions and nail varnish, she found it amazing that she'd kept at it so long. Lawrence said he preferred her without the long, beautifully-shaped and painted nails that she'd been so proud of. It just went to show.

She felt sleepy. Goodness, she thought, if I sit here much longer I shall nod off! And that would be a waste of the morning.

That reminded her of her current preoccupation, ranking second only to How to Help Dory: get herself something to *do*.

It had surprised her that she'd actually had to think quite hard to recall how she had filled her days when they lived in Ewell. There had been the house, of course – a big house, too – and meals to buy for and prepare. But even a few months' distance from that life was making her realise that much of her time had been spent in self-indulgence. Visits to the hairdresser, whole days spent in Kingston, or up in town, wandering round the shops, not because she actually *wanted* anything, more to get an idea of what was available if she had done.

Well, shopping trips were out now. She could, of course, hop on a train and head up to London, but what would be the point? She had done a pretty ruthless hatchet job on the more frivolous of her clothes and possessions when they moved to the country, so she was hardly going to go out and replace them all now, even had she had the means. And there was still that suitcase of designer fashion up in the attic, if she suddenly felt the need to dress up.

I should sell some of that stuff, she thought. Maybe I could ask a few local women in, hold a sort of Tupperware party, but with my own clothes substituting as the merchandise?

It was quite an appealing idea.

How did one crash the local coffee morning circle? *Was* there one, or were these village and country women too busy for such pursuits? She frowned, not knowing how she could find out. The one place where she did rub shoulders with local mothers was waiting outside Banner Primary School for Jacob. She had recognised a couple of women – she'd nodded a greeting to them in the village shop – so why not go up and introduce herself? Now that the days were at last beginning to draw out, there wasn't the same sense that you had to rush home as quickly as you could; there was more inclination to stop for a chat.

And you had to start somewhere.

Lawrence had spent a successful half-hour with the man from the fencing company, who had sized up the chestnut with a professional eye and said it'd be no problem sorting that lot out, and they'd be along Thursday, eight thirty.

In celebratory mood, Lawrence had taken Badger off to the pub for a couple of pints and lunch. Today's special was steak and kidney pie with cabbage and mashed potato, and they both had that.

Taking their glasses up to the bar for Pete to refill them – Lawrence wondered if some ancient village protocol forbade the buying of pints by anyone other than the employer – he nodded a greeting to a very old man sitting in a chair beneath the dart board.

'Afternoon,' the old boy responded. 'That's a spiteful day out there.'

'It is indeed.'

'You're the fellow's bought Oxleat Woods,' the man remarked.

'Yes.' Lawrence was fishing in his pocket for another fifty pence.

'I remember Oxleat Woods.' The man had a dreamy look in his eyes.

Hardly surprising that you should, Lawrence thought, when you must have passed them to get here. 'Really?' he said politely.

'My old granny used to take me for walks there, ooh,

must have been nigh on seventy year ago!' He looked surprised, as if he'd temporarily forgotten how old he was. 'Over the stile we used to go. My granny made me look the other way when she popped over the stile, said it weren't seemly for a young man to watch a lady lift her skirts.' He chuckled, which brought on a rheumy cough. 'I were only a little tacker, too!' He winked at Lawrence. 'I've watched many a lady lift her skirts since, I don't mind telling you!'

'I expect you have.' Oh Lord, Lawrence thought, I've been nailed by the pub bore. But he's all by himself; perhaps this is the only conversation he'll have today. 'Have you lived here long?' he asked.

'All my life. And my father and grandfather before me. Gardener to the big house, Grandfather was, and Granny was in service. Till they married, of course. You didn't keep your position once you were a married woman, not in them days.'

'Quite.' Lawrence perched on a stool and took a mouthful of beer. It looked as if he would be there for some time, so he might as well make himself comfortable.

'Nine children, my granny bore.' The old man nodded in satisfaction, as if this feat of fecundity were somehow down to him. 'All of 'em survived, too. And Granny, she was hale and hearty till she passed on, and that weren't till she was nearly ninety.'

'Good Lord.'

'She were a real old countrywoman, Granny was.' The old man leant forward. 'Work? She seldom stopped! And she'd walk, all over. Into market, to work and back – that's before she married, you know. You didn't go on working when you were a married woman, not in them days.'

'So you were saying.' Lawrence glanced across at Badger, who had picked up an abandoned copy of the *Sun* and was staring intently at a page near the beginning.

'She were lovely to me, my granny. I can picture her

now, leading the way through the sweet young grass, brushing the bluebells with the hem of her long skirt, pointing with her stick to where the wood pigeons were cooing up in the oak trees.'

'It certainly is a beautiful spot,' Lawrence said.

But he didn't think the old man heard. 'I remember one day,' he said, with sudden eagerness, 'I found a bush I didn't recognise. Huge, it was, covered with purple flowers, bloody great things. Course, I know now it were a rhododendron, but, like I says, I was only a little 'un then, and I'd never seen one before. "That's a rhodydendron," Granny says. "It was once part of the gardens of the big house." They had heaps of rhododendrons, you know, all different colours. Azaleas, too, and in some places you could see fruit trees. And roses, gone wild, you know, reverted, all suckers and poor little flowers, but still roses.'

'Really?' Lawrence glanced surreptitiously at his watch. 'Well, er –'

'Pickett,' the man said. 'Harold Pickett.'

'Lawrence Langland,' Lawrence said. Harold Pickett reached up a gnarled hand in which thick dark blue veins stood out, and they solemnly shook hands.

'I won't get up,' Harold Pickett said. 'I'm waiting for my operation. I'm having a new hip.'

Before Harold could launch forth on this new topic – which, from the light in his eyes, he clearly found as absorbing as the history of Oxleat Woods – Lawrence stood up. 'It's been so nice talking to you,' he said quickly, 'but I've got Badger's second pint here, and we really ought to be drinking up and going.'

'Badger, eh!' Harold shook his head.

Not knowing quite what to make of that – and thinking he'd rather not have it explained – Lawrence smiled in reply and went back to Badger.

'Colder here than it is in Moscow,' Badger remarked.

'Crikey.' Lawrence pushed a pint across the little table. 'Drink up, then we're going back down to the stream to think some more about this chicken idea.'

The remainder of Lawrence's day had been so busy that it was only later – much later, when he was in bed listening to Izzy's quiet breathing beside him – that he realised what Harold Pickett's remarks meant.

There had once been a garden in Oxleat Woods, a proper, cultivated garden. And it belonged to a big house.

Excitement racing through him, he thought: I wonder if we can find it? What a thrill it would be to uncover the remains of walls, find cellars long abandoned, shut up, hidden from the light of day! Scrape the undergrowth off slabs of marble terrace, where once elegant men and women strolled in evening dress!

He lay with his eyes open, staring into the darkness, while his mind ran wild. A big house! Where? I wonder. In the valley, surely – the woodland is old, and there's no obvious clearing where a house could have stood.

What a wonderful spot! The stream, the silent woods behind you, sheltered from the east wind by that bank, how they must have loved it.

A house in the valley.

The day finally catching up with him, he closed his eyes and fell asleep.

PART THREE

Spring

CHAPTER ELEVEN

By the end of March, Lawrence had sold two cants of chestnut. The fencing company had sent men to cut and carry away the first load, but Lawrence and Badger had done the second one themselves. Lawrence had spent a couple of sleepless nights worrying about whether or not he was doing it right, and Badger had proved an imperfect helpmate, being less inclined for days of unrelenting hard work than Lawrence had anticipated.

Lawrence occasionally wished that his course at the agricultural college – which was proving wonderfully informative in every other aspect – would dish out some advice on how to chivvy along a recalcitrant workforce. Badger was unreliable, and would often either turn up late or not at all if some other matter claimed his attention. On the plus side, Lawrence only had to pay him a fairly modest amount – which would be surreptitiously handed over as they stood side by side in the pub waiting while Pete pulled them each a pint – and Badger was always willing to give Lawrence the benefit of his long and wide knowledge of country matters. No doubt, Lawrence had concluded, it made Badger feel important to have a townie greenhorn to inform.

In the third week of March, the weather turned mild briefly and the trees responded by beginning to wake up. Lawrence raced to complete the cutting of the second cant, then decided that was enough. Although he wasn't prepared to discuss it with Badger – with anybody, in fact – working with his trees had developed in him a sense of them as living things. And, with their sap beginning to rise, he felt he must leave them alone.

They *were* living things, of course they were. But Lawrence's awareness involved more than that recognition. There were times when, with Badger off on the tractor, trailering another load off to the fencing people, Lawrence was quite alone in the silent woods. Then, with the tall oaks moving gently high above, with the vigorous new growth on the chestnut stools pushing up straight, strong branches, sometimes he was quite sure he felt the souls of the trees reaching out to him. Part of him dismissed it as fancy, but part of him wanted to believe it. The more familiar he grew with Oxleat Woods, the more his fanciful part gained the ascendant.

One thing he'd learnt about coppicing that had surprised him was its antiquity. In Neolithic times, it was discovered that regular cutting of certain trees not only yielded a mass of straight branches roughly equal in size, it also prolonged the life of the tree. Lawrence read of a hazel coppice in which the stools were reputedly fifteen hundred years old. His own tree species, the sweet chestnut, wasn't native to the British Isles but a relative newcomer. From the pollen record, it appeared the Romans had brought it.

He steeped himself in tree lore. Oxleat Woods boasted many oaks, which were the standards that grew among the chestnut: the oak, Lawrence read, was the tree of Jupiter, *quercus robur*, worshipped by the Druids, sacred to the Greeks, the Norsemen, the Celts. In some places, it was still celebrated annually on Oak-Apple Day, 29th May, which was originally a holiday instigated on his restoration by Charles II, to commemorate the fact that he'd made use of an oak tree to hide from the Roundheads.

Those alders by the stream, those water-loving trees dismissed by Badger as useless for anything but pulping, were, Lawrence learnt, traditionally used for any sort of construction that had to survive underwater, the wood being resistant to decay. Venice, Lawrence informed Izzy, was built on piles made of alder.

He was surprised when elements of tree lore rang loud bells of recognition within himself. But, then, what was more comprehensible than the notion that trees, with their roots deep in the ground, provided a channel between Mother Earth and her children? That the branches and the thinnest, highest twigs, reaching up to the heavens, brought something of that rarified, idealised place down from the skies, something that, as you hugged a stout tree trunk, you could almost visualise permeating your body?

Sacred trees, folklore, legends of fairies and witches. Joseph of Arimathea's staff turning into the Glastonbury Thorn. Maypoles, the Cross of the Crucifixion, evergreen boughs to celebrate the Winter Solstice and their modern-day descendant, the Christmas tree. Lawrence read, thought, absorbed. And – since he was still too close to the Barclay Dawson days – he kept most of his thoughts to himself. But he found an old anonymous rhyme about the relative qualities of wood for household fires and, since it was both appealing and practical, he wrote it out and stuck it on the notice board in the kitchen:

> Beechwood fires are bright and clear,
> If the logs are kept a year;
> Chestnut's only good they say,
> If for long it's laid away;
> Make a fire of elder tree,
> Death within your house shall be;
>> But ash new or ash old,
>> Is fit for a Queen with a crown of gold.

Birch and fir logs burn too fast,
Blaze up bright and do not last;
It is by the Irish said
Hawthorn bakes the sweetest bread;
Elmwood burns like churchyard mould,
Even the very flames are cold;
    But ash brown or ash green
    Is fit to warm the hearth of a Queen.

Poplar gives a bitter smoke,
Fills the eyes and makes you choke;
Apple wood will scent the room
With an incense-like perfume;
Oaken logs, if dry and cold,
Keep away the winter cold;
    But ash wet or ash dry
    A king shall warm his slippers by.

'We'd better get some ash, then,' Izzy remarked laconically on reading it. 'Pity you're not in business as an ash coppicer.'

Jacob had been worried in case anyone put a piece of elder or elm on the fire by mistake. Lawrence reassured him that it was unlikely; elder wasn't very common and, since the depredations of Dutch elm disease, elm was even less so.

There were sound reasons to do with the health and vigour of the chestnuts for calling a springtime halt to cutting, in addition to Lawrence's instinctive (and, he had to admit, quite illogical) feeling that he mustn't hurt his trees. For one, the new growth would be more robust if the trees weren't cut when in leaf; for another, trees cut late in the season would be putting out vulnerable new growth in autumn, the very time when rabbits and deer would be on the lookout for green shoots, other sources having dried up. The young branches would, in springtime, provide nesting sites for the woodland birds, and the fast-developing wild flowers – in particular the bluebells – wouldn't be trampled into annihilation by Lawrence's and Badger's booted feet and their tractor tracks. Lawrence found he cared very much about this. He wanted his wood to be beautiful.

With the cutting over until the autumn, Lawrence and his one-man workforce turned their attention to planting. One of Lawrence's contacts at the NFU had helped him with an application under the Woodland Grant scheme, which would donate quite a decent sum provided Lawrence planted broadleaves. He discovered he'd get less for conifers. March was a little late for large-scale planting, especially when you had to depend solely on someone like Badger, but since the minimum area under the scheme was twenty-five acres, there was no option but to bite the bullet and go for it.

Slowly, steadily, the bare acres in the cleared area of Oxleat Woods began to sprout young trees: oak, ash, sycamore, hornbeam, each tied to its stake, each protected by a plastic tube to keep the rabbits away. And the deer: Lawrence had read somewhere that you could deter deer by spreading lion droppings on the boundaries of your land, but, as Badger remarked, fresh lion shit wasn't a commodity you often came across in Sussex.

Extraordinary, Lawrence mused as he dug out the hole for yet another sapling, how an animal's brain worked. The last lion to exist in the wild in England probably turned up its toes in prehistoric times, yet deer living here today retained in their genes a fear of the smell of their ancient predator's droppings. Quite extraordinary.

In the absence of lion shit, he thought, we'd better play it safe and do it by the book. The book advocated a barrier, both for newly planted saplings and for newly coppiced stools, but barriers came expensive. The cheapest method was an electric fence, and even that was prohibitively pricey considering how much was needed. Lawrence, brooding over the problem, recalled someone advising him to get a couple of dogs, and encourage them to run in the woods. Deer, apparently, disliked rushing, barking dogs nearly as much as they disliked electric fences. And, Lawrence thought, Jacob could have a lot more fun with a couple of dogs. They would have to do until he could afford proper fencing.

Moving on to the next sapling, he thought about having a dog with him. He started to smile: Jacob wasn't the only one who was going to be pleased.

Spring was going well for Jacob, even before his father announced they were going to get a couple of dogs. He was now playing regularly in the school football team, at left wing, and the pride he took in carting home his dirty kit every Wednesday evening showed no sign of diminishing. The school shirts were quartered in royal blue and white, and the shorts were plain white. Jacob thought they looked nice hanging over the white stove in the kitchen, and he couldn't resist pointing them out to his family at every possible opportunity.

Mum and Dory were clearly getting a bit bored with football, especially Dory, although Dad could be relied on for an interesting discussion of tactics and technique. He usually came to watch the matches, which made Jacob want to sing. Coming home in the van afterwards, they would have what Dad called a debriefing; sometimes Dad would make suggestions as to how Jacob might have done better, but just as often he would say things like, 'You played well, Jacob. I don't know how you got that shot in past their goalie. I bet even Shearer couldn't have done it.'

Brian Dent didn't bother about football, not unless Mr

Hargreaves really made a big thing about it during games lessons and *forced* him to. Even then, Brian's efforts only lasted till the final whistle went – there was no question of him being up to playing in the school team. Mr Hargreaves said Brian had an attitude.

Jacob was quite sorry Brian wasn't in the team. It meant that on Wednesdays Jacob didn't have Brian's company on the way home because he caught an earlier bus. Still, they travelled home together on the remaining four days of the week, any one of which could lead to that wonderful invitation, 'Want to come back to the caravan?'

Going with Brian to his caravan was one of the highlights of Jacob's life. He didn't really understand about the social niceties of the visits. His mother had said they should check with Miss Hoylake – who turned out not to be Brian's aunt really, just a friend who Brian had to call Auntie Ruth – but, since Miss Hoylake hardly ever seemed to be there, Jacob didn't see how it could matter. Brian's dad worked in the town; he did something for the Council, but, Brian said proudly, he was an outdoor worker and not one of those wimps who sat in an office all day. Jacob had said his dad was an outdoor worker, too. He'd thought it was all right not to admit that Dad had worked in an office until a few months ago. Dad wasn't a wimp, anyway, even if he had.

Brian and Jacob usually had the caravan to themselves. It was big, so big that Jacob had a job imagining it being towed behind a car. He'd asked Brian if they ever did that, and Brian had said crushingly, 'It's not *that* sort of a caravan, it's one you live in permanently.'

Jacob hadn't known there were different sorts of caravans.

You climbed in through the door via a little step, and inside the door a heavy velvet curtain hung, which felt furry on your face and smelt of very old dust. Brian said it was to keep the warmth in, which was funny as there never seemed to be much warmth to be kept in. Not when they got there, anyway, although the first thing Brian would do was to put a match to a tall, cylinder-shaped heater that stood in the middle of the floor. It smelt even when it wasn't alight, and when it was, sometimes it made your eyes water. Brian said it ran on pink stuff – paraffin – which his dad bought in a big gallon drum from the village shop. Jacob thought it was funny that something coloured pink – a colour he associated with pretty things like Dory's hair ribbons when she used to wear them, and sweet peas in big bunches – should smell so disgusting. Why had they made paraffin *pink*? Why not sludge green? Or – this was Brian's suggestion when Jacob mentioned it – shit brown?

That had made them laugh so much Brian had fallen off the bench seat that ran along behind the table where they had tea.

Brian always found something interesting for tea. He knew how to put the kettle on and make a brew, as he called it, which he'd pour from the pot into two big mugs, stirring in sugar and milk that was kept in a real fridge. They had the electric, he said. Dad had run a cable along. From where, he didn't say. With the mugs of tea they'd have things like shop-bought individual trifles in plastic cartons, or a banana, or hunks of sponge cake. Once they'd finished a beef stew that Brian's dad had left in the cup-board – Jacob hadn't liked that – and once it had been biscuits which Brian said were called ladies' fingers. Brian had been a bit rude that day, too – well, they both had – making up names for biscuits and things that featured other parts of ladies' bodies. Jacob had said you could have sponge puddings and call them ladies' bums, and Brian had fallen off the seat again.

After tea, Brian sometimes allowed Jacob to play with his ferret, which lived in a big wooden box with a wire mesh front. The cage fitted under Brian's bed, which was at the door end of the caravan, next to a little room where there was a loo and a very small basin. (Brian said you mustn't use the loo for wee, only for Number Twos, because it was a chemical toilet and his dad had to empty it. For wees, you went outside and did it in the grass.) You made up the other bed by collapsing the table and putting an extra bit of seat between the seats on either side. It made quite a big bed, but that and Brian's only came to two; Jacob didn't know where Miss Hoylake slept. Or perhaps she slept in the big bed, and Brian's dad slept on the floor? He didn't think he ought to ask – after all, Brian didn't ask that sort of question about Jacob's family.

The ferret was extraordinary. It was a pale wheaty colour, and its eyes looked red. It was about ten inches long, and it liked to drape itself round Brian's neck like a soft fur collar. Brian called it Mabel. (It was actually a she.) Brian said Mabel hunted rabbits, which she chased in their warrens till they ran out to where Brian waited with a net. He promised to let Jacob watch her in action one day. Jacob hoped he wouldn't disgrace himself if Mabel caught a rabbit, although he was afraid he might. The idea of her sharp little teeth making short work of a rabbit – Brian said she was a clean killer, when she was allowed to be, and went straight for the throat – made him feel slightly queasy.

They still hadn't been out to look at the badgers' sett. Brian said it was no good in winter, although he didn't explain why.

But that was a minor detail. The football and having as his best friend someone like Brian, who lived in a caravan into the bargain, was enough to make Jacob so happy that, in his prayers when he remembered to say them, he prayed very hard that things would stay *exactly* as they were for ever and ever. Amen.

But they didn't. One day, when Jacob had just finished

his maths homework and managed to make the sum come right, and when Dory was late home because she was doing a play rehearsal, and when Mum had said she'd made a chocolate cake for tea, when, in fact, everything in Jacob's garden was roses, Dad came home and made an announcement.

'Jacob,' he said, trying and failing to suppress a gynormous smile, 'Jacob, old son, what would you say if I suggested we bought a couple of dogs?'

CHAPTER TWELVE

Dory's rehearsal had gone on longer than usual. The girl playing Ariel had protested over Mrs Sawyer saying she had to wear a chain round her neck, symbolising her enslavement to Prospero, which she would fling away with a fine gesture when he gave her her freedom at the end of the play.

'I refuse to wear a chain,' Emma Hardcastle had said flatly. 'It's too like women always having been chained to men. To the sink, and that.'

Everyone knew what she meant, even though her explanation had been less than lucid.

'But, Emma, Ariel isn't necessarily female,' Mrs Sawyer said. 'Nor male either, come to that. It's a spirit. A free spirit, which Prospero has forced to be his slave in return for freeing it from Caliban's mother's imprisonment. Caliban's mother Sycorax, you know, who penned Ariel in a cloven pine.'

Emma waited with obvious impatience for Mrs Sawyer to finish. Then she said with irrefutable logic, 'Well, *I'm* female.'

'Indeed you are,' Mrs Sawyer muttered. Then: 'Suppose we made it a very pretty chain?' She eyed Emma. 'A very precious one? Gold, say?'

You could see Emma was wavering. After another ten minutes' haggling, they agreed that Emma's symbolic chain should be more like a necklace, and that she need tear at it in anguish only twice at the most.

All of this meant Dory missed the bus that went all the way into the village – from where it went on to serve several other villages – and instead had to catch the one that went only as far as the station. She was, she knew quite well, meant to ring home if that happened, so that Mum or Dad could come out in the van to meet her. It wasn't very far – half a mile, maybe – but there wasn't a proper pavement and the road was unlit. That made it dangerous because of cars racing past. Also – this was something Dory didn't admit to anyone except herself – it was scary. There were woods on one side of the road, and the ruins of some old warehouse building on the other. The building had no roof, and all the windows were broken. The interior looked hor-ribly black.

By the time she got off the bus, it was almost dark. It shouldn't have been – it was April, after all, and it was only just past seven o'clock – but the evening was dim with thick, low-hanging cloud. Dory glanced at the telephone box and debated. Then she walked on. She was angry with Dad because this time last week she'd got home to find Jacob over the moon because Dad had said they were going to have dogs. *Dogs!* I ask you, Dory fumed silently. Smelly, raucous things, jumping up and laddering your tights, get-ting on your bed, *drooling*. Dory had a thing about saliva.

The dog-buying expedition was due to happen the fol-lowing weekend. There was a woman out in a village on the opposite side of town who'd had a litter of springer spaniels – 'I suppose you mean her bitch has,' Dory had amended in a superior tone when Jacob told her – and the Langlands were allowed to go and make their selection of a pair of the puppies as soon as they were old enough. That would be, the woman had said, at the weekend.

In vain had Dory thrown into the ring everything she could think of to deter her parents, raking up from her memory every example of poor canine behaviour she'd ever read, been told about or seen in a film. 'They'll tear cloths off tables and all your food'll get ruined!' she shouted.

'That happened in *Beethoven*,' Jacob said smugly.

'We'll go away on holiday and they'll follow us and get lost!'

'*Incredible Journey*,' said her brother.

'They'll leak underneath and leave nasty stains on the hearthrug!'

'That was Granddad's old dog, and he was nearly fifteen. That's a hundred and five in human years,' Jacob added helpfully. 'I expect you'll leak underneath when you're a hundred and five.'

She'd thrown a plate at him – it didn't break – and Mum said that was enough, they were having dogs, whatever anyone said, because Dad needed them. And that was that.

Dory was amazed that Mum had accepted it without putting up a fight, as Mum had always, surely, been a totally un-dog sort of person? Mum's tights cost far more than Dory's did – Mum always bought Christian Dior tights, in lovely subtle colours that went perfectly with whatever shoes she was wearing – and Mum's very smart navy and black skirts were immaculate. Mum would *hate* having dogs!

But then Mum didn't wear tights much nowadays. She wore her jeans, or those overally things she'd got at Baldock's. Dad had them, too. And her skirts only appeared on special occasions, like going to church at Christmas and seeing Jacob's teachers.

Mum was putting on weight. Maybe, Dory thought, her smart, tight skirts were a bit too tight now.

Dory arrested the little stab of pity she felt for her mother by reflecting that Mum bloody well ought to have stood with Dory in the great dog debate. She *ought*!

Dory wasn't going to ring up for a lift home when nobody bothered enough about what *she* wanted, when they rode right over her feelings like they had done. Huh! Serve them right if she got run over. Kidnapped. Stuffed in the back of a man's car and –

It didn't seem a good idea to go on with that thought. She made herself stop, instead running aloud through her lines in Act III, Scene i. She was Ferdinand, and it was the bit where he and Miranda realise they like each other a lot. She wasn't sure how she felt about being Ferdinand – Mrs Sawyer said she'd chosen Dory because she was tall and had short hair and quite a deep voice for her age. At first the others had teased her and called, 'Boy! She's a boy!' after her, but once they'd stopped doing that, Dory discovered she liked being Ferdinand after all.

> '. . . O, she is
> Ten times more gentle than her father's crabbèd;
> And he's composed of harshness! I must remove
> These logs – no that's wrong –
> Some thousands of these logs and pile them up,
> Upon a sore injunction.'

Dory didn't understand that bit.

> 'My sweet mistress
> Weeps when she sees me work, and – '

There was something in the road.

On the bend before you got to the railway bridge, something was lying in the road.

Dory stood quite still. She tried to make her eyes see better, screwing them up, then opening them very wide. But the woods came right down to the road there, and great trees overhung the bend, making it as dark as midnight.

What to do? Go on, have a look?

But that was how they got you. They put bundles in the road that looked like babies, then, when you got out of your car to investigate, bashed your head in and stole your car.

148

But Dory wasn't in a car.

Go back, then, phone Dad, get him to come.

The thing in the road made a soft noise. It went, 'Meh!' and the brief sound made Dory's heart ache with pity.

Whatever it was, it was hurt.

She crept forwards.

It was a deer. Lying on its side, its shoulder and leg somehow stuck to the road, it was trying to raise its head. The huge eyes seemed to plead for help.

Dory flung her schoolbag into the hedge and hurried towards the creature, which flinched. Cross with herself for not thinking, she slowed down, approaching it on tiptoe, holding her breath. But the deer, panicked by pain and the nearness of a human, made a stupendous effort and lurched upright, making a sickening sound as its damaged flesh came away from the road's surface. Then it gave a leap, crashed through the thin hedge and seemed to fall into the short grass under the trees.

Dory ran after it, desperate to help, almost crying at her inability to do so. She fell on her knees beside the deer's head, saying stupidly, 'Don't! Oh, you poor thing, don't!'

She heard running footsteps on the road. A voice said, 'Who's there?'

Friend or foe? It didn't seem very important, somehow.

'It's me. Dory Langland. There's a deer in here. I think it's been run over. Can you fetch help?'

The person pushed through the gap in the hedge that the deer had made. 'Dory? It's Sam. I was on the train – I didn't call out in case I scared you.'

Sam. Of all people, it was Sam. Dory felt quite a lot of the fear and tension leave her. 'Come and have a look.'

Sam was beside her. Very slowly and calmly, he reached out his hand to the deer, running it over the shoulder and the foreleg; the deer had fallen with its wounded side uppermost.

'Is it badly hurt?' Dory whispered.

'Yes, I'm afraid she is.' His eyes were fixed on the deer. 'There, there, poor lass,' he said softly. 'There, there.'

'What . . . Should we get the vet? My dad's got a van, we could take her, we could –'

'Can you stay with her?' Sam asked.

'Yes, but –' It wasn't the time for questions. 'Of course,' she said, more bravely than she felt. The deer's obvious distress, and the sight of her gaping wounds, were combining to make Dory feel sick and faint.

'Good girl,' Sam said approvingly.

'What do I do?' Dory asked.

'Kneel here by her head, where I am.' He moved out of the way. 'Slowly now! Don't alarm her.'

So slowly that she was hardly moving, Dory did so.

'Now, very gently, stroke her neck.'

Dory put out a hand and touched the deer's warm neck. The flesh gave a shudder, but, as Dory stroked, relaxed.

'Good!' Sam said. 'You've got the touch. Now, talk to her, very quietly and steadily.'

'What about?'

There was a quick flash of pale teeth as Sam grinned. 'It doesn't really matter. Just keep up a steady monologue. It'll keep her calm, keep her lying still.'

'Oh, I see. So she won't damage herself any more while you're getting help?'

'I – Yes.'

He crawled away backwards, then, when he was a few yards from the deer, slowly stood up.

'How long will you be?' she whispered.

'About ten minutes. Fifteen at the most. Okay?'

She swallowed. 'Okay.'

There was a crackle of undergrowth as he pushed his way through the hedge. Soon after, she heard him break into a run.

150

Her hand was stroking the doe's neck, almost automatically. As if I were a machine, she thought, watching the movement of her arm. 'Poor deer,' she said. 'Poor dear deer.'

When it came to it, it was actually quite hard to think of anything to say. So she went through her Ferdinand lines again. Then again.

And again, this time putting Miranda's lines in between her own speeches. Still her hand went stroke, stroke. The doe's eyes were open; sometimes Dory saw the long-eyelashed lids flutter down and up again. The animal hadn't moved since Dory started speaking. Perhaps deers appreciate Shakespeare, Dory thought abstractedly.

> '. . . if hollowly, invert
> What best is boded me to mischief! I,
> Beyond all limit of what else i' th' world,
> Do love, prize, honour you . . .'

There was a movement on the road: Sam, carrying a gun.

She jerked in shock, and a spasm went through the doe. 'Sam! No!'

He came into the woods, the gun held behind him. 'We've got to, Dory. I'm really sorry, but we have.'

'Get my dad! We'll put her in the van, and –'

'The littlest movement is causing her agony. Can't you see? And a vet couldn't help her, nobody can. Her shoulder's smashed to bits, her foreleg's only attached by strips of flesh.'

'Can't she be mended?'

'No, Dory.'

She wanted to be sick. Hanging on by bits of flesh. Oh!

'Wh-What are you going to do?'

'I'm going to shoot her.'

'Are you allowed?' The silly, childish question flew out before she could stop it.

151

But Sam didn't laugh at her. 'Yes, it's all right. I'd have got my dad to do it if he'd been home. It's his shotgun. But Mum was there, she said it was okay for me to take it, as it was an emergency.'

'Golly,' Dory muttered. Her opinion of Judith Hearst went up a few notches; not everyone's mother would consider a dying deer needing to be put out of its agony a sufficient emergency to allow your son out with his dad's shotgun. Most of the mothers Dory knew would probably bleat about sending for the police and notifying the authorities. During which time the deer's agony would continue.

'Come here,' Sam said quietly. 'Get up very gently, and walk over so that you're behind me.'

She gave the doe one last stroke. Then she bent over and put a kiss on the soft neck. 'Goodbye, poor, poor deer,' she whispered. The doe's ear gave a slight flick.

She crawled backwards to where Sam stood, then got up, taking up her position behind his broad back. It seemed odd, somehow, for him to be wearing school uniform; a boy about to do a man's job.

As if he knew her thought, he murmured, 'Don't worry. I've done this before. I won't hurt her.'

A sob caught in Dory's throat. She managed to control it.

'Ready?'

She nodded, then, realising he couldn't see, said, 'Ready.'

She shut her eyes tight. There was a blast – *incredibly* loud in the silence – and a smell. Then Sam said – and she loved him for the shake in his voice – 'It's done.'

Dory opened her eyes. The doe's head had a big hole in it. She was, undoubtedly, quite dead.

It was funny, Dory thought, how *quite* dead looks altogether different from *nearly* dead. Something goes, some last bit of vitality. Even if the almost-dead thing hasn't moved for ages, you know it's still alive, because it's –

inhabited, was the best word she could think of.

It seemed strange – majestic, sort of – to be there at that moment when life became death.

Sam cleared his throat. 'Come on. We ought to go home. You can come with me. Mum said she'd put the kettle on, have a cup of hot, strong, sweet tea waiting for us.'

'I don't really like tea.'

'You will tonight,' Sam said. He sounded as if he were smiling. 'Anyway, you'll have to drink it, like it or not. It's the best thing.'

For shock, she imagined. The best thing for shock.

She got her bag and followed him out onto the road – was the poor deer just to be left there? – and he reached out his spare hand to help her. The shotgun, its barrel at a funny angle from its stock, was under his other arm.

'What's that?' There was something in Sam's hand.

'Spare cartridge,' he said. 'In case I – in case it was needed.'

She was glad, so glad, it hadn't been. To shoot a poor wounded creature once was bad enough, to have to do it twice was –

Abruptly she wrenched herself away from Sam and threw up in the ditch.

She waited, but there was no more to come. Wiping her streaming eyes, she straightened up. Mortified, she said, 'Sorry.'

'It's all right,' Sam said. 'I feel a bit like chucking up myself.'

'Do you?' She wiped her eyes again and looked at him.

'Mm. I did just what you did, first time I saw something killed. It was a myxied rabbit – a rabbit with myxomatosis – and my dad picked it up by its back legs and bashed its head against a tree.'

'Ugh!'

'I know, but it was the kind thing to do. The poor little

thing was so far gone, it couldn't move, couldn't see, and it was slowly starving.'

Dory thought with sudden feeling, I *hate* the country! Things – animals – get so hurt!

'Come on.' Sam took her hand again. 'Hot, sweet tea.'

Judith Hearst seemed to take it all in her stride. She sat Sam and Dory down at her kitchen table, and plonked before them the predicted mugs of tea. To her surprise, Dory found that it was the very thing she wanted above all else. Judith, with a quiet smile, silently poured her a second cup.

'You've locked the gun cupboard?' she asked her son.

'Yes. I cleaned the gun before I put it away, although I wasn't very thorough. Do you think Dad'll mind if I don't do it properly till tomorrow?'

'No. He'll maybe do it himself.' She muttered something else: it sounded like, 'He's got bugger-all else to do.'

Sam said, 'Dory did well, Mum. She kept the doe calm while I came for the gun.'

Judith studied them both. 'I reckon you both did well,' she said.

The few words, from Judith, meant more to Dory than a whole speech from someone else.

'More tea?' Judith asked her presently.

'No thanks.' It was difficult to summon the energy to move, but she knew she should. 'I ought to go home. They'll be worried.'

'I phoned them,' Judith said. 'While you were on your way here. Told them what had happened.'

'*Did* you?' Dory found it hard to credit that her parents hadn't come dashing straight over to support her, look after her. She said, in a small voice she was instantly ashamed of, 'Aren't they coming for me?'

Judith looked at her kindly. 'They are. I told them to give

us half an hour, to let you recover yourself.'

How right she'd been. Dory warmed to her even more. 'Thanks.'

'All right now?' Judith asked.

'Quite all right.'

Dory stood up. As she did so, she noticed for the first time that her school skirt was wet with blood. Alarmed, she touched it, then, repelled at its stickiness, stood with her hands away from her.

'Not very nice, is it?' Judith said calmly. 'Put it in soak overnight, salted lukewarm water. It'll wash out tomorrow.'

'What will I wear for school?'

Judith smiled, a sudden sweet expression which, Dory noted, lit up her somewhat heavy face. 'You'll have to wear a non-uniform skirt,' she said. 'Then you can tell them all why, and they'll all know what a heroine you've been.'

The possibility of it happening just the way Judith said it would ran through Dory's mind. She saw herself, the centre of an avid group of girls. Saw her form mistress, Miss Fenton, telling everyone what had happened. Saw them saying, 'Gosh, Dory, well done! *I* couldn't have!'

And, although Dory didn't say so to Judith or her son, sitting cradling his mug in his big, capable hands, the best bit of all was that the girls would know she'd performed her heroic act with Sam Hearst.

They'd know. Dory would make absolutely sure they'd know. She was going to tell them.

CHAPTER THIRTEEN

Isobel stood at the field gate and mentally ran with the opposition's bowler as he made his enthusiastic approach. The ball flew out of his hand, shot down the crease, bounced a few feet from the waiting batsman and came up in a vicious rise. The batsman made a sort of defensive lunge and caught the ball with an edge. The ball shot out at an angle, going wide of the wicketkeeper and straight for Lawrence, at first slip. Lawrence got a hand to it, but couldn't hold it; the ball, deflected, looped upwards again, and the man at second slip ran, put out his right hand and leapt, all apparently in one movement, coming down with the ball securely caught.

Isobel, caught up in the mini-drama, almost clapped. But, since it was cool for April and she seemed to be the only spectator, she changed her mind.

Someone else didn't share her inhibition: from the low wooden hut that served as the village cricket team's pavilion, there was a shout of 'Great catch!' and the sound of clapping. Looking over, Isobel saw a dark-haired woman in jeans and an Indian cotton top standing in the pavilion's doorway. Seeing Isobel, the woman waved in a friendly manner, then turned to go back inside.

Thinking that it would possibly be warmer watching from the pavilion, Isobel waited till the end of the over, then walked round the boundary to join her.

It was Lawrence's first outing for the village team. Badger

had mentioned it. 'They told me to ask you,' were his exact words, and he didn't actually identify who 'they' were, but Lawrence, Isobel could see, was tickled pink. He'd spent all one evening rummaging through the attic for his cricket whites, which had turned out to be cricket yellows, and a little on the short side. Isobel had lengthened the trousers, and Judith had brought some stuff that was meant to restore white things to their original state of purity. In the age-old tradition of his school days, Lawrence was using his house tie as a belt.

Isobel had to admit that, even if he had just missed a catch, he looked the part.

She reached the pavilion and went inside. The dark-haired woman was busy buttering sliced white bread. She turned as Isobel came in, and said, 'I shouldn't hang around if I were you, or you'll get put on the teas rota.'

'Oh.' Isobel wasn't sure whether to stay or go. 'Er – is your husband playing?' Silly question, of course. Disinterested passers-by didn't usually stop and offer to do the teas.

'Yes.' The woman reached for another loaf and tore open the plastic bag. 'He just made that fine catch.'

'It *was* good.' Isobel perched on the end of a trestle table. 'He saved my husband's bacon, too. Lawrence missed it.'

'Sheer bad luck,' the woman said charitably. 'It's all reflex action when you're close fielding, isn't it? And happening to be in the right place at the right time.'

'Yes,' Isobel agreed sagely. This woman clearly knew a lot more about cricket than she did. 'Would you like a hand with the sandwiches?'

'Wouldn't mind. Sally Miller was meant to be doing it with me, but her little girl's got a cold and she's staying at home with her.'

'Oh, Sally, yes.' Sally Miller was one of the Banner Primary mothers; a few weeks ago, Isobel had enjoyed a fascinating gossip with her outside the school gates. Isobel now knew a great deal more than she had done before about the school staff. She went to pick up a spare knife. 'Shall I do some filling while you butter?'

'Lovely. The fillings are over there.' The woman nodded towards a big tray covered with a tea towel. 'I'm Nan Black.'

'Isobel Langland.'

They were in the middle of comparing notes on families – Nan had two girls a few years older than Dory – when, glancing up, Nan said suddenly, 'Oh gosh. Unless you want your name carved on the wretched rota in letters an inch deep, you'd better stop making sandwiches and start looking totally clueless.'

'Why?'

'Mrs Bellyflop's coming.'

A loud voice could be heard from outside: 'Get *under* it, Martin, move your bloody *feet*! It's not likely to fall right into your outstretched hands, now, is it?'

'Mrs Bellyflop?' Isobel couldn't believe she'd heard right.

Nan grinned. 'I'll explain later. She won't stay long, that's the one good thing you can say about her.'

A large person materialised in the doorway, dressed in a navy anorak over a gathered cotton skirt with a pattern like sofa covers. Isobel knew her by sight; they had exchanged good mornings several times. Removing a headscarf from tightly permed grey hair, the woman said, 'What's the score? That idiot of a lad who's meant to put it up has obviously gone off somewhere. They can't possibly be ninety-two for three.'

'They are,' Nan said. 'And it's only just three. Noel made a good catch.'

'Hrmph.'

You might have said well done, Isobel thought.

The woman went over to inspect a plate of finished sandwiches, lifting a corner of crust to peer inside. 'What's this?' she demanded.

'Salmon and cucumber,' Nan said shortly.

'*Salmon*?' Good heavens, Nan, don't spoil them!'

'It was special offer at Safeway.'

'All the same, you shouldn't –'

'This is Isobel Langland,' Nan interrupted. The woman turned, apparently only noticing that there was someone else in the room because Nan had brought her to her attention. She lurched over to Isobel, holding out a hand like a ham.

'Hilary Bellafield,' she shouted. 'How d'you do? Come to help with the teas? That's the idea, we're always short.'

'Isobel has just been telling me she suffers from dermatitis,' Nan said. 'Nasty weeping blisters, all over her palms.'

Isobel hastily put her hands behind her back. Hilary Bellafield, she noticed, wanting to laugh, was trying to wipe the hand that had just shaken Isobel's on the back of her skirt.

'Oh Lord,' she muttered. Then, up to volume again, 'No sandwich-making for you, then.' She glared at Isobel, as if this imaginary dermatitis were a condition Isobel had deliberately acquired in order to get out of cricket club teas. Since it was exactly that, Isobel felt quite guilty.

'She's going to let me know when it clears up,' Nan was saying. 'Then I'll put her on the rota.'

'Husband playing, is he?'

Isobel nodded. 'Yes. Lawrence, playing on the right behind the wicket.'

Hilary Bellafield went to the door and looked out, studying the play for some minutes. Then, coming back, she said accusingly, 'He's the man who bought Oxleat Woods.'

'Yes, we –'

'You're in Mad Albert's cottage.'

Were they? 'We're renting the cottage on the green.'

'Yes, Mad Albert's, just what I said. Like it, do you?'

'It's –' Realising that discussing their home with this rude woman was the last thing she wanted to do, Isobel said, 'We do.'

'You surprise me,' Hilary said. 'Albert lived like an animal. I'm amazed the place wasn't verminous.' Leaning closer, resting the bulge of her stomach on the table where Isobel was perching, she whispered, 'Find anything?'

'No vermin, no.'

'I meant –' She glanced back at Nan, who had still not gone back to her sandwich-making but was staring at Mrs Bellafield with dislike evident in her expression. 'Oh, never mind.'

Nan said, 'Village gossip held that poor old Albert was a closet sexual deviant, whereas in fact anyone who bothered to give him the time of day –' she shot Mrs Bellafield a look that suggested Mrs Bellafield hadn't – 'knew he was merely a slightly simple, harmless old man. What Hilary wants to know, Isobel, is whether or not Albert's cupboards and drawers yielded anything salacious.'

Isobel looked at Hilary Bellafield, who didn't even have the grace to seem ashamed. 'I'm sorry to disappoint you, but no. Unless you're interested in a very old pair of underpants that had been used to block a draught in the bedroom window?'

There was a snort of laughter from Nan. Mrs Bellafield frowned, then said, 'Of course not. Now I must go,' she went on accusingly, as if Isobel and Nan had been trying to detain her. 'Hundred and one things to do, and Lionel will be wanting some tea. Tell Derek he'll be fit to play again next week,' she said to Nan.

Then, with a flurry of chintz skirt, she was gone.

Into the vacuum left behind her, Isobel said, 'What a ghastly woman.'

'Isn't she?' Nan agreed, getting back to her buttering.

'Is she always like that?'

'No, she's fairly subdued at the moment. They've got money worries, poor things.'

'You mean she's usually worse?' It was hard to credit.

'Much worse. How's the dermatitis?'

'It's made an amazingly sudden recovery.' Isobel fetched another bowl of sandwich filling. 'Thanks so much for that.'

'It's okay. I didn't see why you should be roped in for teas on your very first visit.'

'I don't know anything about dermatitis,' Isobel said. 'I'll have to look it up in case she asks me about it.'

'I know all about it. I'm a nurse.' Nan stopped her buttering and looked at Isobel. 'I hope you don't think I was interfering. Noel says I'm always pushing in and deciding things for other people who are quite capable of deciding them without my help.'

Isobel met her eyes. 'I don't think you're interfering, I think you're very kind.'

Nan smiled wryly. 'No I'm not. Noel's right really. I usually think I know what's best for people.'

'Who doesn't?'

'Certainly Mrs Bellyflop does,' Nan said.

'Wonderful name,' Isobel observed.

'My girls called her that because of the stomach.'

'I noticed.'

There was silence while they finished the sandwiches. A companionable silence, Isobel thought; funny how you meet some people and straight away feel easy with them, whereas with others, you –

'Do you like village life?' Nan asked, loading cups and saucers on to a tray.

'I think so. It's too early to say, really.'

'Where were you before?'

'Ewell.'

'What made you move down here? Your husband wasn't made redundant, like poor old Mike Hearst, was he? He's really –' Abruptly Nan broke off, clamping a hand over her mouth. 'Sorry. None of my business. You'll think I'm as bad as bloody Mrs Bellyflop.'

'No I won't. I don't, I mean.' It was, indeed, quite different, meeting Nan's concerned enquiry. 'Lawrence wanted a change, and in fact he'd already made up his mind to hand in his notice when he was made redundant, so we were quite lucky.'

'I can't see that it's ever lucky to be made redundant,' Nan remarked.

'It is if you're planning to leave anyway, because it means you go with a nice fat cheque instead of without it.'

'I see what you mean.' Nan stacked the cups and saucers beside the tea urn. Then she said thoughtfully, 'It was brave of you to agree to alter your life so drastically just because your husband wanted a change.'

Brave. Nobody had said Isobel was brave before. People had said, 'How do you like it?' and, 'How are you settling in?' Even, 'Was the house verminous when you moved in?'

Brave.

Was I brave? she wondered. I might have been, if I'd wanted to go on living the Ewell life. As it was . . .

'It wasn't a question of being brave,' she said, finding that she didn't want to parade in false colours in front of this straight-speaking, kind-hearted woman. 'I wasn't totally averse to a change either.'

Nan studied her. 'For reasons you don't want to talk about,' she said.

Was it so obvious? 'No. Not really.'

'And why should you? Sorry.'

'It's okay.'

The extraordinary thing, Isobel thought as she helped arrange the final stack of cups and saucers and then went outside with Nan to watch the last over before tea, was that she'd almost poured out to Nan the whole miserable story.

Isobel found Lawrence in the crush of players helping themselves to tea, and he introduced her to Noel Black.

'I've been talking to your wife,' she said as they shook hands.

'Oh dear, has she roped you in for teas?' Noel asked.

'Quite the contrary. She saved me from being roped in by your friend Mrs Bellyflop.'

'Yes, we all noticed she'd stopped by. You couldn't really miss her, could you?'

'Was she the creature in the flowery skirt?' Lawrence asked.

'Yes,' Noel said. 'One of her quieter outfits. She has a stripy thing that frightens horses.'

'She told Nan to tell someone called Derek that Lionel will be fit to play next week. She made it sound as if she'd issued an order.'

'She probably has.' Noel made a face. 'For thirty-five years, poor old Lionel hasn't even blown his nose unless Hilary said it was okay.'

'Derek's the captain,' Lawrence informed her. 'That's him, in the hat.'

'Oh.' She looked to where he was pointing, then back to Lawrence. 'I thought I'd stay and give Nan a hand clearing up, then I'm going home. Jacob's at Brian Dent's this afternoon, but he'll be home in time for *Gladiators* and I don't want him to be in alone with Dory. She's still a bit twitchy after her experience with the deer.'

'Who's Dory?' Noel asked. 'Your dog?'

'No, my daughter.'

Noel looked embarrassed. 'Oh dear. Sorry.'

Lawrence was laughing, and Isobel found herself joining in. 'Don't worry about it,' Lawrence said.

'Won't you join us in the pub afterwards?' Noel asked her. 'Nan usually does. I could make amends by buying you an enormous drink.'

'No amends necessary.' She smiled at him. 'Thanks anyway, but I really should go home.'

'Another time, then.'

'Definitely.'

Lawrence said, with reasonably credible innocence, 'Oh, do we go to the pub afterwards?'

He had enjoyed his first game with the village eleven, he reflected, as he stood and sipped his first pint of the evening. It was a pity they hadn't won. It had looked as if they might, and, gratifyingly, it was his own partnership with Derek that had got them anywhere near the visitors' total. Lawrence had made seventy-seven; not bad considering it had probably been twenty years or more since he'd lifted a cricket bat.

'Another pint, Lawrence?' Someone was waving a jug in his direction. Lawrence hadn't room in his glass for a whole pint, but he accepted a top-up.

He hoped he'd played well enough to be kept in the team. There would be long-standing regulars to consider.

Some time later, when quite a lot of the cricketers had gone home, the village elderlies started to drift in. One of the first was Harold Pickett, who elbowed his way to the bar, ordered a brown and mild, and then demanded his usual little table under the dart board with the determined single-mindedness that once won Britain an empire.

The displaced cricketers who had been sitting there seemed not to mind; they were, Lawrence assumed, used to Harold Pickett.

He went over to say hello.

'Been playing, have you?' Harold Pickett asked.

No, I always dress like this, Lawrence wanted to say. 'I have.'

'Do anything useful?'

'I made seventy-seven.'

'Not bad, not bad,' Harold acknowledged. 'How are things in Oxleat Woods?'

'Funnily enough, there was something I wanted to ask you,' Lawrence said, sitting down. 'Seeing you has reminded me.'

Harold took a very long drink of his brown and mild. 'Thirsty weather,' he observed.

Lawrence got up and went to order him another pint.

'Now then,' Harold said, when he had polished off his first drink and made a start on the second, 'what was it you was wanting to know?'

'You were telling me a couple of months or so back about how you used to walk in the woods with your grandmother,' Lawrence began, 'and that –'

'My old granny,' Harold said lovingly. 'My dear old granny. Had nine children, she did. She were that good to me, my granny.' There was a suspicion of moisture in Harold's bleary blue eyes.

'Yes, I'm sure,' Lawrence said, biting down his impatience. 'My granny was quite nice, too. But what I wanted to ask was, could you explain where it was you saw the rhododendrons?'

Harold gave him an assessing look. 'Want to go looking for the old house, do you? Hunting for buried treasure? There won't be any of that, I can tell you. You'd be wasting your time looking.'

'I'm not interested in buried treasure. Well,' Lawrence amended honestly, 'no more than the next man. I just thought it'd be so fascinating to discover the ruins of an old house in the woods.'

Harold watched him for a few moments, then said, 'Fair

enough. Reckon I'd feel the same. Now, then,' he wriggled around in his seat, making himself more comfortable, 'let me see.' He screwed up his face in concentration. 'We used to go in from the other road, not where you go in now, through that gate on the main road. Granny used to take me along the footpath. Know where I mean?'

'No,' Lawrence said baldly.

'Hm. Maybe it's not there any more.'

There was a long pause, during which Harold didn't say anything at all. Lawrence had an idea. 'I suppose,' he said tentatively, 'you wouldn't come and have a look? Refresh your memory, so to speak?'

'What, me with my hips?' Harold sounded incredulous.

'Well, we could go in the van.'

'Not all the way, we couldn't. Can't go driving among overgrown rhododendrons, stands to reason.'

'I thought we could drive along the tracks, and you could tell me if anything looked familiar.'

'Hm.' Harold had another long think.

'Perhaps,' Lawrence said craftily, 'you would allow me to make it worth your while. After all, you would be giving up some of your valuable time.'

'Valuable to you, it seems,' Harold replied quickly.

Not so dozy as he likes to pretend, Lawrence thought. 'Indeed it is,' he said equably. 'Shall we say a tenner for an afternoon out in the good fresh air?'

'Make it twenty.'

'Fifteen, and I'll buy you lunch and a pint in here.'

'Done. Tomorrow suit you?'

'Monday would suit me better.' Lawrence was committed to puppy-buying the next day.

'Monday,' Harold said. 'Collect me at ten o'clock. Know where I live?' Lawrence shook his head. 'Holly Lane. Number Five.'

'I hope you won't let me down,' Lawrence said, only half jokingly, as he got up to return to the bar.

Harold eyed him. 'I won't,' he replied.

CHAPTER FOURTEEN

Lawrence didn't get the smooth start to Monday morning that he had anticipated. The puppies had produced lakes of widdle on the kitchen floor – a generous stream of which had run under the Rayburn, producing an awful smell of gently simmering dog urine – and Lawrence had done the lion's share of the clearing-up. Isobel had been making ominous retching noises, so it hadn't seemed a good idea to enlist her help. Jacob, to Lawrence's surprise and delight, hadn't minded the smell in the least, cheerfully helping to swab the flagstones, reaching in under the stove with a Flash-soaked rag, and even singing as he did so.

'They can't help it,' he explained to the disgusted Dory. 'They lived in a shed before, with a fenced-in run where they did their wees and stuff.'

'Not over breakfast!' Dory said with a shudder.

'They'll be house-trained soon,' Jacob said confidently. 'The lady said they nearly are now, it's just the strangeness of being in a new house. I expect they miss their mum.' He picked up the two puppies – which had been christened Rosie and Millie – and held them up so he could nuzzle them. Their plump brown and white bodies wriggled in delight, and they licked all the bits of his face that they could reach.

Lawrence, catching Izzy's expression, muttered, 'It's all right. Mrs Hall said they've been wormed.'

Lawrence was nearly as taken with Rosie and Millie as

Jacob was; he suspected Izzy, too, wasn't immune to their charm. It was difficult to see how anyone could be. One of them, released by Jacob, was nibbling at her shoe, pulling at the lace as if determined to get it undone; Izzy started to smile.

The puppies were pedigree springers, and, although it was hard to tell at eight weeks how they'd be as adult dogs, they seemed to have the friendly, affectionate nature typical of the breed.

'Dad, we don't have to have their tails cut off, do we?' Jacob was asking anxiously.

'No, Jacob, I shouldn't think so.' Mrs Hall had explained that you always used to dock springers because, when they were running through thick undergrowth putting up game, their tails got full of burrs, dead thistle heads and other detritus. Nowadays, however, she said, you'd be lucky to find a vet who'd do the operation. Lawrence didn't fancy doing it himself, so it looked as if Rosie and Millie would remain as Mother Nature made them.

When Jacob and Dory had left to catch the bus into school, Lawrence tucked the puppies up in their box in the corner of the kitchen.

'They won't stay there,' Isobel remarked. He glanced at her; she was looking down at the puppies with an expression almost as soppy as Jacob's.

'No. You may spend a fair part of your morning falling over them.'

'I'll try not to hurt them. Can't we make a run of some sort outside, like Mrs Hall had? I'm sure it can't be good for them to be inside all day.'

'I agree. I'll see what I can do this afternoon. There's some chicken wire in the shed, and I expect I can find some posts or something.' He went over to her, putting a hand on her shoulder as she stood at the sink finishing the washing-up. 'Izzy, are you sure you don't mind?'

He'd meant did she mind about the puppies. But as he said the words, it occurred to him that there were a great many things to which the question could equally be applied. Are you sure you don't mind living in a cramped, dark little rented house, in a village where you hardly know a soul? Are you sure you don't mind not having shops, lunch parties, friends to gossip with? Are you sure you don't mind country life, married to a financial manager who, virtually overnight, has turned into a woodsman?

He almost asked her the whole lot. But he was sure he felt her shoulder stiffen under his touch, as if she knew what was in his mind and didn't want to hear it.

The silence extended; the moment passed.

She said, 'I don't mind.'

I wish, Lawrence thought as he went to find the van keys, that I could talk to my wife. Find out what she's thinking. How she really feels. Only I'm half afraid of what she'll say.

On the way out through the kitchen he paused. He wanted to go to her, take her in his arms, tell her he appreciated the effort she was putting in to making this new life work. To tell her, even, that he loved her. He couldn't remember when he'd last said it. It was something you assumed your wife knew without being told.

Wasn't it?

He watched her back as he laced up his boots.

Perhaps it wasn't.

'Izzy?' he said.

'Hm?' She turned round.

Their eyes met across two yards of kitchen.

His nerve failed. Whatever was the right moment, it certainly wasn't in an untidy kitchen that smelt of puppy, when Izzy was hard at work and he was in a hurry.

He just said, 'I'll be home after lunch, and I'll make a better arrangement for the pups.'

She gave him a smile. 'Thanks.'

Then she went back to her washing-up.

Harold Pickett must have been watching out for him; as he drew up outside Number Five, Holly Lane, Harold emerged from the house, closing and locking the door, then trying it at least three times. Then he stepped carefully up the short path, making elaborate use of his walking stick, securing the gate behind him as conscientiously as he'd fastened the front door. Which, Lawrence thought, was pretty silly as the gate was only about three feet high, and anyone intent on committing a felony in Harold Pickett's little house would simply have stepped over it.

'You're late,' Harold said as Lawrence helped him into the van.

'I know. Sorry, I had to clear up after our new puppies.'

'Tsk. In the house, are they?'

'Yes. For the time being.'

'I don't hold with dogs in the house. Yard's the place for a dog.'

There didn't seem much point explaining; he just said, 'Quite.'

He noticed that Harold had dressed up for the outing. He had a maroon waistcoat under the jacket of his grey suit, and he had polished his old-fashioned black shoes till they shone like a soldier's toecaps. It touched Lawrence that the old boy had bothered.

'Lovely morning,' he said.

'Aye.'

'Just the day for a jaunt in the country, don't you think?'

'Ye-es,' Harold said guardedly. 'As long as my hips can take it.'

'We'll drive as far as we can.' They were approaching a junction just outside the village. 'Now, where did you say I should go?'

Harold leaned forward in his seat, grimacing out through the windscreen. 'Reckon it must be along there.' He waved in the direction of the lesser road. 'This ain't it, not the little lane my granny and I used to walk along. But the lane goes off this road.' There was a pause. 'It *must* do.'

'We'll have a look,' Lawrence said, putting the van into gear and moving off. 'If it's wrong, we'll look somewhere else.'

He'd said it to be reassuring; Harold had seemed anxious. But he heard the old man give a quiet chuckle, and, turning briefly, saw that Harold was regarding him with an amused expression. 'Now, there's an idea,' Harold murmured. 'Never have thought of that meself, I wouldn't.'

Biting back the retort that sarcasm was the lowest form of wit, Lawrence drove slowly off up the lane.

'That's it!' Harold shouted suddenly, after about half a mile. 'See? That there stile, with the oak tree beside it. Got it?'

Lawrence, stopping, stared. The oak was plainly visible, but a stile . . .

'That?' he said. 'That broken bit of fence?'

'That's a stile,' Harold insisted. 'Leastways, it used to be.' His eyes went dreamy. 'I can see my granny now, lifting her skirts, hopping up on the step like a young girl . . .'

'Where do we go from here?' Lawrence asked. It seemed a good idea not to let Harold wander too far off down memory lane. Getting him back again might prove difficult, and there was work to be done.

'What? Oh.' Harold stared glumly at the stile. 'See what you mean.'

'Even if we manage to get over –' Lawrence had almost said, get you over, but, in the interests of diplomacy, managed not to – 'there's not much of a path the other side. It's dreadfully overgrown.'

'Don't suppose anyone's used it in years,' Harold said.

'They don't. People won't walk any more, they take their cars, park up somewhere and eat their picnics leaning up against their own front bumpers.'

He was absolutely right.

'Isn't there a track a bit further up, on the same side?' Lawrence said. 'I'm sure there is.' He edged the van forwards.

'Track? I don't know about any track . . . oh.'

There it was. Only a vehicle's width, deeply rutted, almost as overgrown as the path beyond the stile, but a track. Definitely.

'Good God alive, you ain't going to drive up there?' Harold, clutching at the door handle as if about to throw himself out, looked aghast.

'Yes. But I'll go gently, I promise.'

Lawrence put the van at the track. There was a lurch as first one front wheel, then the other, went down into the ruts. But after that, progress, although bumpy, was steady.

'Watch out!' Harold yelled as the low branch of a beech tree loomed ahead.

'Got it,' Lawrence replied calmly, as the van went under the branch with probably no more than six inches to spare.

'Steady!' Harold shouted as an enormous puddle spread before them.

'I think we can make it.' Lawrence kept the revs high, slipping the clutch as they drove very slowly through the water.

'Oh, my dear Lord,' Harold said piously, covering his face with his hands as the track went past a steep slope that fell away to the right.

They came to what looked like a meeting of the ways; from the left, a narrower track met and crossed the one they were on. It seemed highly likely that it was the path leading up from the stile.

'Harold?' Harold didn't reply. 'It's all right, we've

stopped.' Very slowly, Harold took his hands away from his face. 'I think that's the path you would have walked up,' Lawrence said. 'What do you think?'

Harold stared. He looked to the right, then straight in front of him, then back at the path. Then, turning to grin at Lawrence, 'Reckon you're right.'

Trying to control the excitement, Lawrence said casually, 'Drive on a bit, do you think?'

But Harold shook his head. 'No. The rhododendrons were that way.' He waved towards where the path dived off to the right, under a stand of fir trees.

'Shall we try walking, then?'

Harold was grinning again. 'Reckon we might.'

The path was fairly clear under the trees. Many years of fallen pine needles had made a pleasant surface for walking; footsteps fell with a muffled sound, and there were few brambles to clutch at the ankles.

Then the belt of trees ended, and the path became much more overgrown. 'Let me go ahead,' Lawrence said. 'I'll try to beat a way for you.'

But Harold was lost in his memories. Swishing his stick at nettles and low branches, he was muttering to himself. '"Long way for a little feller like you," she'd say. "You'm earned your tea, my laddie," and she'd fish out a piece of lardy cake, or a gert slab of gingerbread, and we'd sit there on that very branch, and . . .'

It was, Lawrence concluded, the right path.

He had noticed a change in the woods even before Harold said anything. Oak, birch, beech and chestnut had, slowly but steadily, lost their predominance, and given way to other sorts of trees. There was something with pretty coppery leaves, heavy with blossom as yet in tight bud . . . something else which, even to Lawrence's inexperienced eye, was surely an apple tree? And then a whole clump of the same trees, perhaps an ancient, long-forgotten orchard, whose trees, unpruned, had reverted to the wild and now only yielded a meagre harvest . . .

Then, right in front of them, an enormous rhododendron, grown to the height of a tree, spreading right across the path.

Harold turned to Lawrence, a look of triumph on his face. 'Rhododendron,' he said unnecessarily. 'This here's the wild one – it'll have lovely mauve flowers before much longer – but if I remember right, we'll come to some cultivated ones if we go on down the path.' He pushed aside a swathe of rhododendron with his stick, and led the way.

They were, Lawrence realised, at the top of the bank above the stream, but at a place he hadn't really explored yet. They must be about half a mile from where the stream met the road, deep into the wood.

Harold was inching forwards, holding on to tree branches. Only a few yards in front of him, the slope dropped away towards the little valley through which the stream ran.

'Steady,' Lawrence said. 'That's quite a drop in front of you.'

'I can see that,' Harold said with some asperity. 'I'm not blind.'

Lawrence wondered how he stood as regards insurance, if someone walking in the woods with him fell and half-crippled himself.

'The path goes down there, see,' Harold said, waving with his stick. 'It zigzags down the slope.'

He was right. The terraced path wound backwards and forwards across the slope leading down into the valley, so that its gradient was quite gentle. All the same, it still didn't look like the sort of thing an elderly man with a stick and dicky hips ought to be tackling. 'Shall I go on by myself?' Lawrence suggested.

'Not on your nelly!' Harold pressed on along the path,

apparently without a thought as to how he was going to get back up again. 'Look! What did I tell you?'

There were other rhododendrons, smaller bushes with leaves of a different green. Azaleas, too, and something that looked like a clump of nightmarishly huge rhubarb. And, clinging to the steepest part of the slope, a structure that could once have been a rockery.

Harold pointed at a large, rambling bush with big, glossy leaves and a mass of tight, pointy buds. 'Magnolia.'

Lawrence's excitement bubbled over. 'This was a garden, wasn't it?' he said. 'A planned, carefully laid out, lovingly tended garden.'

Harold looked almost as excited. 'It was that. And it's exactly where my old granny used to bring me. There were a bench, once upon a time . . . where was it, now?' He stared in front of him, frowning. Then: 'There. Where the path makes its final bend before it goes out into the valley.'

Lawrence ran on down the path, bounding over obstacles, not even noticing the brambles whipping at his face and hands.

Yes. On the bend, just where Harold had said, was an ancient wooden bench, covered now by a mass of under-growth. Lawrence called out, 'It's still here.'

There was silence. Turning, Lawrence saw that Harold was standing quite still, a soft smile on his face.

It must be, Lawrence thought, quite a moment for him.

Lawrence went on into the valley, only half aware of the sounds of Harold's progress down the path. If that was the garden, he was thinking, then the house must have been . . .

'You're standing in the hall,' Harold's voice floated down. 'The house was right there.'

Lawrence whipped round. 'How can you be so sure? You never said you knew where the house was!'

'You never asked,' Harold replied. He negotiated the last few yards of path and came to stand beside Lawrence.

'Course, I didn't know it as a house, like, only as a ruin. But my granny knew it. She were in service there, before she married. Women didn't work after they married, not in Granny's day. Anyway, she couldn'ta gone on working in the house, because it burnt down. Round about 1890, would have been. In the old Queen's day.'

Lawrence waited for him to go on, but he was lost in his dreams. 'So your granny brought you here for your picnics? To the place where she'd been in service? And showed you where all the rooms used to be, the hall, the kitchens, I suppose, and –'

'Stable block were over there.' Harold pointed. 'Kitchen garden, down there in that big flat bit, where the stream bends round. This 'ere were the ornamental garden. Stands to reason, it were what the main rooms looked out over. Grandfather was the head gardener. He used to keep it looking something beautiful, Granny said. Roses, that was his speciality. We'd probably find some if we looked.'

'Hm.' Lawrence wasn't really listening. He was picturing a house – Georgian? Or older? Jacobean, or Tudor, per-haps? A house that stood in a quiet valley in the woods, where people had lived down through the centuries . . .

'My hip's giving me gyp,' Harold announced. 'And I'm spitting feathers.'

'You're – oh, you're thirsty. Okay,' Lawrence smiled, 'hint taken.'

Turning, they began the formidable task of getting Harold back up the zigzag path, along beneath the rhodo-dendrons and the firs, and back to the van.

CHAPTER FIFTEEN

Dory was singing as she ran across the green towards home. Sam hadn't been on the bus today – he had CCF on Fridays and stayed after school – but she was going to meet him later.

The episode with the deer had changed things. Changed a lot of things, some of them very profound, although Dory wasn't ready yet to think about those. Her whole attitude to living in the country, for example. But, on the Sam front, now that it was clear he liked her too, she could admit to herself that she'd fancied him from the moment he'd offered her fourteen pence to get her out of the embarrassment of not having enough bus fare. Well, she'd fancied him before, really. Seen him larking around with his friends and liked the look of him, the fair hair and the eyes that sometimes appeared blue, sometimes green. The strong shoulders, the well-developed muscles in the neck. She hadn't known who he was, then.

'Sam,' she said softly as she set off up the path to the house. 'Sam.'

The morning after they'd helped the stricken deer, Sam had been waiting at the bus stop when she got there, which was unusual as he rarely caught the bus in the morning, more often getting a lift in with an older friend who'd passed his test and had the use of the family's spare car. Dory could hardly wait for the day when such freedom was available to her, although she prayed with all her might that her parents would have something more elegant than the crappy old van by then; it would do her street cred no good whatsoever to go calling for her friends in a van with a sliding door and rolls of wire and a dozen fence posts in the back.

'I wanted to make sure you were okay,' Sam had said. 'If I'd waited to see you on the bus this afternoon, even if you weren't okay now, you would be by then. If you see what I mean.'

She did. And her heart was jumping about like someone on a bouncy castle at the thought of his being so concerned.

'I'm fine,' she said. Which wasn't what she'd told them all at breakfast – the drama and the attention were too good not to milk for all they were worth – but Sam wasn't to know.

'Did you sleep all right?'

She risked a look at him. He was staring out across the road, as if suddenly riveted by the wheelie bin that someone had just put out in front of the imposing entrance to the Bellyflops' house. 'Yes, eventually.' She hesitated. Then, because his asking seemed to make it all right to confess: 'Actually I kept waking up. I couldn't stop seeing the poor thing's head, after – well, you know.'

'Yes. I'm sorry.'

'You had to do it. I only hope –' goodness, it was difficult! 'I just hope I have the courage to do what you did, if I ever have to.'

He made an awkward sort of noise, which could have been acknowledgement or denial. Then, after a moment, he said, 'Would you like to learn to shoot?'

'*Me?*' It came out as a squeak. 'Me? Golly, I don't think I'd be allowed!' What her parents' reaction would be to herself, standing brandishing a gun, didn't bear thinking about.

He smiled. 'It's not so alarming. And it's not against the law, if that's what's bothering you, provided it's on your

179

own land or you've got the landowner's permission. My dad taught me. He got me a four-ten – that's a small shotgun,' he explained, 'and took me out rough shooting.'

'What's that?'

'Rabbits, pigeons.'

'Why?' she demanded. 'You said last night that killing things made you feel funny, so why did you go out shooting pigeons and rabbits?'

Her voice had suddenly got strident. Not for the first time, she wished she had a bit more self-control.

But when he spoke, he sounded as if he understood. 'Dory, killing things is part of the whole scene. My dad has an allotment, which he works hard on, and if he let the birds and the rabbits have unlimited access, there wouldn't be anything left for us. He does his best with netting, and with old plastic bottles on sticks to make a noise and scare the birds off, but it's never enough. We only kill to keep the numbers down. Believe me, there are always hundreds more than we ever take. And we eat them. My mum makes a great rabbit casserole.'

'Oh.'

She stood staring at her shoes, weighing up the conflicting claims of her lifelong stance as a defender of animals – which, she had to admit, had usually been more for the sake of having something to argue with her parents about than from any profound conviction – and her huge desire to let Sam and his dad teach her how to shoot.

'Think about it,' Sam said. 'Dad often takes me out on Friday evenings. You could come with us, if you like. You could just watch, the first time.'

'I'd have to ask Mum and Dad.'

'Of course. Would they let you, d'you think?'

'If your father's in charge, I should think so.'

The bus came round the bend into the village. Sam said, 'Let me know?' and she nodded.

As if by silent agreement, they didn't sit together on the bus. Sam went to the back, where one of his friends punched him and said, 'The Gunners lost last night! They're a load of wankers, your team!'

Dory found an empty seat next to Emma Hardcastle. Emma said, almost before Dory had settled, 'I didn't know you knew Sam Hearst.'

It sounded like an accusation. 'Actually, yes.' Dory bit down hard on the words that implored to be spoken: we shared a very important event last night. And he's going to teach me to shoot a four-ten.

Emma hissed, 'He's not bad, is he?'

Dory's first instinct was to say something dismissive, both of Sam, and of Emma Hardcastle's curiosity. But her first instinct gave way before a second one. One that said gently, Emma's trying to be friendly. Do I really want to reject friendship?

She leant her head towards Emma's and whispered back, 'He lives quite near us.'

'He does CCF on Fridays,' Emma said. 'I like their uniforms. They make them look dead smart.'

'Yes. But not that little feller who gets on the bus at the crossroads. He looks more like a pudding than a soldier.'

Emma giggled, more generously than Dory's feeble joke deserved. But Dory took it as a gesture of tentative new liking. 'That was a good rehearsal last night, wasn't it?'

'It was all right,' Emma agreed. 'Mrs Sawyer says I can borrow a gold chain that she's got, a really thick one with little jewels hanging on it.'

'Great! You were right to make your point,' Dory said, with the experience of one who had spent a good fourteen years making her point at every possible opportunity.

'That's what I thought. What's your costume like? Has Mrs Sawyer said yet?'

'Dark tights and a silver-grey doublet with purple bits,

because Ferdinand's royal. And a silver band round my head, like a coronet. And she says can I have my hair trimmed just before the performance.'

'Hey, that's drastic! Will you?'

Dory had been going to refuse – she'd thought she'd try her hair long for a while – but then, if she were going to go rough shooting with Sam, maybe a short boyish haircut was more suitable. 'Might,' she said.

As the bus disgorged its load, Sam came up behind her and gave her a nudge. 'See you later,' he said.

She didn't know if he was aware of how perfect his timing was. She and Emma had just been spotted by four other girls in the class, who, running across to join them, couldn't possibly have missed Sam's gesture, even if Emma had, which didn't seem very likely.

As Dory set off up the road towards the school, for once the centre of a group instead of on her own, the other four girls wanted to know about Sam. And this time, Dory was ready. She dropped her first hint as they went in through the school gates, her second as they were dumping their bags in the classroom, her third as the bell went for assembly.

By the time break came, most of the class knew that Something Had Happened to Dory Langland on the way home from the play rehearsal last night. Dory, inwardly smiling, decided she'd spin it out till lunchtime before she told them what it was.

Now, running the last few yards home, she was bubbling with the excited anticipation of going out with Sam later. Okay, his dad was going to be there too, but that was fine. It was better, maybe, that they weren't going to be alone together – this first time, anyway. She had a quiet conviction that it wouldn't be the last. And her parents undoubtedly wouldn't have let her go just with Sam; they weren't too happy about the shooting anyway, and had only said yes because she'd promised she'd watch to begin with, and because Sam's dad had come round to say he didn't allow any nonsense, and Dory would be safe with him and Sam.

Sam's dad had proved to be a formidable man, tall, broad-shouldered, and unsmiling. He looked as if he'd just had bad news. Dory was actually a bit nervous about him, and had to keep reminding herself that he couldn't be that bad, since he'd agreed to her going with him and Sam on their Friday evening shoot.

She liked calling it a shoot. It made it seem important, conjuring up images of hip flasks and plus fours, eager dogs rushing into undergrowth and people talking about beating and Purdeys, whatever they were.

She flung open the back door and said, 'Mum, can I eat early because –'

Then she noticed her mother wasn't alone: Auntie Maude – no, not Auntie! – Maude was sitting at the table with her, and they looked as if Dory's entrance had interrupted a right old gossip.

'Maude! I didn't know you were coming!' Dory chucked her school bag into the corner and went to give her aunt a kiss. Maude was wearing a suede jacket the colour of toffee, over a cream sweater and a black skirt; she had a silk scarf knotted round her neck that perfectly matched the jacket. She smelt divine.

'Hi, Dory.' Maude kissed her in return. 'How's tricks?'

'I'm going shooting this evening.'

'Shooting?' Maude raised an eyebrow. 'Good Lord, child, has country life made a convert of you so soon?'

Dory glanced at her mother, waiting for her to say something crass about Sam. But she didn't, merely smiled encouragingly.

'Not exactly,' Dory said. 'There's this boy I know, and

the other night me and him had to kill this deer I found in the road. It had been run over.'

'Ghastly,' Maude murmured.

'I got blood all over my skirt, then Sam shot it. In the head. The deer, I mean.'

'Good God.'

It was lovely that Maude was reacting so much. 'It was the kind thing to do,' Dory pontificated. 'The poor thing's leg was only hanging on by the skin, and –'

'Dory, I applaud your compassion in putting a creature out of its misery, but –'

'Her misery. It was a doe.'

'– but I really don't think I wish to hear the gory details. What else is new?'

'I'm Ferdinand in the play, and Emma Hardcastle says I can go to her house tomorrow and look at videos.'

'Emma Hardcastle?' Mum said. 'Who's she?'

'A girl in my class.' Dory helped herself to a cake; they were very attractive cream ones, with bits of kiwi fruit and stuff on the top. Maude must have brought them.

'Have a cake, Dory,' Maude murmured.

'She's invited you over?' Mum was asking.

'Yeah.'

'That's nice. Will you need a lift?'

Dory could tell that Mum was pleased but trying to be cool about it. The old familiar irritation rose up like indigestion, but then she thought, Mum's being pleased for me as much as for herself. More, maybe. She said noncommittally, 'I can catch the bus over. But you or Dad could pick me up.' As an afterthought, she added, 'Please.'

Isobel looked astonished. Then she said, 'I expect that'll be all right.'

'We could all go,' Maude said. 'You, Piers and I could have a drink in some quaint country pub on the way. I can play yokel-spotting.' She glanced at Dory. 'We'll go in my

car, then whoever gets put in the back won't have to disen-
tangle themselves from rolls of barbed wire.'

'It's not barbed wire,' Isobel said. 'But I take your point.
Dory, have you got homework and what time are you going
out?'

'No, and half-past seven.'

'We're eating at eight. I'll give you yours with Jacob.'

Dory smiled at her mother, who resumed her astonished
look. Then, turning to include Maude as well, she asked
her mother and her aunt if they'd come upstairs with her
and tell her what you wore to go shooting.

Isobel set the table for Maude, Lawrence and herself in a
daze, still trying to adapt to the fact that her daughter had
said *please*. Plus she'd smiled. Looked happy.

She and Maude had gone upstairs with Dory to help her
get ready. Maude had said you didn't dress up for anything
in the country, did you? To which Dory had said no, it
wasn't a question of dressing *up*, more of selecting something, then making absolutely sure you didn't look as if
you'd bothered. Then she'd turned to Isobel and asked if
she could borrow Isobel's Barbour, 'but only if you haven't
been hanging it up again. Honestly, Mum, you just *don't*,
Barbours are meant to look as if you've slept in them for
about a million years.'

Isobel had fetched her Barbour, which had in fact been
hanging up, but which was still damp from when she'd
walked the puppies before Maude arrived. Maude oblig-
ingly rolled it up all anyhow and sat on it while Dory
struggled into her jeans – the ones with the rip in the knee
– and pondered over which shirt went best with which
sweater. By the time Maude and Isobel had persuaded her
that the ginghamy shirt and the plum-coloured sweater
were best – especially if Isobel lent her a pink and mauve
scarf which she never wore because it had been a present

from Douglas, who didn't understand that they weren't Isobel's colours – the Barbour had cooked in the heat from Maude's bottom and was now satisfactorily creased and aged-looking.

'How do I look?' Dory had said as she stood in the door of her room, body tense and coiled up ready for racing off down the stairs.

Isobel had wanted to hug her. To say, in that poignant moment, you look beautiful. My lovely daughter, you're confounding me by the speed at which you're changing.

But hugs and meaningful statements weren't what Dory would want to hear, so she'd just said, 'You look very nice, darling. Casual, but as if you'd made a very small amount of effort.'

Dory grinned. 'A *very* small amount.'

'Minuscule,' Maude agreed. 'Have fun. And keep your head down.'

Dory sighed, but she was still smiling. 'I'm not doing any shooting tonight, I told you. I'm just going to watch.'

'All the more reason to keep your head down,' Maude said.

Isobel made herself not say, be careful. Or even, what time will you be back? She just said, 'We'll leave the back door open for you, Dory. Will you lock up, if we've gone to bed?'

'I won't be late,' Dory said. 'But I'll lock up, yes.'

Isobel and Maude listened as Dory's feet thumped down the stairs. Then Maude, folding up discarded jumpers and putting them back in the drawer, said, 'Going shooting. Whatever next?'

It had been, Isobel reflected as she put out wine glasses, very decent of Maude not to remark on the far more remark-worthy aspect of Dory: the sea change in her character.

'Want a hand?' Maude asked, coming into the room and stretching. She smothered a yawn. 'God, why is it that reading aloud always makes one yawn? I'm not in the least tired, but I could hardly get through the last page for yawning.'

Maude had been reading to Jacob, which was, Isobel thought, kind but totally unnecessary, Jacob being perfectly capable of reading to himself. Jacob had been fed, been allowed to take the puppies into the garden for a run, been told for the tenth time that no, he couldn't take them up with him because they had to learn that downstairs was puppy territory, upstairs was out of bounds, and then sent up to bed. Maude's kind offer of reading to him had, Isobel was sure, been intended to soften the blow of the puppy ban.

'Could you get the salad?' Isobel asked. 'It's behind you, on the sideboard.'

'Sideboard,' Maude repeated. 'Nobody has sideboards any more, do they? Not like this brute. Not yours, is it?'

'Of course not, it comes with the house.'

'Thank God,' Maude said, deftly folding paper napkins into shapes that looked like the Sydney Opera House. 'Not your style, darling, stained old dark wood sideboards.' There was a pause as Maude finished the third napkin, then she said, 'Seriously, Isobel –'

'I can't bear it when you begin by saying "Seriously",' Isobel said. 'It reminds me of far too many occasions in the past. Like, "Seriously, are you going to hand in that essay with all those spelling mistakes?" and "Seriously, you're not giving Mollie *that* for Christmas?"' Maude always called their mother Mollie. 'Even, "Seriously, Isobel, you're not really going to marry Lawrence Langland?"'

'There, I have to admit I was wrong,' Maude said. 'You and Lawrence got on far better than I'd expected.'

'Got?' Isobel repeated. 'Was that use of the past tense intentional?' A shiver of dread ran through her at the thought that the happy days she and Lawrence had shared were firmly in the past. They're not! she protested silently. It's not too late, we can have more happy days! *Are* having them!

They were. Weren't they? She had unwisely fluttered right up to the flame, back in Ewell, but she hadn't got burnt. Not too badly. Hadn't done irreparable damage.

Had she?

Maude had paused in her napkin folding and was staring at Isobel, her expression intent. 'Darling, what's wrong? It's not what it was, you and old Piers, is it?'

Isobel said in a rush, 'Yes, it is! It's fine! We're just very busy, that's all, it hasn't been easy, finding our feet down here. No time for fun!' She tried to laugh, but even to herself it sounded false.

'Fun,' Maude mused, placing a napkin on a side plate. 'Yes, you used to be such fun together.' She, too, appeared to be making an effort, moving away from the dangerous ground of the present to the safer waters of the past. 'I remember leaving your flat in the early days with my ribs aching from laughing so much. Do you remember that night when Piers insisted we played sardines, and that idiot man from the penthouse went and hid on the flat roof outside your kitchen, and his friend fell off into the dustbin?'

'Vividly.' Isobel was grateful for Maude's tact. 'Lawrence had to find him a shirt, because his was covered in tea leaves and potato peel, and he gave him a rugby club one that said "Onanist of the Month", and the chap obviously didn't have a clue what an onanist was.'

'And,' Maude was laughing, 'ages later Piers met him in the street still wearing it, and he said, "I really must let you have your T-shirt back".'

'And Lawrence said, "Oh, you can keep it, it's more suitable for you."'

'And,' they said in unison, 'he *still* didn't know what it meant!'

They were laughing when Lawrence came in. 'Give me a huge gin,' he said. 'Obviously I've got some catching up to do. Hello, Maude, nice to see you.' He gave her a kiss.

'Hi, Piers. I'll get your drink.' She headed off towards the kitchen. 'I could do with a refill.'

Lawrence went over to Isobel and put his arm round her. 'What were you laughing about?'

'That chap who fell off the roof at the flat. The one you gave the rude T-shirt to.'

'Terry Price,' Lawrence said, beginning to smile. 'God, I'd forgotten all about him. Wonder if he still wears it?'

Isobel reached out for the bread, removing herself from Lawrence's embrace. Then, because the mood of fun and the happy memories brought back the good days, deliberately went back to him and, taking his arm, put it round her again.

'That was nice,' he said quietly, hugging her with both arms. They stood for a few moments, close together, not speaking. Then Maude came back with the drinks.

Over supper, Lawrence told Maude about the house in the woods. 'It's in ruins,' he said, 'more than ruins, really. You can only see the stumps of the walls if you know where to look.'

'What age?' Maude said, munching on lasagne.

'Jacobean. Built in 1625 for a local Wealden ironmaster. Huge central chimney stack part of the original house, then wings and a bigger kitchen block added later.'

'You can tell all this from your stumpy walls?' Maude asked, amused.

'He's been looking it up in the local reference library,'

Isobel said. Her sister, she thought, mustn't be allowed to get away with the idea that she was the only member of the family who could find their way through cross-references and microfiches. 'The house has quite a history.'

'Which Piers can't wait to relate,' Maude said. 'Go on, then, Piers, I'm all ears.'

Lawrence filled their three glasses, then said, 'It was called Oxleat Place, and the original inhabitant, who probably built it, was one Joshua Middlecombe, who had made his fortune in iron. He had a furnace on the far side of the village, in fact, which operated up till the end of the eighteenth century, when the Midland coalfields were discovered and demand for Wealden iron ceased. The Middlecombe family went on living at Oxleat Place, but without the income. It gradually started to go into decline. It didn't help matters when a son and heir went off to fight for Wellington at Waterloo, contrary to his wise old dad's advice, and got himself killed. The old dad, apparently, never got over it, and left the running of the house and the whole estate to his daughter, who was half-dotty already and made more so by the demands of looking after the place with hardly any money and a father who, as he got increasingly senile, kept asking when Georgie was coming home.'

'Georgie being the son killed at Waterloo?' Maude said. 'Yes.'

'Poor, poor old man,' Isobel murmured. How sad, to think of him, sitting waiting for someone who would never come back.

'Poor daughter,' Maude remarked. 'Then what happened?'

'The old man finally died, and, because the daughter was more or less certifiable by then, was persuaded to leave the place to the son of his cousin, a young man called Jeremiah Middlecombe. This would have been around the middle of the century – about 1860. The cousin, who had seen which way the wind was blowing and had apparently been itching to get his hands on Oxleat Place for years, brought an injection of serious cash and made the estate hum again. It was he who added the new wings and the kitchen when he finally married and started a family. He also built a stable block and a rockery – you can still see the rockery.'

'Which makes me think you're going to tell me something awful happened to everything else, which of course it obviously did. Yes?'

'Yes.' Isobel saw Lawrence flash Maude a quick smile, like a reward for a clever deduction. 'This is where looking things up in the reference library starts to combine with primary source material – well, secondary, in fact, since it's the grandson of someone who was living at the time that I've actually spoken to. My friend Harold Pickett's granny was in service at the Big House, as he calls it, up until she married, which Harold thinks would have been about 1887, when she was twenty-one. Three years later, fire coursed through the whole house, Jeremiah's new wings and all, and razed it to the ground.'

'Granny wasn't to blame, then,' Maude said. 'Not a question of her dropping the warming pan, or letting the fat get too hot.'

'According to the book in the library, contemporary opinion was that Jeremiah himself might have been the engineer of his own downfall. His daughter, Amelia, wanted to marry a young man who was eligible in every way, except that he was the son of Jeremiah's head groom. Amelia was doing everything in her power to make her father change his mind and let her marry the chap – which in those days can't have amounted to much – and rumour had it that Jeremiah was feeling the strain and hitting the bottle. Apparently he fell asleep in front of the fire one night, having stoked it up to see him through another bout of brandy-drinking, and didn't wake when a log rolled out and set fire to the hearth rug and Jeremiah's chair. By the time anyone else noticed the blaze, it had a firm hold. The servants raised the alarm, the rest of the family got out, and the fire polished off the house.'

'What about Jeremiah?'

'What was left of him was discovered lying in front of the fireplace, underneath a large chunk of beams and ceiling.'

'So Amelia got her man after all,' Maude said.

'Probably. History doesn't record.'

There was silence in the room. Isobel, thinking about Jeremiah and Amelia, imagining those hundred-year-old events happening down there in the valley in the woods, guessed that Lawrence and Maude's thoughts were running on similar lines.

But then Maude said, 'I could be wrong – I'll check – but I think this discovery of a ruined house may have significance for you lot.'

'Significance?' Lawrence said.

'It's interesting,' Isobel said, 'quite fascinating, in fact, and we're planning to have a thorough nose around once the weather's better, but –'

'Naturally,' Maude said. 'That's not what I meant.' She toyed with her almost empty glass; Lawrence, taking the action as a hint, topped it up again. 'Thanks. I don't want to raise any false hopes, but this reminds me of some friends of mine who have a strawberry business in the Vale of Evesham. They bought the land and started the business, living in a caravan all the time they couldn't afford a house. Then, when they were starting to make a go of it, they applied for planning permission to turn a derelict old barn into a house. They got it, on the grounds that, for one thing, they needed somewhere better than a caravan to live in and run their business from, and for another, because of the precedent. There had been a dwelling there before, as evidenced by the barn.'

'You're saying we might be able to rebuild Oxleat Place?' Lawrence said. 'But it'd be far too big for us! Far too expensive, at today's prices. We'd just about be able to pay the architect for a place of that size!'

'You wouldn't have to build the same house, nit.' Maude smiled at him. 'Nor even in exactly the same place.'

'Oh, we'd build there, all right.' Lawrence, Isobel noticed, had a dreamy look. 'It's the perfect location. Joshua Middle-combe knew what he was about.'

Isobel said, 'A house in the woods? Are you serious, Maude?'

'As I say, I'd have to check it out. But I know these friends of mine got permission to build, no problem, and it seems to me your case is almost exactly like theirs. Growing business, need for somewhere to live – you can't possibly be planning to stay in this hole a moment longer than you have to – and precedent, there having been a house on the spot before.'

Isobel was watching Lawrence. Now he didn't look so much like a man in a dream, more like a man who has just been informed his dream might be about to come true. Sensing her watching, he met her eyes. 'Izzy?'

She stared at him for a long moment. Several thoughts ran through her head: all the time we're renting, we can stop renting, abandon this new life and go back. Buying – building – your own house is a commitment. If I agree, it means there really is no going back. Ever.

Ewell. Shops, glamour, social whirl, friends, money.

Versus the simple life.

Inside her head a little voice cried, don't ask me, *I* don't know!

She said carefully, 'Let's ask Maude to check. Do some enquiring ourselves. There's no point in getting worked up about something that may be impossible to bring about.'

'Then?' Lawrence said. His eagerness tore at her.

'Then,' she said, refusing to be drawn, 'we'll see.'

In bed, when at long last they'd finished all the booze, done the washing up, heard from a thrilled Dory what a wonderful time could be had stomping round in a wet wood looking for things to shoot at, Isobel was just beginning to drift off when Lawrence put his arms round her.

She wasn't sure, but she thought that what he murmured indistinctly into her ear was, 'Izzy, I do love you.'

CHAPTER SIXTEEN

Maude was not a woman to let the grass grow under her feet. In the middle of the week following her visit, she phoned to ask if she could bring her friend Bill down, because Bill was an architect and also knew all there was to know about planning permission, and in what situations one was likely to be granted it.

Isobel, putting the phone down after saying yes, please bring him to lunch, and, yes, today's fine, sat down in the kitchen to wait while the kettle boiled. 'Bill,' she said aloud. Did they know about Bill?

She wasn't sure. Maude had many friends, lots of them male, and she scattered their names in her conversation without usually bothering to say who they were, what they did, or – most importantly if you were her sister – what was their relationship to Maude.

The kettle boiled. Well, Isobel reflected, Maude having a friend who's an architect might prove useful to us. He can advise us, perhaps tell us whether this whole idea's practical, maybe give us an idea of costs.

The house-in-the-woods concept appeared to have developed a momentum all of its own. Which was very frightening, when you hadn't really decided whether or not you were in favour.

She took a cup of coffee through to Lawrence, who was working in the living room.

'That was Maude,' she said, putting the mug down

between the Playskool boot and Lawrence's calculator. 'On the phone.'

'Hm?' He didn't look up.

'She says can she and her friend Bill the architect come to lunch.'

Then he looked up. 'What, today?'

'Yes.'

She watched the excitement flood his face. 'Oh, Izzy, that's great. Isn't it? I mean, to have a professional look at the site so soon, give us some advice.' She didn't answer. 'That *is* why he's coming? So we can take him to look at Oxleat Place?'

'Oh, yes, he's not coming purely for the pleasure of my toad-in-the-hole.'

Lawrence was staring at her, looking anxious. 'Izzy, what's wrong?'

It touched her that all the excitement had left his face because she hadn't shared it. For his sake, she tried to sound as if she were eager, too. 'Nothing. You're right, it's great that he's coming. Nice of Maude to arrange it. I'll go and peel some more spuds.'

They didn't linger over lunch. Bill was as keen to get out on site, as he kept calling it, as if it were his own house he was proposing to build. As Bill and Maude pushed back their chairs and got up from the table, Lawrence thought they'd all paid scant attention to Izzy's meal.

'That was lovely, Izzy,' he said. 'I love toad-in-the-hole.'

She flashed him a smile. 'You hate it,' she said. 'I only did it to use up those sausages Dory didn't want.'

'Oh.' He couldn't recall ever having told her he didn't like it. 'Well, yours was jolly nice.'

'Are we going to this old house or what?' Maude called from the hall.

'Coming,' Lawrence said. He helped Isobel stack the

plates in the sink, and then ran hot water over them in the bowl. 'I'll do them later,' he said.

She smiled again. 'No you won't. But thanks for the thought.'

They shut the puppies up securely in their new outdoor pen, and went down to Oxleat Woods in Bill's car, which was a very clean Saab. When they got to the track that Lawrence had driven down in the van, with Harold Pickett, Bill said he didn't think he wanted to take the car down there and did they mind walking?

Bill and Maude had taken wellies out of special zip-up bags in the Saab's boot. Lawrence, catching Izzy's eye, saw that she was as amused as he was. 'Ready?' he asked when Bill had at last finished tucking his trousers into his yellow silk socks and put his long, slim feet into his boots.

'Ready.'

It didn't take much longer to walk to the old house than it had done to drive, since Lawrence had had to inch the van forwards so slowly. Leading the way down the zigzag path, he said over his shoulder, 'It's down there, in that level bit between the stream and the bank.'

'Wonderful spot,' Bill said. 'Superb view down the valley, and the bank behind you to give shelter. You'd have to cut back a lot of woodland, though, or it would keep out too much light. Nothing'll grow, and the house will feel gloomy.'

Lawrence wondered if he was the only one who had noticed the change from 'would' to 'will'.

Isobel and Maude were edging down the slope, Isobel giving Maude her hand because Maude was wearing a straight skirt and could only take small steps. Lawrence waited till they were at the bottom of the path, then went across to show Bill where he and Harold had found the ruined walls.

Bill spent a good twenty minutes exploring, throwing out

the occasional 'Good Lord! Fancy that!' and 'Wow!' while the rest of them stood patiently waiting. Then, rejoining them, he said, 'This was some house. Porched hall, inner hall where the staircase was, and beyond it the kitchens. Two wings leading back from the main building, probably later additions.'

'They were,' Lawrence said.

'Right. Over there,' Bill waved his arm, 'courtyard, stabling and outbuildings, I imagine. Some place,' he said again.

'Could we rebuild here?' Lawrence asked. He tried to sound cool and laid back, but he didn't think he'd succeeded.

Bill paused, apparently considering. 'When did the old place burn down?'

'In 1890.'

'Hundred years,' Bill muttered, 'plus a few.'

'Is that significant?' Maude asked.

'Reasonably,' Bill said. 'The land being used for housing relatively recently can't hurt, when we're talking planning permission. But the important thing is really that you and your family –' he looked at Lawrence and Isobel – 'need a place to live and run your business. And, as I saw for myself, there aren't any houses for sale nearby.'

'We've been on the lists of most of the local estate agents since October,' Isobel said. 'Nothing's come up in the village. There have been some suitable houses in the town, but Lawrence wants to live nearer than that.'

Lawrence wished she'd said *we* want to.

'Quite, quite,' Bill was saying. 'Near the job, and all that.'

'Well?' Maude said. 'What do you think, Bill?'

'Why not apply?' he said. 'Suck it and see, as they say.'

'Yes, but what do you *think*?' Maude repeated.

Bill frowned. 'If you really want an opinion, I think you'll get it. Permission. But don't hold me to that, because I don't know what your own planning people are like, and I don't know what factors they may take into account that I'm unaware of.'

'Could you build a house here, given that permission was granted?' Lawrence asked.

'Me personally?' Bill's tone was neutral.

'Oh, I didn't mean that!' Lawrence, afraid Bill would think he was asking for favours because of the family connection, spoke quickly. 'I meant, could a house be built here?'

Bill said quietly, 'It's the perfect spot. I would give my eyeteeth to design a house in this valley.'

There was a silence while they all considered the implications of that.

Then Maude said, 'On that positive note, perhaps we should call it a day and go back. My feet are freezing.'

Maude was destined to spend quite a lot of her week with her sister: the next morning, Isobel received a phone call from Mollie to say she was coming back from Belgium the next day, and would Isobel see about getting her house ready and come to meet her at Gatwick? The moment Isobel put the phone down, it rang again.

'You were engaged just now,' Maude said. 'Was that Mollie?'

'Yes.'

'She phoned me before she phoned you. Isn't it *typical* that she should announce, with scarcely any warning whatsoever, that she's coming home, and expect you and me to drop everything to get her house in order and fetch her from the airport!'

'Utterly typical,' Isobel agreed. 'Shall I meet you at Mum's?'

'I suppose so. But not today, I can't possibly get away. We'll go to the house in the morning, then go on to meet her. What time did she say her flight got in? I didn't write it down.'

'Half-past three.'

'I wonder why she didn't come on Eurostar?'

'Perhaps she's claustrophobic. Lots of people are.'

'Not Mollie,' Maude said with certainty. 'See you in the morning, then, at Church Road.'

'Okay.'

Lawrence needed the van the next day, so Isobel got the train to Reigate. It was an awkward journey, necessitating two changes, but not taking the van meant she could wear something smart; even a second-class carriage was cleaner than the van.

Doing up the waistband and zip of one of the suit skirts, Isobel realised she'd put on weight. Quite a lot of weight.

Premenstrual, she told herself, trying to recall where she was on her cycle. Just a bit of water retention, that's all.

Refusing to get panicky – what did it matter if she couldn't wear her smart suits? She didn't have occasion to often – she took a pair of leggings and a long jacket out of her wardrobe and hurriedly put them on. Then she carefully made up her face and wondered what to do with her hair.

Her mother would notice, and no doubt comment on, a less than immaculate coiffure, which was a bit of a problem as Isobel hadn't had her hair cut for at least seven months. Put it up? She twisted her hair into a pleat, but too many short ends stuck out. She tried securing it in an elastic band, which was better, and then wound it into a bun and tied a thin silk scarf round the bun. That looked good. In fact it looked *very* good.

She got a taxi from the station to her mother's house. Bill's Saab was parked in the drive. Hurrying inside – oh dear, why did Maude have to bring him? We'd have got on much better on our own – she discovered her sister in the kitchen, struggling to light the boiler.

'Where's Bill?' Isobel asked after they'd exchanged an abrupt kiss.

'Bill? Oh, *sod* this thing, I thought I had it that time.'

'His car's outside.'

'Oh, yes. He lent it to me.'

No more explanation was forthcoming. Isobel adjusted her understanding of Maude and Bill's relationship: a man who cared about his car, yet was willing to lend it to someone, must be quite close to them. Pretty fond of them, probably.

'Let me have a go,' she said, crouching down in front of the boiler. 'You have to hold the white button down for ages more than the instructions say, otherwise the pilot light goes out.'

'Hurry up,' Maude said – ungratefully, Isobel thought, since Isobel had relieved her of a clearly onerous chore – 'it's freezing in here.'

'You don't wear enough clothes,' Isobel remarked, still holding down the button.

'I should get myself a nice vest, perhaps?' Maude said caustically. 'Woollen pants?'

Isobel grinned. 'They'd suit you.' Then: 'There! Listen – that roaring sound's the gas jets. The boiler's alight.'

'Well done. I've put the kettle on, coffee in a minute. Mollie's special Kenyan blend – I think we've earned it.'

They drank their coffee wandering round their mother's house. It smelt slightly stuffy, but otherwise it was immaculate, with the bed made up with clean sheets, the bathroom sparkling, fresh towels on the rail and blue stuff in both loos.

'I don't know what she wanted us to do,' Isobel said as they returned to the kitchen. 'She left it spotless.'

'She wanted it warmed,' Maude replied. 'And hot water

for a bath, the moment she steps through the front door. Mollie always says travelling makes one filthy.'

'It probably did, when you went on steam trains. But she's arriving on an aeroplane, and she'll only have been in the air about half an hour.'

Maude shrugged. 'Well, that's how she is. You won't change her.'

They refilled their cups from Mollie's cafetiere.

Maude said, 'Bill's really keen about your house. He wants to design it, given that you get planning permission. Can you afford him?' She smiled wryly. 'Can you afford the house?'

'Yes,' Isobel said. 'Yes to both, unless Bill charges the earth. We may have toad-in-the-hole for lunch, but we're not on the breadline. We're just being careful, till we see what sort of an income Lawrence will clear on the coppicing.'

'Being careful,' Maude repeated. 'God, Isobel, seriously, I can't get used to the change in you. You got your degree in wild, unnecessary extravagance, and now look at you.' She glanced at Isobel's leggings and jacket. 'You're putting on weight, too.'

'No I'm not.' She drew her jacket closer round her; trust Maude to notice the moment it dropped away to reveal the soft new bulge of tummy. 'Nothing that won't dissipate in a day or so.'

'Oh. Well, you're different from what you used to be.'

There seemed no easy answer to that, so Isobel didn't make one. After a moment, she said, 'Is Bill a good architect?'

'Superb,' Maude said instantly. 'You should see his work. He did this beautiful conversion for some people in the Weald. Honestly, it's out of this world. And his own house is all his own design. It's small, but so imaginative, you have no idea.'

Isobel was watching her. 'You're fond of him, I see.'

Maude drew breath to comment – to deny? – then said, 'I admire his work. I would anyway, and I'm not alone – a lot of people speak highly of him. But yes, I am fond of him.'

There was a companionable silence. Isobel was just about to ask how long Maude and Bill had known each other when Maude said, 'And what about you and old Piers? Do I take it that this new house project indicates a fresh start, a general burying of hatchets?'

'No hatchets to bury,' Isobel said shortly. 'I *told* you, there's no problem.'

'You told me no such thing. I remarked that you and Piers were different together, and you changed the subject.'

'Oh.'

'Well?'

'Maude, give it a rest, will you? I'm fine. Lawrence is fine, too.' Suddenly she had a vivid memory: Lawrence putting his arms round her in bed, saying, 'Izzy, I do love you.' It made her feel like crying. 'It's just that we're adjusting to a new life,' she went on, swallowing the tears. 'It's bound to take some time.'

'Hm.' Maude managed to put a lot of scepticism into the brief sound. 'I don't mean to pry, but I'm concerned about you. You seem *so* different that I've almost been worried in case you were ill or something.'

About to snap, to say, leave it! Isobel detected the real concern behind the lightly delivered remark. She reached out, briefly touched Maude's hand. 'I'm not ill, I promise you. It's just – oh, a lot's happened. Things that have made me have to think everything out all over again. Reassess my life, if that doesn't sound pretentious.'

'It doesn't if it's true,' Maude said. 'And I imagine it is.'

'It is.'

203

After a while, Maude said, 'What, exactly? What happened?'

'Moving to the country, getting the children into new schools, meeting new people, adapting to –'

'That's all *since* you moved, and all perfectly understandable. What I want to know is, what happened before you left Ewell?'

Isobel wished that her sister was not so perceptive. Or, failing that, not so inquisitive.

'I – I misjudged something,' she said eventually. 'Made a real idiot of myself. Other people knew – at least, I think they did. They *must* have done, it was . . . Well, I was quite sure they were all talking about me, laughing at me, and it was getting to me. Affecting me so I didn't want to go out.'

'Mild agoraphobia,' Maude remarked. Then: 'Oh, Isobel, why didn't you say? Couldn't I have helped?'

It was nice of her, Isobel thought, to have offered instant sympathy instead of straight away demanding to know the sordid, shaming details. *Could* she have helped? Isobel wondered. Could I have saved myself this whole bloody upheaval by simply opening my heart to my sensible, strong elder sister and having her say, you're overreacting, don't be so silly. Don't even *think* about moving, it'll all blow over in next to no time.

She could almost hear Maude saying the words. Almost feel herself being comforted, reassured. Deciding that staying in Ewell wouldn't be so dreadful after all. In fact, would be absolutely wonderful, just like before.

Only it was too late, now.

She felt like crying again. But for a totally different reason.

Abruptly she got up, collected Maude's mug, and went to rinse it and her own at the sink.

'Time to go,' she said. 'We don't want Mum hanging around and thinking we're not coming.'

Maude opened her mouth, then closed it again.

But, all the same, Isobel had the feeling she wasn't going to get away with leaving it at that.

'Tell me about this place in the country,' Mollie said as Maude drove them back to Reigate. Isobel was sitting in the back, trying to keep away from the main beam of her mother's stare. 'I could scarcely believe it when you wrote and told me. I was fully expecting you to be back in town by Christmas. But here we are in April, and you're still sticking it out!' She sounded amazed, as if Isobel were enduring some awful sort of self-imposed hardship. Which in a way, Isobel reflected, she was.

'Lawrence was thinking of leaving Barclay Dawson anyway,' she said wearily, 'and then they had another round of staff cuts and he was made redundant.'

'Redundant!' Mollie breathed, as if Isobel had said Lawrence had caught plague.

'Mum, I told you all this,' Isobel said.

'Ah, but it's different hearing it face to face,' Mollie said obscurely.

'You don't hear with your face,' Maude remarked.

'Don't split hairs,' her mother ordered. 'Isobel, darling, how *could* you?'

'We had no option. I just told you, Lawrence was made redundant.' Horrible word, she thought, feeling a sudden fierce stab of angry loyalty to Lawrence. How dared they say he was redundant! He wasn't, never could be. Not to her, not in things that mattered.

'But he could have found a similar job with another company!' Mollie wailed theatrically. 'Why bury yourselves in the country? And woods, for heaven's sake! What does Lawrence know about woods?'

'Rather a lot now,' Isobel said. 'Don't get so upset, Mum. He knows what he's doing. He's not stupid.'

Her mother muttered something. Isobel didn't catch it, but Maude said, 'He's not, Mollie. You don't know what you're talking about.'

Oh God, Isobel thought, we've only been together half an hour and there's a row looming already.

There was a taut silence for a mile or so. Then Mollie said, 'I suppose you're downshifting. Exchanging comfort for simplicity. Getting back to nature, as if anyone would want to, having managed to escape. Fran was telling us about it – Harry's friend Fran. She's American, and apparently it's the latest fad over there.' She made it sound as if it couldn't possibly be anything but a temporary madness.

'Downshifting,' Isobel repeated softly. It was a good description.

Mollie was turning round in her seat, fixing Isobel with a penetrating gaze. 'Darling, shouldn't you talk about this to someone who understands?'

'Mum, there's no need. I told you, Lawrence has gone into everything thoroughly. We're fine.'

'I didn't mean that.' There was a pause: Mollie had always liked to milk situations for every last drop of drama. 'I meant you, Isobel. I have a close friend who's a psychiatrist, and I think it would be a good idea for you to talk to him. It's probably nothing, just your time of life, but it won't hurt to check. Shall I telephone him, and see if he'll give you an appointment?'

Isobel was so angry she couldn't speak.

Into the breach Maude said, 'Mollie, Isobel doesn't need a psychiatrist. Don't exaggerate.'

Fuming silently, Isobel wondered yet again if it was being two years older that made Maude so much better at dealing with their mother.

'I still think she should see him,' Mollie said. 'He's charming, so kind.'

'Thank you, Mother, but no,' Isobel managed to say.

'*Mother* now,' Mollie said, sounding hurt. 'I was only trying to help.'

'No you weren't, you were interfering,' Maude said, but kindly. 'Now, tell us some more about life in Brussels. Is the food as good as people say?'

Deflected, Mollie went off into a long description of a restaurant where they served nothing but mussels in a variety of mouth-watering ways.

Isobel, leaning back in the corner and waiting while her heartbeat gradually slowed down, stopped listening.

Mad. Her mother thought she must be mad, to have left the luxurious, elegant Ewell life and gone to live in the country. Well, perhaps that was only to be expected, given Mollie's nature and the fact that she hadn't an inkling as to the secret reason for Isobel's compliance.

But, not an hour previously, Isobel thought miserably, Maude put the idea into my head that a brief chat with my down-to-earth sister would have put everything into perspective, so that, when Lawrence said he wanted a change, I'd have had a suitable counterproposal to moving away, and suggested instead that he merely found a new job. He'd probably have given in without much of a fight, he always did seem amazed that I agreed to go to the country.

She sat looking out at the suburbs passing by the car window. Shops. Houses. Lights, people, cars, buses, taxis, the reassuring bustle that she'd left behind her.

Mad.

Am I mad?

Oh God, I think I must be.

CHAPTER SEVENTEEN

Dory faced the prospect of Fourth Form Parents' Evening with secret alarm. Not *public* alarm, of course – it would be distinctly sad to be like the swots, who were crapping bricks at the prospect of their parents getting together with the teachers, even though, in the swots' case, the general atmosphere could only be one of mutual congratulation.

Dory and Emma Hardcastle – now definitely in each other's 'best friends' slot – allowed the apprehension to show when they were alone.

'Mrs Nugent's going to flay me with sarcasm,' Dory said gloomily as they sat in their special place behind the netball courts making a desultory – and far too belated – attempt to prepare for a history test. 'She'll tell Mum and Dad I haven't done any work whatsoever, and that I'd stand a chance of turning in intelligent essays if I'd only *listen*. But it's so *boring*, all that stuff about the build-up to the First World War and how the end of that one led to the start of the next one. I mean, it's all bloody wars, and one's just like another.'

'Yeah.' Emma had found a picture of the Kaiser in her text book and was busy Tippexing out the ends of his moustache. 'Oh, look! I've made Kaiser Bill look like Hitler!'

They both started laughing. Then Dory remembered her dad's story about someone playing Trivial Pursuit being asked what was Hitler's first name, and answering 'Heil', and they laughed some more.

'Oh, shut up,' Emma said finally. 'We've just *got* to learn this stuff.'

Dory opened her book and frowned in concentration. She fixed her attention on the War Guilt Clause and the Treaty of Versailles, trying to memorise Article 231.

Somewhere near at hand, a thrush was singing (Jacob knew most birdsongs, and some of his knowledge had rubbed off). She could smell some sort of flowery smell: the tree they were sitting under was covered in pink blossom (Jacob didn't know so much about trees). It was so hard to keep her mind on 1919 Europe.

She thought about the poem they'd done in English. It was called 'Naming of Parts', and it was a man having to learn what the bits of his rifle were called and being distracted by lovely natural things. She muttered some lines under her breath.

'What?' said Emma.

Dory hardly heard. 'Nothing.'

She sat with her mouth open, amazed not only because she'd just recited a whole verse of a poem she didn't think she'd learned, but more so – *much* more so – because suddenly she completely understood what the poet was saying.

What was his name? Something Reed. Henry Reed. Born 1914, so the war he was involved in had been the Second World War.

She sat gazing out across the distant hockey pitches. They'd done poetry of both wars – lots of things by someone called Wilfred Owen, who Dory remembered particularly because he was killed just a week before the Armistice, and also by an officer called Siegfried Sassoon, who, Mrs Sawyer said, had very nearly been court-martialled because he believed in pacifism.

Lines from their poetry marched through her head, in the way 'Naming of Parts' had done. And the breakthrough of understanding she'd had with Henry Reed applied to Sassoon and Owen, too.

Something important seemed to have happened. With new clarity, she saw what the *point* of it was. You experienced something, it moved you profoundly, and that made you able to find the words so that, when other people read them, they felt it too.

Dory thought, *I* could have written a poem about the deer, about how what happened made me feel so close to Sam, because he was involved too. I could have said – or tried to say – how the whole thing sort of *changed* me, made me feel I could understand the suffering of other creatures.

Other people, too, she added to herself. Wasn't she even now feeling sad about Wilfred Owen?

With an effort, she brought herself back to the present task; unfortunately, it wasn't English she was meant to be revising. Still, history had people in it too; that was called Social History. Could the same breakthrough happen with history?

She bent over her book with a sudden, urgent need to know.

Isobel and Lawrence were both going to the Parents' Evening. Changing out of her jeans, aware of Lawrence singing in the shower, Isobel thought of past such events which she'd attended alone. Having Lawrence around so much more was still strange, she reflected as she put on her lipstick. It was almost as if they didn't know each other and were starting out.

And sometimes, he –

'Do I have to wear a suit?' He was out of the shower, and had interrupted her train of thought.

'No, don't think so.' She looked at him in the mirror. His face was tanned – well, weatherbeaten was more accurate, since there hadn't been much sun yet – and what she could see of him above the towel round his waist looked muscly. Unaware of her watching him, he let the towel fall as he reached in the drawer for clean underpants. She felt a strange little surge of sexual desire pulse through her at the sight of his naked body. Good Lord, she'd forgotten just how well put together he was . . .

'I could wear my jacket and grey flannels,' he was saying. He was safely inside his underpants now, and she felt herself relax. This was daft! She'd been married to him for nearly seventeen years, knew him inside out, and here she was feeling aroused, damn it, as if she'd just copped her first glimpse of him in the buff!

'Izzy? Are you listening?'

'Sorry. Yes, jacket and flannels. Absolutely.'

He came and stood behind her, putting his hands on her bare shoulders. Meeting her eyes in the mirror, he smiled, and she responded. Then, breaking the mood, he bent to give her a quick kiss on the top of her head and said, 'I feel like a generous gin to get me through the ordeal of Dory's teachers, but we'd better not. Had we?'

'No,' she said firmly. 'But we'll have a nightcap when we get back.'

Dory was sitting at the kitchen table, totally ignoring the puppies clamouring for attention in their box by the Rayburn, and pretending to do her maths homework. 'Can Sam come over while you're out?' she asked.

'Yes, providing you do your homework,' Isobel said.

'He's coming to *help* me do it,' Dory said.

'He's not to do it,' Isobel protested. 'It's no good for you if he –'

'I know, I know. Don't get *taut*, Mum. He tells me the method, then I have to work it out for myself, and if I go wrong, he tells me where.'

'You're lucky to have him,' Lawrence remarked. 'He sounds a better teacher than any maths master I ever had.'

'Where's Jacob?' Isobel asked.

'Gone off with Brian.' Dory sounded disinterested.

'When's he due back?'

'*I* don't know!' Dory looked as if it couldn't possibly be any of her business. 'Does it matter?'

'It depends,' Lawrence said. 'If he comes in at eight, it doesn't matter. If he rolls up at four in the morning, it does.'

Dory sighed.

'Come on,' Isobel said. 'Time we weren't here.'

Lawrence wondered why parents' evenings made him feel vaguely guilty. Because he knew there was more he could have done to help his children along the thorny path to being educated? Or merely because going into a school – any school – brought back uncomfortable memories?

They saw four or five teachers whose opinions of Dory's efforts were depressingly similar. Then they were admitted to the presence of Mrs Nugent; waiting outside the room, Izzy had told him in a whisper that Dory hated Mrs Nugent worst of all because she kept making her retake substandard tests.

'Dory, yes, Dory,' Mrs Nugent said, finger running along the relevant line of marks in her book. 'It hasn't been easy for her, has it, settling into a different life?'

She was the first teacher to put any sympathy into the remark. Lawrence thought that was a good sign. 'No,' he agreed. 'Mind you, she was never a piece of cake, even before we moved.'

Mrs Nugent smiled. 'A mind of her own,' she said.

'Tell me about it!'

Mrs Nugent raised her eyes, meeting first Izzy's gaze and then his. 'Dory seems to have had some sort of a breakthrough just recently,' she said.

Izzy said, 'Breakthrough or breakdown?'

Mrs Nugent smiled again. 'Break*through*. Suddenly she seems to have discovered the whole point of history, with the predictable result that, in her last test, she achieved one of the highest marks in the class.'

'Christ!' Lawrence exclaimed before he remembered where he was.

'I, too, was surprised.' Mrs Nugent took his blasphemy in her stride; perhaps she was used to that sort of thing on parents' evening. 'Some of her essay answers were a little uncontrolled – for example, there was no need to go into the putative emotions of the Kaiser as he faced Allied punitive measures after the Armistice – but, with some guidance, I see no reason why she should not achieve an A in the GCSE.'

'An A,' Izzy breathed.

Lawrence was speechless.

Mrs Sawyer was last on the list, and she, too, spoke of Dory's mysterious epiphany (Lawrence resolved to look it up when they got home). Dory's feel for poetry, she said, was excellent; she understood instinctively, apparently, and had an ability to put herself in another's shoes. And, Mrs Sawyer concluded, she made an excellent Ferdinand, and could Mrs Langland please persuade her to keep her hair short until after the performance?

'We ended on a high all right,' Lawrence said as he turned the van round in the school drive, managing to miss all the posh cars. 'I feel really proud of her.'

'Even though seventy-five per cent of her teachers said she didn't try?'

'Yes, even though. Don't you?'

'I do, I do,' Isobel said. 'It's such a huge relief to see

213

something, at least, going right for her.' She sounded as if she were near to tears.

'Lots of things are,' he said, reaching out to grasp her hand. 'Think of Sam, and having that Emma girl as her friend.'

'I know,' Isobel said. 'But you get the feeling with Dory that it's all so uphill. And she *did* so hate leaving Ewell, and having to go into a state school. I'm so afraid that this thing with Sam's going to blow up in her face, that Emma'll find another best friend, and Dory will revert to being permanently morose and she'll stop working, even in English and history.'

It seemed a lot of things to reassure her about, and he wasn't sure he knew how. Fumbling for some sort of response, he said, 'Maybe she'll grow out of it.'

'What? Which bit?'

She sounded angry. But then she let out a suppressed snort of laughter.

'What?' he said.

'I can't think why I'm laughing,' she said, doing so again. 'God knows, there's not much to laugh about. But I was just thinking, you've been offering the same palliative remark since she was born.'

'Have I?'

'You have. Everything from her refusing to sleep at night to throwing her potty round the kitchen.'

He grinned. 'She doesn't do that any more, which goes to show how right I was.'

He was picturing the baby days. They'd been in his mind anyway – he'd dreamt last night of Izzy when she'd just had Jacob, when she still carried the laid-down fat of pregnancy which hadn't yet been used up in milk. He'd loved her particularly like that. The disadvantage had been that it was virtually impossible to make love without getting soaked in milk.

'What do we tell her?' Isobel said, interrupting his thoughts. 'She's bound to be waiting to hear, for all that she'll pretend she isn't.'

'We need to get the right balance between giving her a kick in the pants for not working hard enough, and a huge pat on the back for her English and history.'

They were pulling up outside the house. 'Me or you?' Isobel said.

'You can give the pat, if you like.' He was quite proud of his magnanimity.

Isobel smiled. 'Thanks, but it's okay. She's more used to rockets from me. I'll have my say first, then you can lavish praise on her.'

Dory responded with sullen indifference to Isobel's remarks – which Lawrence thought was ungrateful, since Izzy had toned down considerably Dory's teachers' opinions. But then, he reasoned, Dory wasn't to know that. More surprising was her lack of delight at what he had to report from Mrs Nugent and Mrs Sawyer.

'Aren't you pleased that they said you're doing so well?' he asked.

She shrugged.

'Dory?' Isobel said.

Dory was stuffing books in her school bag, and still didn't answer.

'Did you get the maths prep done?' he asked.

'Dad, it's *homework*. Calling it prep's just *sad*.'

'Did you, though?' Isobel said. 'Did Sam –'

'No,' Dory said. 'He didn't come.'

She was out of the room, door slammed behind her, before either of them had a chance to detain her.

Lawrence met Isobel's eyes. 'Oh Lord,' he said.

'Oh Lord, indeed.'

Without asking her if she wanted one, he went and made them both a large gin. Then they sat down at the table and

215

he took her free hand. They didn't speak, but he guessed that, like him, she was contemplating the disintegration of the fragile structure that Dory had painfully been becoming.

Outline planning permission came through quite quickly: Lawrence's contact in the planning department said they'd been lucky, because a meeting had taken place very soon after the Langlands' submission was put in.

Being granted permission to build, although a *sine qua non* (that was what Maude's Bill called it), was really the start of their worries, Lawrence thought. All the time you hadn't been given the go-ahead, you were just indulging in pipe dreams, in wouldn't-it-be-lovelies. Having that vital permission meant you had to stop dreaming and get down to it.

Lawrence was inwardly quaking at the responsibility of it all. He wasn't sure if Izzy felt the same. She had greeted the news with a neutral expression, but later he'd thought he heard her weeping. She denied it, but a few days afterwards she put out two rubbish sacks of her smarter clothes. When he asked if she was really chucking the stuff out, she said yes, there was no earthly point in keeping things that no longer fitted either her waistline or her lifestyle.

When she said her mother was coming to visit, Lawrence's heart sank even further. Mollie had a way of undermining Izzy – he'd always thought so. And, right now, she didn't need any more of that. He tried to suggest gently that they put Mollie off, but when Izzy said, 'How, pray?', he'd been stumped and had to fall back on some contagious illness in the house. Izzy had replied dejectedly that it wouldn't work, her mother had had virtually everything and claimed to be immune to the few things she'd so far escaped.

'Shall I try to get back early?' he said on the morning of the day Mollie was coming.

'You can if you like.' She sounded as if she didn't care either way.

'I will,' he said decisively. He bent to kiss her; her face felt cold. He wanted to hug her, put his arms round her and fold her inside his jacket the way he'd done in their courting days when a trip to Wimbledon had been colder, wetter and windier than either of them had anticipated.

But she didn't look like the Izzy he'd courted. Her expression was closed, and she looked distant. A stranger.

Feeling excluded, he walked out and shut the door.

Isobel heard the van start up, and wished she could rerun the last few minutes. Wished she could convince herself it was okay to lean on Lawrence, to accept gratefully when he offered support. Especially when, like today, she so much needed it.

But a part of her held the rest of her back – a part of her that resisted the temptation of getting closer to Lawrence because it feared she might not be able to go *on* being close. Feared she was on the point of discovering she couldn't go on with this new life, that she'd have to leave him to it on his own.

She stood up, wearily clearing the breakfast things from the table. Under Lawrence's chair, she found his notebook. At the top of the page he'd written 'Oxleat Place', with his own version of one of Bill's rough sketches. Lawrence wasn't nearly as good a draughtsman as Bill; she was touched. Painfully so.

Too soon it was time to go and meet Mollie's train.

They walked back from the station. Isobel had offered a taxi, but Mollie said she'd worn her country shoes specially, and was perfectly capable of walking.

Isobel led the way up the path to the house and opened the back door, standing aside to allow her mother to precede her into the kitchen. She was used to it; she tried to see it through Mollie's eyes.

'You *live here?*' Mollie said, accentuating each word separately, as if to question both the fact that anyone could live in the place as well as doubting the place itself. 'But, darling, it's damp! And it's dirty! Did you *have* to have dogs?' She seemed as immune to the charms of Rosie and Millie, greeting her from their box with little grunts of pleasure, as her granddaughter. 'You've got mice, I'm absolutely certain.' She was opening cupboards and drawers, as if about to embark on a one-woman extermination programme.

'The occasional one, usually a fieldmouse,' Isobel said lamely. Then, picturing her own and Judith's efforts, she protested, 'It's *not* dirty.'

Her mother shrugged, turning it into a shudder. 'Have it your own way.'

'This is a rented house, Mum. It's only a temporary measure. We'll be moving into the new house within the year.' She had no idea how long it took to design and build a house and have it fit for habitation, but a year sounded reasonable.

'Another year here?' her mother said faintly. 'Dear God.'

'We've been through a winter already,' Isobel said, trying to stay calm. 'We can face another one.'

Mollie was looking at her, shaking her head slowly. 'Isobel, I hardly recognise you as my daughter,' she said. 'Make us a coffee, or something, I must talk to you.'

Feeling as if she had no choice – her mother always had that effect – Isobel did as she was asked.

Elbows on the table – Mollie made an exception to her own rule when there was serious talking to be done – she launched into what sounded to Isobel like a prepared speech. Unfortunately, it contained all the elements Isobel herself couldn't stop thinking about: how happy she'd been in Ewell, how much more suited she was to the smart-set life than to this rural squalor, how unwise it was to commit herself to this false move – that was Mollie's expression – by agreeing to the new house.

Mollie threw in a lot more in the same vein. When she had finished, and Isobel felt more desperately miserable than she'd ever done in her life, Mollie concluded with the suggestion she'd made before. 'Darling, why *not* see my tame psychiatrist? I'll pay, if that's what's holding you back.'

Isobel felt too defeated even to protest at the patronising tone. Dropping her head on to her folded arms, she said, 'I don't want to see a psychiatrist.'

There was silence in the kitchen. It was, Isobel thought absently, the first silence since her mother had walked in through the door. She was beginning to quite enjoy it when Mollie said, 'You can't stay here, darling. You're absolutely *not* a country person. You're my daughter, I know you, and believe me, you don't *belong*.'

They had lunch. Isobel hardly ate anything, bringing down on herself her mother's comment, 'If you typically eat as sparingly as that, darling, I really can't understand why you've put on weight.' Then they had some more coffee. Shortly after that, Mollie helped Isobel do the washing-up; then she said she ought to be going so as to avoid the rush hour. Isobel forbore to say that the rush hour didn't start for a good two hours yet, and, anyway, any rushing was on the down line and not the up; she was as eager to see the back of her mother as Mollie undoubtedly was to go.

Walking slowly back from the station – aware of a smudge of lipstick on her cheek where her mother had kissed her – Isobel stopped on the edge of the green and stood looking across at the house.

She admitted to herself – for the first time – that she wholeheartedly regretted having agreed to move out of Ewell.

'Filthy, damp house,' she muttered. 'I'm absolutely *not* a country person.' Then – for there was a protesting part of her loyal to Lawrence and his enthusiasm, although she didn't trust it – 'I'm going mad. I should see a psychiatrist.'

She trudged on across the green.

Why, she asked herself, did I seem to be managing? I felt for a while that I was becoming a true rural person, a village dweller. I coped with winter in a tacky little house, with dressing sensibly – awful concept! – in unsmart, practical clothes, with hauling logs in, even with two puppies, for God's sake. I started to make friends with village people. I really believed I could make the adjustment.

Was it an illusion? It must have been.

She had been so relieved, she decided, at having made her escape from the shaming situation she'd left behind that it had coloured her reaction to the new life. It had seemed a refuge, its very safety giving it the appearance of something attractive, something to be desired. And for that, she had accepted the removal of herself and her family from their natural habitat to this frightening place called The Country.

They were outsiders. They'd joked about the traditional village attitude – that, when you'd been there fifty years or so, people might grudgingly accept you – but oh, she thought, rapidly becoming illogical with distress, how true it was. They weren't wanted.

'Outsiders,' she whispered, ignoring the fact that nobody had suggested it, even in fun. Ignoring Judith. Sam. Nan Black, even, God help her, Mrs Bellyflop, none of whom had suggested, even obliquely, that the Langlands didn't 'belong'.

The prospect of going on – even with thinking about

what to do for supper, never mind anything as vast as building a house and making up her mind whether or not she could live in it – suddenly seemed quite out of the question. Hurrying on into the house, she scribbled a note for Lawrence: 'Gone to bed with a migraine, food in fridge, PLEASE DON'T DISTURB' – then went upstairs.

She threw her coat and jeans on the floor, unwound her hair from its bun, drew the curtains. Then she crept in under the duvet and pulled it right up over her head.

The world was shut out; had shut her out.

She wasn't at all sure she wanted to be readmitted.

PART FOUR

Summer

CHAPTER EIGHTEEN

Jacob tried to adjust his position crouched under the hedge without making any noise. It wasn't easy. But it was necessary, because a bramble was sticking into his leg and it was becoming more and more difficult to ignore the small pain.

'Stop wriggling,' Brian hissed.

'Sorry.'

Jacob tried to control his breathing, but his heart was beating heavily with excitement, and he wanted to pant. Staring out across the moonlit field, he kept *thinking* he saw movement, only it would turn out not to be.

The badgers' sett was in a bank on the uphill side of the field, under a thick hedge which, according to Brian, was very *very* old. You could tell, Brian said, by counting the number of tree and bush types per ten yards and multiplying by something. Brian hadn't been too sure what the something was – he'd said seven hundred, but since that would have made the hedge six thousand, three hundred years old, Jacob thought he was probably wrong.

Jacob and Brian had made a hide in the corner where the old hedge joined the more modern fence. They'd draped an old bit of tarpaulin – Brian referred to it as a 'tarp' – across between a fence post and a low branch of a holly tree, and covered it with bits of bracken. Jacob was very afraid the hide was all too visible, but perhaps it wouldn't be to a badger.

It was a great night for badger-watching, which Jacob decided must go among his top five favourite things, even if Dory did say it was boring. *He* thought *she* was boring, anyway, always going on about Sam Hearst and looking sort of droopy. Everyone had thought it was all over between them a few weeks ago, because Sam had been supposed to come round and do Dory's maths and he hadn't turned up. In fact there had been a misunderstanding: Sam had thought Dory was going *with* Mum and Dad to parents' evening, when all the time she'd been in, sitting at home chewing her nails and getting ratty with Jacob, waiting for Sam.

Dory had been even worse about Sam since they'd been friends again.

Jacob and Brian had been planning the badger trip for ages. Brian had been out with his dad the previous week and reported back that the badgers' young were now old enough to go out at night with their parents. After that it had just been a matter of waiting for a fine night; even Brian and Jacob's enthusiasm had limits, and neither of them fancied lying under the 'tarp' in pouring rain.

Today had been a lovely day, sunny, warm, not a suggestion of so much as an occasional shower nor even a 'spotterto' of rain, as Dad said when he was being Michael Fish. During geography, a note had arrived on Jacob's desk; opening it up, he read, in Brian's unmistakable hand, 'We go tonnigh.' Brian wasn't very good at spelling.

Jacob had called in at home to tell Mum he was going to Brian's for tea and might be quite late. She'd seemed almost not to hear, so he'd said it again and she said okay. He had been very tempted to take Rosie and Millie – they'd sat on his feet while he was talking to Mum, and Millie had got the frayed bit on his sock between her teeth and pulled out about a mile of grey thread. But he knew they'd be useless on a badger-watch. It wouldn't be fair to take them on a wonderful, exciting journey out into the darkness then forbid them even to wriggle.

There had been nobody in the caravan when the boys got there. Brian did them mugs of tea, and they had Bovril sandwiches made with some rather old bread. There was a small green spot on one of Jacob's slices, which smelt musty. He picked it off when Brian wasn't looking.

They'd had to think of things to do till it got dark. They did their spellings – honestly, Brian's were really *awful*, and in the end he got cross when Jacob kept saying he'd got things wrong, so Jacob suggested they do something else. They did some work on the tree house Brian was building, and had another cup of tea sitting up on the platform. Then Miss Hoylake came back, and Brian lied and said, 'Auntie Ruth, we haven't had anything to eat and we're *starving*,' and she cooked them beef stew with peas. Both things came out of tins, and Jacob thought they were delicious. For pudding they had an individual fruit pie each. Jacob thought the fruit in his was plum, but he wasn't sure.

Brian's dad came back, and the caravan started to feel a bit crowded. Brian's dad was in a good mood – he'd put a pony on the horses (Brian said it meant betting) and won two hundred pounds, and he'd brought a bottle of champagne back with him. Jacob thought he must have drunk something else before he came home with the champagne, as he kept starting to sing weird songs like 'Chirpy Chirpy Cheep Cheep' and 'I've Got a Luverly Bunch of Coconuts'. Then he sat down rather abruptly on the bench that turned into a big bed and pulled Miss Hoylake down on to his lap, saying, 'Come on, Ruthie, give us a kiss.'

It seemed a funny way to behave with your sister. Then Jacob remembered that Miss Hoylake wasn't actually Brian's real aunt. Brian was getting a bit embarrassed over his father's behaviour – Jacob could tell, because his ears had gone bright red – and suddenly stood up and said gruffly, 'C'mon, Jake, time to go.'

It wasn't anywhere near dark enough when they left the caravan. They'd sat under the tarp watching the last of the sunset, and soon after that, the first stars had popped out.

That had been an hour and a half ago.

Jacob was just beginning to doubt whether badger-watching was actually all it was cracked up to be when he saw another movement under the bank. He stared, rubbed his eyes, stared some more. This time, the movement went right on being a movement.

At the same instant he was about to whisper to Brian, Brian nudged him and said, so softly it was more like breath on his ear than words, 'Look, under the oak. Three of them.'

There were two big badgers and a little one. One of the big ones turned, looking behind it in a manner that was so nearly human that Jacob wanted to laugh. He could almost hear the badger saying, 'Oh, *do* hurry up!' just like Mum and Dad did when they were out shopping and Jacob had stopped to look into an interesting shop. Sure enough, two more little shapes came flopping out of the hole in the bank, one of them losing its footing and bumping against its parent's ample rear end.

Now it wasn't hard at all to keep still. He was lying on his tummy, elbows dug into comfy dents in the earth, hands supporting his face. Beside him, he heard Brian breathe a sigh of contentment. He felt like doing the same.

As the badgers went about their business, the moon slowly rose high above the quiet fields.

Both Brian and Jacob had already forgotten all about the time.

Lawrence heard the back door slam and thought, thank God, Jacob's back.

He hadn't told Izzy that he was getting worried. Had been worried, in fact, since first the *Nine O'Clock News*, then *Newsroom South East* finished without a sign of Jacob. Izzy had sat hunched in her chair, apparently absorbed in a film he was quite sure she'd seen at least twice. Had she been worried, too?

Getting up, Lawrence saw her glance at him. 'Jacob's back,' he said.

She smiled briefly. 'Thank goodness.'

He was obscurely relieved that she *had* noticed: she was becoming increasingly distant. He didn't know what to do.

He went through to the kitchen, about to give Jacob a bit of a lecture on keeping reasonable hours and not worrying his parents. But it wasn't Jacob, it was Dory.

'I've had a *fantastic* time,' she said, face alight with joy. 'It was a *wonderful* film, even Sam said so, although he and Dan said Emma was daft to cry and – What's the matter?'

'I thought you were Jacob.' He sat down heavily on a kitchen chair.

'Jacob? Isn't he back?'

'No.'

'*God!* But Dad, it's nearly *eleven*!'

'I know.' He stood up again. 'We'll have to go and find him.'

Dory raced to the door. 'I'll get Sam to help, and his mum and dad. Well, his mum anyway, his dad's unlikely to want to.'

'Hold on, Dory, no need to –'

But she was already running down the path. He could hear her calling, 'Sam! *Sam!*'

Lawrence went back into the living room to tell Isobel that he appeared to have instigated a search party.

Isobel, paired with Judith Hearst, discovered that Judith's natural walking pace was faster than her own. Pride giving way in the face of discomfort, she said, 'Could we slow down a bit?' and Judith said, 'Sorry.'

It was more than forty-five minutes since the search had started. As a first step, Sam, Lawrence and Dory had gone to the Dents' caravan, and while they were gone, Isobel and Judith had sat in Isobel's kitchen reassuring each other that Jacob would undoubtedly have been with the Dents, and the others would be bringing him in any minute.

He hadn't been, and they didn't. Lawrence reported that Mr Dent and whoever it was with him – 'Ruth Hoylake,' Judith supplied with an expression that said exactly what she thought of Ruth Hoylake – had been fast asleep, lying half-dressed on the bed with an empty bottle between them. When Lawrence's banging on the window had at last woken them up, they'd said they had no idea where Jacob was, nor Brian.

'They didn't even seem concerned!' Lawrence had said, his incomprehension plain on his anxious face. 'Bloody man, I wanted to hit him.'

'Dad was great,' Dory said. 'He would have, too – hit Mr Dent, I mean – except Sam held him back!'

'It wasn't quite like that,' Sam said. Isobel saw him exchange a comradely glance with Lawrence, who smiled briefly.

'Mr Dent, when he'd shaken himself half-awake, muttered something about badgers,' Lawrence said. 'The trouble is, Sam says there are any number of setts round here, and we have no idea which one they've gone to. *If* in fact they've gone to look for badgers.' He ran his hands through his hair.

Isobel went over to him and hugged him. 'We'll split up into two parties,' she said, 'and go searching for them.'

'Sam and I know most of the setts,' Judith said. 'Want to come with me, Isobel? Sam can take Dory and him.' She nodded at Lawrence; she still didn't seem to be able to accustom herself to calling him Lawrence.

Since then, Isobel and Judith had walked to two setts, neither of which was being watched by a pair of small boys. They were now deep in the woods on the far side of the village, and Isobel was feeling queasy with anxiety.

'All right?' Judith said.

'Yes.' It sounded absurd. 'But very worried.'

'Naturally. It's always bad, first time it happens.'

'You mean I've got to go through a repeat performance?'

'Several, probably. By the time they're about twelve, you don't worry so much.'

'But your Sam seems such a steady, responsible boy.'

Judith snorted. 'Now he seems steady. Wasn't always that way.'

There was a silence, and they trudged on for several paces.

Then, as if she'd made up her mind to elaborate, Judith went on, 'We had to move out here, see, when Mike was made redundant.'

'Like us.'

She saw Judith turn to look at her. 'Not much like you. Your husband's got involved in something else, straight away, and now you're planning this new house of yours.'

Her meaning was obvious. 'You mean, not like us because we've got it cushy.'

'That's about it.' She could hear the smile in Judith's voice. 'No offence.'

'None taken.'

'Mike took it bad, being out of work. He'd been in a good job, we were doing all right. It all had to go, the car, the house, the lot. Sold my new three-piece suite. We were lucky to find the house in the village.'

Isobel remembered the burst pipe, back in the winter. And Judith had said they had damp seeping down the walls. Oh Lord. 'But Mike couldn't find work?'

'He'd tackle anything that turned up at first. Pump attendant, shelf-stacking in the shop, a bit of gardening. But he got demoralised. Said, why should he bust a gut doing odd jobs when it only led to them cutting his benefit when they found out? Now, he won't even go looking. Just stomps around at home, getting in my way and shouting at me when I say so.'

Isobel bit back a sympathetic comment; somehow she knew Judith wouldn't want to hear it. 'Is there work?' she asked instead. 'I mean, if he were to look?'

'Dunno. I suppose so. It's hard on Sam, see. He used to idolise his dad, and now his idol sits around reading the *Sun* and complaining.'

'Sam's all right,' Isobel said staunchly. 'We really like him, all of us. He's done Dory a lot of good.'

'Reckon she's done him good, too. He needed someone as erratic as your Dory to stop him taking life so seriously. She's made him lighten up.'

Isobel wasn't sure she liked Dory being described as erratic. But, thinking it over, she had to acknowledge it was accurate. 'Erratic,' she repeated.

'She's settling down, mind,' Judith went on. 'When Sam first used to bring her round, she was a stiff little thing. But she relaxes with us now. Doesn't mind getting her hands dirty helping out.'

She minds at home, Isobel thought. She wondered what Judith's secret was, how she managed to get Dory to give her a hand.

Unexpectedly, Judith said, 'And what about you? Why can't you relax?'

'Me?' The question stunned her. 'What do you mean?' Isobel hedged.

'You know perfectly well,' Judith said calmly. 'When you first moved in, you were quite chipper about it, set about your new life with courage. I admired you, when it was so clear it wasn't what you were used to. But then you started to close in, sort of.'

'Close in?' Isobel feigned surprise but she knew only too well what Judith meant. They'd been growing closer, until Lawrence had started talking about building a house, making the move to the country a permanency. And then, Isobel was well aware, she had withdrawn. From everybody. Judith included.

'Yes. I couldn't make it out,' Judith was saying, 'when you'd just decided you were going to build yourselves a lovely new house in your woods.'

Isobel had to admit, it must have seemed unreasonable. And to Judith, struggling with a damp, poky house and a morose husband in the throes of severe depression, she knew she must appear deeply ungrateful, her petty problems nothing compared to what Judith had to contend with. Judith wasn't to know she was tearing herself apart over problems that were just as happiness-shattering as Judith's.

They walked on for another few paces. She's given up her time to come and help find Jacob, Isobel thought. She's just confided in me, told me something about her own anxieties. Couldn't I tell her something of mine in return?

Why not?

Without even having to think about it, Isobel was quite certain that anything revealed to Judith Hearst would carry the seal of the confessional.

'I'm unhappy because I don't think I belong here,' she began. 'Lawrence does, he loves it, and he'll make a success of it. The children, too. Jacob' – it gave her a stab of pain to think about Jacob, out there somewhere, possibly in danger, and she waited a second for it to subside – 'Jacob's always loved the country, and, although we had our troubles with Dory, she's happy here now. The thing is, building our house makes it all absolutely concrete. Certain. And I'm not sure I shouldn't go back to town.'

'Why did you agree to leave?'

It was the expected question, but still Isobel reacted to it with a jolt, as if a small current had been run through her.

She took a deep breath.

'Out of shame,' she said. 'I believed someone had expressed interest in me, and I went to fairly elaborate lengths to return it. Then I – well, I was wrong.'

Having at long, long last put her humiliation into words, she considered it.

It didn't actually seem so dreadful.

'So, you saddled up and headed out of town?' Judith said. 'Because you couldn't face the repercussions?'

'That's about it. Lawrence came home one day and suggested we move, not because of what I'd done – he didn't have an inkling, I'm quite sure – and I was so low, so miserable, that I thought *anything* would be better than going on living in Ewell.'

'But, with distance, the problem doesn't seem so bad, and you're now wondering what the hell you're doing here?'

'Exactly.' Oh, she thought, the relief of speaking of it.

'No wonder you're down,' Judith said. 'What are you going to do?'

'I don't know! I can't make the family go back. They won't want to. And Lawrence has burnt his bridges – we all have. If I went back to the old life, I'd have to go alone. And I don't want to. I feel it's a choice between them or what I really want.' She felt a sob rise up. 'And now Jacob's lost, and we haven't found him, and I don't know what I'll do if anything's happened to him!'

The sob broke out of her, followed by several more. She felt Judith come up to her, felt strong arms go round her. Then she was clinging on, her face pressed to Judith's anorak-clad shoulder, crying out all the sorrow, the anxiety, the pain of conflicting desires that just couldn't be reconciled.

'First things first,' Judith said gently as Isobel's storm of tears showed signs of ceasing. 'Let's you and me finish this loop – another mile, that's all it is – then, if we haven't found them, we'll go back, see if the others had better luck. Okay?'

'Okay,' Isobel sniffed. 'God, I'm sorry. I hate crying.'

'Not keen on it myself,' Judith agreed. 'But you have to let it out, sometimes.'

'Thanks for listening.'

'You're welcome.'

They trudged on through the woods, and Judith pointed out another sett. The boys weren't there, either.

On the last quarter of a mile back to the village, Judith said, 'Know what I think?'

'No, what?'

'Reckon you should go back to the place you used to live.'

'Back to Ewell? What, for good?' When somebody else suggested it, it sounded an awful idea.

'Not for good, no. I meant, go for the day. Do the things you used to do – shopping, and that. Let yourself remember what it was really like. Could be you're seeing it through rose-coloured specs, like. Being back there might remind you of the less good aspects, then living here mightn't seem such a bad idea.'

A day in town, Isobel thought. Up to Ewell, have a look at Cedar Holt. On into Kingston. It had a certain appeal. And it was unlikely she'd run into *him*, as long as she was careful.

But would it act the way Judith seemed to think it might? Wouldn't her visit be more likely to make her want to go back permanently?

There was no way of finding out unless she tried. And, really, she had to do something.

They reached the village, and crossed the green. Approaching the house, she could see that lights were on, just about every single one.

'Do you think –' Isobel began. 'Do you think it's a sign? To tell us all's well?'

'Hope so. C'mon, let's see.'

As if Judith, too, couldn't wait any longer, she started running, grabbing Isobel's hand and pulling her along. Breathless, they burst into the kitchen.

Lawrence had made a huge pan of porridge. Sitting at the table, with steaming bowls of it and golden syrup, jam, sugar and hot milk arrayed before them, sat Dory, Sam, Jacob and Brian.

Lawrence looked up as Isobel and Judith came in. Looked straight into Isobel's eyes. His face glowing, he said, 'They're fine.' Then – and he must have read her mind – he said softly, 'Don't.'

She bit back the furious, anxiety-born exclamation: where the *hell* do you think you've been!

Instead, staring down at Jacob's white face, eyes huge with alarmed anticipation, she went to stand behind his chair. Putting a hand on his shoulder – a casual hand, denying the impulse to take him in her arms – she said, 'Did you see any badgers?'

Lawrence took Brian home, and came back to report that nobody seemed to stir when he'd let himself quietly in, turning to mouth 'Goodnight' to Lawrence as he did so. It didn't seem much of a life for a child, Isobel thought.

Sam and Judith had gone, too. Dory and Jacob were in bed. She and Lawrence went up, although she anticipated taking a long time to drop off to sleep.

Lawrence, beside her, had relaxed, his breathing

deepening. But she didn't think he was quite asleep. Before her nerve failed, she said, 'Lawrence?'

'Hm?'

'I'm thinking of going up to town for the day. To have a reminiscent look at Ewell, then into Kingston for some shopping.'

Was it her imagination, or did she feel him go tense?

'I'll drive you.'

'No, no, don't bother. I know how busy you are. And I'd be better on my own – you know how I am when I'm shopping.' She gave a laugh which, even to herself, sounded false and forced.

He said, 'When are you going?'

'Oh, perhaps the day after tomorrow. Tomorrow, even.'

There was a long silence. Then he said, 'It has to be the Kingston shops, does it?'

'Not really, I suppose. Only I know where I am in Kingston.'

'Oh.'

They lay side by side, not touching. Then suddenly he said quietly, 'Oh, Izzy,' and, rolling towards her, took her in his arms.

Arousal happened without her having been aware of feeling in the least like it. If she'd thought about it, she'd have said that the events of the evening were the last thing that would have led to making love.

But, clinging to him as his climax, closely followed by hers, surged through them, she felt that it had been the one thing she really needed.

He said something, but she didn't hear. 'What did you say?'

'Nothing. Just I hope – oh, nothing.'

She hugged him, feeling very close to him. I must go soon, she thought. It's not fair to live with my uncertainty while he doesn't know about it. It makes me feel deceitful.

Either I've got to overcome it, or, if I can't, tell him, so he can start planning the future without me.

The thought of that, of Lawrence making plans that no longer included her, made her want to cry again. Strange, it felt as if he was crying, too. But it must have been her imagination.

CHAPTER NINETEEN

Lawrence wished he was the kind of man who would think it perfectly reasonable to spy on a wife of whom he had become suspicious. But he wasn't. Putting sliced bread in the toaster, he recognised the dismal fact that he was in for a rotten day.

Why was Izzy going on this sudden trip to Ewell and Kingston? Surely not just for shopping: for one thing, there was nothing unique about the Kingston shops which, as far as he knew, had equivalents in many other towns; for another, in the past, when Izzy had gone for a day's shopping, she'd always gone up to London.

Why wasn't she going to London today? It was a much easier journey, for God's sake – one train from their local station to Charing Cross – whereas she'd have to make at least one change to get from there to Ewell.

Was she meeting one of her girlfriends for lunch? If so, why hadn't she told him? And wouldn't he have been aware of the preliminary manoeuvres, the phone calls making the suggestion and firming up on the arrangements?

Izzy, as far as he knew, hadn't had any contact with any of her former friends since they'd left Ewell, which, bearing in mind his unpleasant recollection that she hadn't been seeing much of her girlfriends before the move, wasn't really surprising.

Had she had contact he *didn't* know about? With some person he equally didn't know about? A man?

The toast was burning, and he didn't notice till Jacob came into the kitchen and said, 'Pooh, Dad, something's on fire.'

Lawrence lunged for the toaster, tripped over Rosie, who was calmly chewing the fat white lace of his trainer, said, 'Oh, *fuck*,' and tried to change it into 'Oh, fiddle,' even though he knew it was too late.

'Dad said *fuck*,' Lawrence heard Jacob confide to Dory when she sat down to breakfast.

Dory took no notice. Her eyes were shining, and before either her father or her brother could think of any distracting topics of conversation, she'd launched into a blow-by-blow account of how Sam had led the hunt for the lost boys.

'We *know* what happened, Dory, we were *there*,' Jacob said when at last she paused for breath; Lawrence reflected that she seemed to have bigger lungs than most people.

'*You* weren't,' she retorted. 'Not till we found you.'

Before she could recount yet again the moment when Sam led the way to the sett on the hillside and said quietly, 'I think we're in luck,' Jacob piped up, 'Dad, where's Mum?'

'She's in the shower. She wanted to get her turn in early today because she's going up to town to do some shopping.'

'*Is* she?' Dory said, distracted from Sam. 'She didn't tell me! And there's *heaps* of things I need. I could have made her a list if she'd let me know earlier!'

'I expect that's exactly why she didn't,' Jacob said with a sagacity beyond his years.

'I think it was a spur-of-the-moment decision,' Lawrence said pacifically; it was nearly too late, Dory was shooting a furious look at Jacob and seemed to be on the verge of hitting him. '*Children*,' he shouted suddenly, making all three of them jump, 'just once in your sweet lives, *stop* it!'

Jacob was staring at him with his mouth open. Dory was too, but she recovered more quickly. 'I expect you're still feeling the aftereffects of last night's drama,' she said charitably. 'Is that why Mum suddenly decided she needed a day in town, to get over the shock?'

Lawrence hadn't thought of that. Was it? Was Izzy's abrupt need to be back in Ewell – back on safe, well-known territory – really nothing more than a perfectly understandable response to having had her younger child missing for several hours last night?

Wouldn't it be just like her, to give herself a little treat after the ordeal?

He strode across to the table. The children flinched slightly, and he smiled. 'It's okay, I'm not going to shout at you again.' He bent down and put his arms round Dory, kissing the top of her head. Her glossy hair was still slightly damp, and smelt of Izzy's expensive shampoo. For good measure, he gave Jacob the same treatment; Jacob's hair was tangled and had bits of twig in it, and smelt of earth.

'You don't need to go overboard, Dad,' Dory said, but she, too, was smiling. 'You don't often shout at us, so you don't have to grovel when you do.' She added magnanimously, 'I expect we deserved it, anyway.'

'You did,' he said, returning to the toaster to do another four slices. 'And I wasn't grovelling.'

Leaving the children discussing – reasonably amicably – when was the last time he'd shouted at them, he went to pour himself more tea. Then – for suddenly he needed to be with her – he poured another cup and took it up to Isobel.

'Tea,' he said as he went into their bedroom.

'Thanks.' She was sitting at the dressing table applying mascara. 'What was all the shouting?'

'I burnt the toast, tripped over a puppy and Dory was about to hit Jacob.'

'Nothing new there, then.'

He met her eyes and they both smiled.

After a couple of sips of tea, she stood up and went across to the wardrobe. Then – she was dressed in her housecoat over her underwear – she turned to him, looking slightly awkward. 'Lawrence, was there something else?'

'What? Oh – no, I suppose not.'

She smiled at him again, a warm, loving smile. 'It's just that I was going to try on a few different outfits before I decide what to wear, and I don't really like doing it with an audience.'

'No, of course not. Sorry.' He turned and went out on to the landing, pulling the door closed.

But she came after him. Catching hold of his holey old working jersey, she pulled him back. Then she put her arms round him and, reaching a hand up to push his head down towards hers, kissed him. Very thoroughly.

'What was that for?' he panted when she'd finished.

'You looked hurt when I asked you to leave me in peace.'

'Oh.' Then, wanting to say more but not knowing what, he said softly, 'Izzy.'

'Now I'm going to get dressed.'

She shut the door firmly in his face.

Isobel sat in the van's front passenger seat, wishing she'd been firm about Lawrence running her to the station. Or rather *not* running her, since she really hadn't wanted him to. The van's front seat was permanently grubby, probably because Badger often sat there in his working overalls, and Badger was, as Mollie used to say of a less than fastidious neighbour, a stranger to soap and water. Isobel had brushed the seat vigorously with an old J-Cloth, but she was still apprehensive about what must be rubbing off on the seat of her black skirt.

She'd spent half an hour trying to find an outfit whose waistband didn't threaten to cut her in half before she was a third of the way to Ewell. In the end, she'd settled for her favourite straight skirt, which fitted so well over the hips that she could manage to persuade herself it didn't matter that she'd had to put elastic through the buttonhole to loop over the button. Anyway, her pale amber long-line jacket covered her waist, and she was wearing her cream shirt untucked (Dory had always called it 'tucked out' until she was old enough to know that it sounded wrong).

It was lovely to wear sheer tights again (although she'd cut her shin shaving her legs, leaving Lawrence's styptic pencil bloody at the end). Her black patent shoes probably hadn't been a good idea; they only had two-and-a-half-inch heels, low by her previous standards, but she'd spent nearly three-quarters of a year in flat shoes – slippers, boots, trainers – and even this height of heel made her feel that she was walking as if leaning into a gale.

At least, she thought, as Lawrence pulled up in front of the station, my hair's gone well. It was long enough now to make a bun that didn't feel as if it were coming down if she turned her head too fast.

Lawrence said quietly, 'You look lovely. I'd forgotten you when you're launching a commando raid on the shops.'

'My heels are too high and my skirt's tight round the waist.'

'You're still lovely.' He pulled her to him, and she thought he was going to kiss her. But he didn't, merely buried his face in the junction between her neck and her shoulder. 'Nuzzle, nuzzle,' he muttered. 'You've got scent on.'

'Mm. The Chanel you gave me two birthdays ago.'

'That long? What did I give you last birthday?'

'A skillet, so the kettle doesn't boil all the time when it gets left on the top of the Rayburn.'

He sighed. 'Oh dear. The last of the romantics. No wonder you're leaving me and running back to Ewell.'

She laughed. 'It's all right, I asked for a skillet.' Then

she took in properly what else he'd said. 'I'm not running back to Ewell,' she whispered.

There was dead silence in the van. Then he said: 'Aren't you?'

I'm not, I'm not! she shouted silently. But she couldn't shout the denial out loud, just in case . . .

In case such a vehement rejection of the idea proved to be an overstatement?

'I'll be back tonight,' she said gently. 'I absolutely promise.'

He stared at her, his brown eyes fleetingly full of some deep emotion she couldn't read. Then – and she could almost feel the effort – his expression lightened. 'Well, if you *absolutely* promise –' it had been one of Jacob's phrases, used only when he wanted particular emphasis – 'then I suppose it'll be all right.'

'It will.' She didn't know what she was reassuring him about. 'Honestly, it will.'

She got out of the van.

'You've got fluff on your bum,' he called.

'*Bugger.* I was afraid of that.' She brushed a hand furiously across her buttocks. 'Better?' She craned round to look at him.

He was staring at her bottom, grinning. 'From where I'm sitting, impeccable. Have a good day.'

Then he put the van into gear – rather clumsily – and drove away.

She bought herself a copy of *Vogue*, then went along the platform to wait for the train. It was late. Settling in an almost empty carriage, she had just opened *Vogue* when the door opened again and Nan Black got in.

'Isobel! Hello. I thought I was going to miss it – thank God it's late.'

'It's the only time we're ever glad a train's late, isn't it?'

244

Isobel said. If asked, she would have said she didn't want company; her pleasure at seeing Nan get into the carriage quite surprised her. 'When we're late too.'

'Right.' Nan sat down with a sigh. 'I'm worn out even before I've left home. Can't think why I'm going, really. What's your trip for? Goodness, you look nice! Love the jacket. Perfect with both your hair and your amber beads.'

'Thanks.' It was, Isobel thought, doing her ego no end of good to have been told twice in ten minutes how nice she looked. 'I'm not actually going to London, I'm going to Ewell.'

'Whatever for? Oh – you used to live there, didn't you? How lovely. Going back to see friends?'

Isobel was about to say yes. But, as she'd discovered over the cricket teas, Nan Black wasn't the sort of person you wanted to tell a lie to. Even a white lie.

'I'm going to lay a ghost,' she said. 'At least, that's the intention.'

Nan watched her for some moments. Then she said, 'And you don't want to say any more. Fine, I don't blame you.' There was a pause. Then: 'Nice of you to say that much.'

Isobel met her level stare. Suddenly they were both smiling, as if something had been recognised between them. 'Shall we meet up for lunch or something one day?' Isobel said on impulse. 'Not coffee – too Ewell, to meet for coffee.'

'Too frivolous?' Nan suggested. 'Smacking of people with nothing to do?'

'Yes. Lunch, on the other hand, being an essential part of the working day, is all right.'

'Lunch'd be great,' Nan said. 'In the pub, then neither of us'll have to cook. What day suits you?'

'Any. Let me know when you're free. Here's the number.' Isobel tore a corner off an inner page of *Vogue* and wrote her phone number.

'*Vogue,*' Nan observed. 'Can I have it when you're done?'

Isobel got off at the next station to catch the first of her connections to Ewell. Part of her – quite a big part – would have liked to go on up to London with Nan, chatting, laughing, comparing notes on village life. But it wouldn't have done, not today: Isobel had a job to do.

She read her magazine – it was strange, but she didn't find the glamorous photography and the fashion articles as all-absorbing as she'd expected to – and was about to discard it when she remembered she was going to pass it on to Nan.

Reaching her destination, she stopped outside the station to gather herself. For the first time since she'd decided on this pilgrimage, if that was what it was, she was faced with the question of what she should do. Go and look at the house? See how the new people are settling in, whether they seem to be looking after the place?

In the absence of any better idea, she did that.

It was quite a hike to the house, and, by the time she was walking up the road to it, she was getting used to wearing higher heels again. Suddenly she thought: what if they see me? She felt silly, striding along past the house where she used to live.

She walked past quickly, casting only a couple of sidelong glances towards the house. No cars in the drive, windows all shut – it looked as if everyone was out.

She stared at the name. Cedar Holt. *Stupid* name, she thought with sudden vehemence, sounds like a very small railway station.

She walked on, turning right and right again so she could peer into the back garden. Again, no sign of people at home. The garden was being well looked after – better, she had to admit, than in their day – and the new people had built a pond and placed a very luxurious swing seat beside it. They had also, as Isobel discovered when she leaned forward against the fence to get a better look, installed some sort of burglar alarm; lights flooded on, flashed off, then on again, and she thought she heard a distant beeping.

Horrified, she shot back from the fence as if it had pulsed out an electric shock. Affecting a nonchalant saunter, she retraced her steps and walked back past the front of the house. The beeping seemed to have stopped; staring at the front door, she saw a face appear at the window beside it. An elderly face, anxious, pale . . .

Isobel quickened her stride and returned to the anonymity of the busy town streets.

She caught a bus up to Kingston, and went into all the shops where she'd once been a regular customer; looked at furnishing departments, linens, household goods, bought a few small purchases for the kitchen. Then, with the departments mentally labelled 'duty' got out of the way, just as she'd always done, she embarked on shoes, accessories and fashions.

She treated herself to a very comfortable pair of Timberland loafers, and – trying to block out the label that said 'Size 30″ waist' – a smart pair of jeans. One of the shops in the Bentall Centre had a sale of pure lambswool sweaters; she bought a gold-coloured one for herself and a sugared-almond-pink one for Dory. Then she had to get Jacob something as well; spurning clothes as something he wouldn't thank her for, she got him three Tintin books which she knew – or hoped she knew – he didn't already have.

Lawrence's needs were different from what they'd been before; he no longer wore a suit, and most of his ties had gone to the jumble sale. After much thought, she bought him something called a gillet, a sleeveless, hip-length jacket with masses of pockets. He was always complaining that he hadn't got enough pockets.

She was coming out of the Bentall Centre, heading for her favourite wine bar where she was planning on having lunch, when she saw him.

Her first thought was that she must be mistaken. Here, in the middle of town, in the middle of the day? No! He'd be in his consulting rooms. Or, if by some chance he'd finished his morning consultations early, on his way to somewhere elegant for lunch. No high street wine bar for him – he'd be off to the golf club. Or the big, expensive restaurant where he and his fellow Rotarians habitually met up.

She stood in the entrance to the Centre and watched. The man was standing in front of a cash dispenser, intent on what he was doing, frowning slightly as he stared down at the array of buttons. A pillar of the Establishment, drawing a modest amount of spending money from an account that *never* went into the red.

Tall – well over six foot – and, as always, immaculately dressed. Pale grey suit, double breasted, beautifully cut. Shirt that was *just* off-white (white was so formal!), with the faint glint of heavy gold cufflinks, showing in the cuffs that extended the regulation inch and a half beyond the jacket sleeves. Old school tie, a discreet navy, gold and bottle-green stripe. Black silk socks, hand-made black shoes – the cobbler up in London kept a last of his narrow feet.

He was counting the notes which the cash dispenser had just yielded, putting them away into the expensive black leather wallet. His face was faintly tanned, as you'd expect of someone who often went on holiday but was too sensible to lie in the sun and get really brown. The light eyes were narrowed in concentration, the perfectly cut, greying brown hair seemed to dare the breeze to lift it out of place.

It *was* him. Of course it was.

Isobel took a deep breath and prepared to move.

CHAPTER TWENTY

Isobel had met Matthew Fairburn at a dinner party given by Dinah and Archie Pope-Cooper. Isobel was in a bad mood: she'd reminded Lawrence about the party on Monday, when he left for four days in Chicago, but he'd forgotten about it, and was anticipating a quiet Friday evening in the peace of his own home which he was reluctant to relinquish.

They'd had a bit of a row. Isobel said it was all right for Lawrence, he'd been jet-setting across the Atlantic and whooping it up in Chicago all week while she'd been stuck at home with the kids, her only excitement having coffee with Kristen Hughes and going to Bentalls to see about the new rug for the landing. Lawrence said her week sounded a damn sight more fun than his, and if she imagined you whooped it up on a four-day high-powered business trip to visit Chicago packaging factories, she must be daft.

'If I'm daft,' she said, turning her back so he could zip up her new and very sexy black sheath dress, with the low-cut neckline that made her breasts swell above it, 'it's because I never get the chance of any conversation more challenging than discussing with Dory what she wants to eat – what she *doesn't* want, actually, she's so damn picky – and reading the instructions out loud to Jacob on how to make papier-mâché animals. It took me *hours* to get the paste off the table top. Goodness knows why Jacob's projects always have to involve mess.'

She got her way and they had gone to the dinner party. Lawrence had hardly been at his best; he'd sat next to some dull cousin of Archie Pope-Cooper who'd just been on a walking tour of Suffolk. Lawrence said afterwards the cousin had managed to avoid walking anywhere near anything in Suffolk that was remotely interesting, which must have taken some doing. The few times Isobel spared him a glance, he'd either been accepting some more wine or yawning.

Isobel had been seated next to Matthew Fairburn. 'He's a doctor, darling,' Dinah had gushed as she introduced them, 'only we mustn't call him *Doctor* Fairburn – oh dear me, no!' And she flung up her hands as if to ward off anyone foolhardy enough to do so. 'He's a *consultant*, and so we call him *Mister*.' Dinah Pope-Cooper had a way of emphasising important words, as if determined to etch them indelibly on her listeners' minds. 'Matthew, darling, this is Isobel Langland.'

Apparently Isobel didn't warrant any lengthier introduction. And there didn't appear to be anything about her interesting enough to require emphasis.

'Dear old Dinah,' Matthew said in a quiet, cool voice as Dinah hurried away to rearrange two other guests rash enough to sit down without first asking her where she wanted them. 'She faces the challenge of her dinner parties like Wellington arranging his troops before Waterloo.'

'Quite. But is Archie Napoleon or Blücher?'

'An enemy or an ally?' He looked at her with real interest, in which she read respect. 'Blücher when he's looking adoringly at her and saying, "Yes, dear", Napoleon when he starts looking fed up and says, "Anyone for a last refill before carriages are called?"'

'He once said I was a topper,' she said. 'And that he liked a gel with a sense of fun. I can't think why he insists on talking like one of Bertie Wooster's coterie when he can't be more than a decade older than the rest of us.'

'If you are including me in that "rest of us",' Matthew said quietly, 'I'm flattered.'

She turned to look at him, studying him for a moment. Deliberately she widened her eyes in what an early boy-friend had once called her fast-lane seduction look. 'I am.' He had, she noticed, the most handsome face. Lean, with a sort of hollowed-in effect under his cheekbones. Smooth skin, well-cut hair, which was dark and contrasted with his pale eyes. He looked a little like Robert Powell.

He returned her appraising stare. He kept his eyes on hers – not just *on* them, she thought, feeling a small shock of excitement, it's as if he's looking right inside me. She was mesmerised by his wide pupils, so dark within the light irises: for a silly moment she felt she was falling into him.

Suddenly Dinah clapped her hands and bellowed, 'I'm just about to bring the hors d'oeuvre, everybody! Now, have you all got rolls and butter?'

Matthew passed Isobel one of the several glass butter dishes set out along the table. The butter was in curls, and stood in iced water.

The back of his hand stroked hers – surely not accident-ally? – and another of the small shocks ran up from some-where between the base of her spine and her pelvis. *God!* Did he *know* the effect he was having?

'Butter,' he said quietly. 'Dinah will send you to your room if you haven't got your roll and butter when she brings the starter.'

With a hand whose trembling she was trying to control, she helped herself to two curls of butter. Then, holding out the dish to him, she murmured, 'You don't want to be sent to your room as well. Do you?'

His eyes met hers again. He gave her a very slight smile – no more than a brief quirk of his well-shaped mouth – and said, 'Most certainly not.'

She could remember little of the meal afterwards. They'd had something salady to begin with, followed by something beefy; Matthew had been given something different because he was a vegetarian. Instantly she wanted to be one, too. Then Dinah had served a very rich chocolate log pudding, accompanied by fruit salad and cream, and finally, cheese; Matthew confided to Isobel that he deplored the English habit of serving cheese after dessert, and that personally he adopted the French method, where you ate cheese with the last of your dry wine, and finished the meal with the sweet.

It was when he was saying it that, for the first time, it occurred to Isobel to wonder if he was married. Too impatient to be subtle, she said, 'Is your wife here?'

She had been so sure, so absolutely certain, he'd say, actually I'm not married, that it was vaguely hurtful when he replied, 'Yes. Veronica's down there, sitting next to Archie.'

Isobel turned to look. Veronica Fairburn appeared as cool as her husband, and indeed had the same pale eyes; hers were subtly made up in beigy colours, with what looked like blue mascara. Her blonde hair was swept into a smooth French pleat, and she wore a pale mushroom-coloured silk outfit with a high cheongsam stand-up collar.

Isobel immediately felt coarse in her low neckline that emphasised the swell of her breasts. And suddenly it seemed that he, too – Matthew – must think her so, for surely his remarkable eyes had not once descended to stare at her exposed flesh?

Oh, *oh*, she thought, resisting the temptation to tug at the top of her dress, how humiliating, to display my breasts before a man who doesn't want to look!

But then Matthew leaned across her to refill her mineral water glass, and, watching intently, she saw the brief downward slide of his eyes.

Inside her head she let out a silent cheer of triumph.

Over coffee, Matthew returned his attention to her. He had previously been speaking to the woman on his left for some time, and Isobel, left in the lurch, had tried to do the same with the man on her right, only to find that he was deep in a vociferous discussion with *his* neighbour about the pros and cons of time-sharing on the Algarve.

She had sat isolated for a good ten minutes. It was an enormous relief when Matthew said softly, 'I've done my duty and listened to a shallow and ill-thought-out exposition on why the United Kingdom should leave the European Union. Now, where were we?'

She felt another of the silent cheers explode in her head.

She could have wept when the evening finally ended, without him having said anything about when they might meet again. He could suggest *something*, surely! she thought wildly. Say, we're going to the Hugheses' party next week, will you be there? Or, why don't you and your husband come for drinks with us? Even, why don't you and I meet for coffee one morning?

She was on the point of proposing something herself – for, without a doubt, he'd given her enough come-ons, was clearly as attracted to her as she was to him – when he said casually, 'I see our local oil painters are exhibiting again, in their usual venue. I have a ticket for the private showing; we Rotarians feel it our duty to support such enterprises.'

'Yes, of course.' Where was the usual venue? How could she get a ticket to the private showing? What did one wear to a do like that?

'Will you be attending?'

She was flattered by his assumption that she would have been invited. 'I expect so,' she said, trying to speak normally, trying to ignore the effect his light, intent-eyed stare was having on her.

'I expect I'll see you there,' he said. Then he smiled – making her knees shake – and went to claim his wife.

Isobel moved heaven and earth to get her ticket; she'd never have imagined it would be so difficult. She'd finally got it from a friend of Kristen Hughes, who was herself a painter and implied that she was doing Isobel a *huge* favour. She'd said, 'I can only let you have one, you know,' and Isobel bit back the reply, I only *want* one, and said instead, 'Oh dear. My husband will be desolate.'

The private viewing was packed with people jawing at full volume, drinking the free wine and stuffing down the vol-au-vents, and hardly looking at the paintings. It was, Isobel thought, a shame because many of them were wonderful. She didn't want to talk, and anyway she didn't know any of the people. She wandered round, giving each canvas her full attention, making herself *not* keep looking over her shoulder to see if she could spot Matthew.

And suddenly he was beside her.

'Oh dear,' he murmured, his breath caressing her ear. 'Spaniels.'

Isobel, who had thought the painting rather good, said, 'I know. So drooly,' and briefly felt like Judas.

They wandered on round together. Again, the accidental touch of the back of his hand against hers. Again, the quiet voice in her ear, as if the comment were secret, only for her. And, as they came to the last exhibit and accepted glasses of wine, which they took over to an alcove with a wide window seat, again the pale, wide-pupilled eyes staring right inside her.

'How are you?' he said.

'Fine.' She tried to adopt his low, breathy delivery, but it sounded absurd. 'Dreadful weather, isn't it?'

He smiled his slow smile. 'And have you read any good books lately?'

She felt herself flush. Crazy, when she hadn't blushed for years. 'Actually, no.' She wanted to say, I couldn't have paid attention even to the best novel ever written, since meeting you. I am in turmoil.

She lowered her head, watched the wine in her glass as she swirled it around. Then she felt his hand on her chin – the briefest of touches – and, responding, looked up.

He was watching her, eyes full of emotion as if he understood. 'Isobel,' he said. It was like a caress.

Too soon, he said he must go. 'A full day tomorrow,' he sighed, with a rueful smile.

She wondered what his day would be like. He would sit behind an expensive desk, she thought, and those wonderful eyes would gaze compassionately across at his patient, sharing her pain, absorbing her distress, promising relief, healing, freedom from all anxiety.

For of course he was a consultant in the private sector; she had looked him up, found the address of his consulting rooms, been to see for herself and been impressed to speechlessness – had there been anyone to speak to – by the elegant brick-fronted Georgian building, with its fresh white paint on windows and doors, and its ancient and very beautiful wisteria climbing up over the conservatory. A Victorian conservatory, she was sure, weathered, authentic.

And Matthew's field – wouldn't you just have known? – was gynaecology. Women's matters. How superb he would be, how sympathetic. How reassuring, to have him at your side in the distress of sickness!

She gazed at him, not caring that the longing must be visible in her face. For didn't he long, too? Hadn't he mentioned this private viewing – virtually *asked* her to be present – because, like her, he couldn't wait until they could be together again?

She said, 'When shall we see each other?'

There was a moment's surprise in his eyes – surely *pleased* surprise, that, a true woman of the nineties, she had felt able to speak rather than wait for him to propose what they both wanted – and then he said, 'Perhaps we could meet for an early evening drink. I often go to the Crown – one doesn't have to dine, they have a very pleasant cocktail lounge. Let's say Friday?'

'Friday.' She wanted to shout, why wait till then? Why not tomorrow? Or Thursday? She restrained herself.

He came with her outside to the street, walked with her to her car. Then he took her hand, raised it to his lips – such firm lips! – and kissed it.

She leaned back against her car.

He said, turning to go, 'Until Friday. Seven thirty.'

She got into the driving seat. But it was a good ten minutes before she felt sufficiently calm to drive home.

For the next three days, she worked on the details of Friday. Early evening was, in fact, the worst time for her; both children would be there, and it was right in the middle of the tea, homework, arguing over TV, preparing things for the weekend activities routine. Lawrence would probably not be back by then; he'd gone to Birmingham. Or was it Bradford?

She contemplated phoning Matthew, asking if they could make it lunchtime instead; the children would be at school. She got as far as dialling the number, listening to the clipped voice of his receptionist saying, 'Mr Fairburn's rooms, may I help you?' then put the phone down.

She didn't dare.

Instead she phoned Maude, and, grudgingly, Maude agreed to sit in. 'It can't be for long, Isobel, I'm going out myself later, and I'll need time to get back to Richmond and change. I can't go out to dinner in what I've worn to babysit, for your two, I'll get irreparably damaged in the general mêlée.'

Isobel protested that the children weren't that bad. And promised no, she wouldn't be late.

Dressing – she'd bribed the children, with a special tea and two videos, to leave her in peace while she showered and got ready – for the first time she thought about Lawrence.

Lawrence.

She tried to picture him, but Matthew's face was all she could see.

Lawrence isn't here, she thought. He's never here. We hardly have any contact any more. He's too busy. And when he *does* come home, he's too tired. I no longer mean anything to him.

She wanted to cry.

Nerves, she told herself. That's all.

She put Lawrence even further out of her head and started to put on her make-up.

The Crown was a very up-market place, famous not only as a first-rate hotel but also because it had been awarded a star in one of the top good-food guides. Isobel, drawing up in the car park ten minutes too early, was relieved Matthew hadn't suggested dinner, because she felt so queasy with apprehension that she couldn't have swallowed food, even if it did come bearing the accolade of a good-food guide star.

She sat in the car for twenty minutes. To be exactly on time would smack of eagerness. Ten minutes late might make him think she wasn't going to turn up, so that he would be extra glad to see her when she did.

Smiling to herself, she got out of the car, smoothed the tight skirt of her new peach-coloured suit, glanced down to see that her high-heeled black patents were pristine, then strolled across the gravelled drive to the cocktail bar entrance.

There was a confusing jumble of people in the bar, and at first she couldn't see him. Then, as if he sensed her presence, he raised his head and looked straight at her.

Their eyes met, and she felt a great smile of delight spread across her face. Holding his gaze, not noticing anyone else, she began to walk towards him. Those pale eyes, that deep, searching stare . . . she felt her body begin to melt in readiness for him, as if already they were crossing the hall from reception, going up in the lift to a room, taking off each other's clothes, slowly, so slowly . . .

'Oh! Here's Isobel!' Matthew said, as if it were a surprise. 'Darling, you remember Isobel Langland? We met at the Pope-Coopers' last week. Isobel, good to see you again. Can I get you a drink?'

Darling.

It took Isobel a few seconds to readjust. *She* wasn't darling. He was speaking to his wife.

Dear Christ, he'd got Veronica with him.

Did she find out somehow what he was up to? Did he have to bring her, to allay her suspicions?

Isobel stood shaking, the freezing sweat breaking out all over her, making her tremble.

'Mike, Sue, another one?' Matthew was saying. 'Roger?'

There was a whole group of them. Friends, good friends, engaging in what appeared to be a regular early Friday evening get together.

He hadn't invited her to a wonderful, thrilling, secret tryst. He'd merely agreed to her coming along to his regular wind-down session with his wife and their friends.

More humiliated than she'd ever been in her life, Isobel pulled her annihilated dignity round her and said, 'Actually I'm meeting Lawrence. Is he here?'

Matthew made a pretence of looking round. It must have been pretence: surely he knew?

'He doesn't appear to be here yet,' he said. He looked

slightly amused. 'Will you join us while you wait?'

'I –' Could she? Could she bear to? 'No, I think I'll wait outside.'

It sounded absurd. It was chilly outside, and nobody in their right mind would wait out there when they could stand in a warm bar with a large gin. She caught Veronica's eyes on her. Veronica, too, seemed amused.

Without another word, Isobel turned and hurried out of the bar.

Driving home, blinded by her tears, she wondered what she was going to say to Maude.

She saw him once more. Once more to speak to: for a while, it seemed she couldn't go anywhere without seeing his tall, elegant figure striding across her line of view. She'd even seen him on the dreadful day she'd gone with Lawrence and the kids to look at properties in the country: they'd been stuck in traffic and he'd walked past the car. She had slid down in her seat and covered her face with her hands; she didn't think he'd seen her. She'd wanted to be sick.

She met him one day on the platform waiting for the London train. Her first instinct was to hide, pretend she hadn't noticed him.

But some devil inside her made her go up to him. Say, 'Hello, Matthew.'

And, when he turned to look at her, staring at her aghast as if questioning her sanity in speaking to him, she said, 'I believe you owe me an explanation.'

He glanced up and down the platform, presumably checking to see if there was anyone he knew within range. Apparently there wasn't. A patronising expression on his face, he said quietly, 'You misunderstood, that was all. No explanation is necessary.'

She tried to work out what he meant. Good grief, she

realised, he's acting as if I said I owed *him* an explanation!

'You humiliated me,' she said angrily. 'You led me to believe that you wanted – that you were interested in me, then you showed me that you weren't in a most shaming way! How do you think I felt, coming into that bar and finding you ensconced with your cronies and their wives – *your* wife, for Christ's sake – when you'd made me think we were going to be on our own?'

'Made you think?' His voice was suddenly icy. 'I think not.'

'Oh yes you did!' Too angry to take any notice of the threat she could feel coming off him in waves, she plunged on. 'Don't lie. All those deep stares, those accidental touches? Come off it!'

He changed tactics. Now the patronising look was back, the menace veiled. 'Isobel, my dear,' he said smoothly, 'this sort of thing is *always* happening to a man in my position.' He smoothed his hair, a superior smile stretching the lean face. 'You are not the first lovely lady – and you certainly won't be the last – to believe herself in love with the doctor. It tends, I am afraid, to go with the job.'

She was speechless. In love with the doctor. It goes with the job. Lovely lady. Did he throw that in as a sop to her bruised vanity?

In *love*? Who the hell did he think he was kidding?

'Don't insult me,' she said coldly. 'Love had nothing to do with it, as well you know. Lust, perhaps. A roll in the hay with someone who fleetingly takes your fancy. That's all we were speaking of.'

'*You* were speaking of,' he corrected her quickly. 'There was never anything of the sort in *my* mind.'

He managed to make her feel like a slut. As if the very idea of physical contact with her made him shudder with revulsion. As if, for heaven's sake, he was afraid he'd *catch* something.

She said, unable to think of anything better, 'You make me sick. Does anyone else realise what a total shit you are?'

The urbane smile was back. 'That, my dear Isobel, is an opinion I suggest you keep to yourself. Your appearance in the bar of the Crown – and, may I add, your abrupt and inexplicable departure – didn't go unnoticed. I was forced to make a comment, and I admitted that I was very afraid you might have taken a fancy to me. It would not, therefore, sound unreasonable if I were forced to enlarge on the details of your – unfortunate and inappropriate infatuation.'

'You – *what*?'

He fixed her with a hard stare. 'I have a position to maintain. An important place in local society. Should you be sufficiently unwise to try to blacken my name, you will find things very unpleasant for you. Very unpleasant indeed.'

She sprang away from him as if he'd hit her.

She was still standing staring at him, mouth open, when the train pulled into the station. He said pleasantly, 'Good afternoon, Isobel,' and got into a first-class carriage.

Stumbling down the train to second class, she stood on shaking legs all the way to London.

CHAPTER TWENTY-ONE

Isobel waited until Matthew had turned away from the cash dispenser and set off along the pedestrian precinct. Then she shot out of the Bentall Centre doorway and hurried off in the opposite direction.

Her heart was pounding, and she felt sick. It came as a shock, to realise what strong emotions could still be engendered by a brief sighting of Matthew Fairburn.

She went into a café, ordered herself a cappuccino.

She sat for half an hour, sipping and thinking.

It was absurd, to feel the way she did. She should have put him firmly in the past, where he undoubtedly belonged.

But she couldn't. He was getting in the way of her adjustment to her new life.

She was going to have to do something.

She found a phone and dialled Maude's number, crossing her fingers and praying that Maude was home. She had some days when her lectures finished early, and Isobel thought today was one of them.

'Hello, this is Maude Adair,' said Maude's answerphone. 'Please leave your name and number, and I'll phone you back.'

'It's me, Isobel. I need to see you! I'll call later, I –'

'Isobel, I'm here,' Maude cut in. 'What's up?'

Thank *goodness*. 'Nothing. Well, nothing life-threatening. I'm in Kingston. Can you possibly meet me?'

'It's going to be difficult.' Isobel could almost see the frown on her sister's wide brow. 'Can't you come here?'

'I – No.'

'Okay. Where are you?' Isobel told her. 'Right. Twenty minutes – say half an hour, I'll have to find somewhere to park the car.'

'Thanks, Maude. I won't forget this.'

Maude laughed briefly. 'Curiouser and curiouser. See you.'

They had another cappuccino while Isobel told her sister what had brought her up to Kingston. 'So I just got on the train this morning, and I've spent the day remembering.'

'And?'

'And I was wrong. I don't think I do want to come back after all.'

'Piers'll be relieved,' Maude said drily. 'Especially now you're on the point of going ahead with your gin palace in the woods.'

'It's not a gin palace!'

'I know. Go on.'

'Go on?' She felt apprehensive.

'Yes. I know there's something more. You wouldn't have interrupted my afternoon and made me drive from Rich-mond to Kingston in all the traffic just to tell me you didn't want to return to town life.'

'How perceptive,' Isobel murmured. 'There *is* something else.'

Briefly, but trying to be strictly honest, she told Maude about Matthew Fairburn.

Maude listened in silence till she'd finished. Then she said, 'I know Matthew. I could have told you he was a shit. I wish you'd said something at the time.'

'Oh, come on! I was hardly likely to do that, when I was all set to plunge into a torrid affair with him! I know you're fond of Lawrence; it would have put you in a rotten position.'

At the thought of Maude being loyal to her and keeping the secret from Lawrence – poor Lawrence! – her eyes suddenly filled with tears.

Maude watched her. 'It hurts to think of betraying old Piers, doesn't it?' She smiled briefly. 'Maybe it's just as well Matthew turned out to be such a bastard,' she observed.

Isobel dried her eyes and blew her nose. 'I feel better now,' she said. Then: 'How do you come to know him?'

'A friend of mine works for him. She's in charge of what Matthew refers to as Patient Relations. What she really does is tell everyone how great he is so that he can justify charging so much.'

'It doesn't sound like much of a job.'

'It's not. She's had enough and is about to jack it in, only he doesn't know yet. She's just waiting to hear whether or not she's got the new post she's after, then she'll give in her notice. I first met him at a dinner party at her house. I've encountered him several times since.'

'What did you think when you first met him?'

Maude eyed her. 'This is going to sound very big-sisterish.'

'When did that ever stop you?'

'Okay. Well, I saw straight through him. He did what would appear to be his usual act – the accidental touches, the murmuring voice in your ear, the asides that are meant just for you. He said something about Philippa's *boeuf en croute* – that the pastry obviously didn't realise it was meant to be puff.'

'Typical!' Isobel remembered how he'd run down poor old Dinah's efforts. 'How unkind.'

'In fact he was right, Philippa's no great shakes as a cook. But she'd gone to so much trouble, and he should have known better.'

'What did you say to him?'

Maude smiled briefly. 'I said obviously he hadn't appreciated that Philippa and I were friends, or he wouldn't have made such a silly, schoolboyish comment. He didn't like the inference that he was immature.'

Isobel laughed. 'I imagine not!' Then: 'Do you think he knows we're sisters?'

'I very much doubt it. We have different surnames, and Philippa doesn't know you so she can't have told Matthew we're related.' Maude eyed her intently. 'Why? Isobel, you're plotting. Tell.'

Isobel sat for a few more moments, working it out. Then she told Maude what she had in mind.

Maude insisted that they go through it enough times to make it perfect. Then she said, 'You'll have to be well out of the way. You'd better wait at the station, or something. It won't work if he knows you're involved.'

'But I want to watch!' Isobel wailed.

'Hm. All right. But you're to keep hidden. And borrow my scarf.' She removed the Liberty scarf that she wore round her neck. 'Put it on your head, and pull it well forward so it hides your face.'

Isobel did so. The scarf smelt of Maude's perfume. 'You're a great sister,' she said suddenly.

'I know. Come on, my car's in the multistorey.'

They drove out to the Crown, and Maude parked in the far corner of the big car park, as far away from the hotel as possible.

'Let me just check . . .' She rummaged quickly through the bag on the back seat. 'Right. Let's go.'

'Is he here?' Isobel asked as they crossed to the hotel. Her heart was thumping again.

'That's his car.' Maude nodded towards a gold Daimler with the registration number MSF 3.

'I wonder what S stands for?' Isobel said.

'Shit?'

They went into the reception area. The bar was off to the left. Isobel remembered, with sick dismay, her fantasy about crossing from the reception desk to the lift, going upstairs with Matthew . . .

'You could wait there.' Maude pointed discreetly to a corner unit set around a coffee table on which was a fan of glossy magazines. 'It'll look as if you're waiting for someone. You'll be hidden by the castor oil plant.'

'Okay. But I'm coming out when you go. Yes, I know,' she said as Maude started to protest, 'don't worry, I'll stay out of sight. Are you sure your hands are dirty enough?'

Maude looked down at her oil-coated fingers. 'Yes. Any more and I'll risk getting it on my clothes.'

Without another word, she sauntered into the bar.

Isobel managed to position herself so that she could see, although she was too far away to hear. Maude approached the bar, going to stand near Matthew but not right by him. He was talking to two other men, one about his own age, one older. All three had grave faces and were apparently engaged in some serious discussion. Isobel wondered if the others, too, were pillars of the Establishment. They certainly looked like it.

Maude said something to the barman, holding out her oily hands. He pointed towards the ladies' cloakroom, and Maude smiled at him. To get to the cloakroom she had to pass by Matthew. He looked up, saw her, greeted her and, in his turn, was shown the filthy hands.

He took her hands in his, and said something to her, eyebrows raised in enquiry. Then, as she answered, a condescending look came over his face; he said something to the two men, then, his arm under Maude's elbow, he escorted her from the bar and out into the car park.

Isobel slipped out behind them.

267

'. . . really no need, Matthew,' Maude was saying. 'I was just going in to wash my hands, then I was going to call the breakdown people. The last thing I want to do is disturb an important meeting of you and your fellow Rotarians.'

'Maude, I assure you it's no trouble,' Matthew replied. 'I'm quite sure the problem can be fixed in a moment by anyone with an ounce of mechanical knowledge.'

'Oh, Matthew, how convenient for me that you happened to be in the bar,' Maude said. Steady on, Isobel thought, panicking slightly. He'll start smelling a rat.

'I'm only too glad to help, Maude.' Matthew released her arm and approached her car. 'It stinks of oil, doesn't it? I begin to see what you mean. Now, then, open the bonnet, there's a good girl. Do you know how?'

'I think I can manage,' Maude said. Isobel smothered a giggle. 'Is that it? Oh no, I've set the hazard flashers going. Sorry. Have I found the right thingy now?'

There was a clunk as the bonnet catch was released. Matthew raised the bonnet, securing it with the rod. 'Well done. Now, you said the engine was spraying oil? That suggests to me . . .' He leaned further over the engine, going 'Hm' in concentration. Then he said, 'Have you had her serviced recently?'

He was, Isobel thought, exactly the sort of person who referred to a car as 'her'.

'Yes,' Maude said meekly.

'And would you happen to know if that service included an oil change?'

'I've no idea.' Maude widened her eyes.

'I think it probably did.' Matthew was bending under the bonnet again, legs braced against the front bumper. 'I can't find anything wrong, my dear. What appears to have happened is that whoever put the oil in has been a little heavy-handed. There's oil all over the top of the cylinder block. All over the engine, in fact.' He released the rod holding

268

up the bonnet, letting the bonnet slam shut. Then he stood back, looking at his hands, now as dirty as Maude's. 'I imagine you haven't got a cloth or you would have used it on your own hands, and – What's the matter?'

Maude was staring aghast at Matthew's legs. 'Oh goodness, Matthew! Look at your *trousers*!'

Across the front of Matthew's long, pale grey-clad legs were wide bands of thick black oil.

'*Jesus,*' he hissed.

'Matthew, I'm *sorry,*' Maude moaned. 'There must have been oil spilled on the front bumper as well. I did say I thought it had been sort of spraying out of the engine.'

Isobel wanted to applaud her sister's acting ability. She sounded so convincing, not at all like someone who had spent fifteen minutes spreading engine oil over exactly the place where it would do the most damage to Matthew's trousers.

'God, what am I going to do?' Matthew muttered. 'I can't go back into the Crown like this, I look frightful.'

'Couldn't I go in and explain for you?' Maude pleaded. 'After all, it is really my fault.'

Matthew shot her a hard glance. 'Don't make me look even more of an idiot than I already feel,' he growled. 'No, I don't want *you* going in there and telling them what's happened.' He glanced down at himself again. 'Haven't you got *anything* I can get it off with?'

Maude frowned. 'I've got some nail-varnish remover in my overnight bag,' she said. 'Would that be any good? But no cloth. Perhaps you could take off one of your socks?'

'Dear God,' Matthew muttered. 'All right. It's worth a try.'

'Oh, good,' Maude beamed. 'I'm so glad I'm going to be allowed to make amends.' She plunged into the car, coming out with a toilet bag, which she put on the roof. 'I'm sure it's in here . . . yes! Now, you'd better take your trousers off, Matthew. This is nasty stuff on the skin.'

'Oh no,' he said, 'give it to me. I'll do it with my trousers in situ.'

But Maude held tight to the bottle. 'I really don't recommend that,' she said, sounding worried. 'This is some remover I got in France. It really is powerful, the label warns you not to get it on your skin, and to wash your hands thoroughly after use. Really, I don't think you should risk having it seep through on to your legs, especially . . .' She glanced down at Matthew's thighs; one of the oil streaks was almost up in his groin.

'I'm not sure,' he said doubtfully.

'We're right in the corner of the car park,' Maude pointed out. 'Nobody'll see. I'll be done in a flash. The stuff evaporates quickly – as soon as it's dry, you can have your trousers back.'

He stood a moment longer. Then, as if abruptly making up his mind that it was the lesser evil, he said, 'Very well. I'll bring my car over – I can sit in it while you do the cleaning up.'

Maude said quickly, 'Oh, Matthew, is that wise? You really are *covered* in oil – won't it go all over that lovely leather upholstery?' Before he could think about that, she hurried on, 'Look, there's nobody around, and your car's only just over there – why not give me the trousers so that I can get going, and you sprint over and get in?'

He hesitated once more. Then swiftly he took off his shoes, unfastened his trousers, slid down the zip and stepped out of them.

'For God's sake, be quick,' he ordered, setting off at a lope towards the Daimler.

'Yes, of course.' Maude held up the trousers. 'Oh – and I'll need a sock.'

He stopped, took one off, balled it up and tossed it to her.

'Thanks.'

Maude looked up, caught Isobel's eye and nodded. Isobel ran out of her hiding place behind the nearest car and slid into the passenger seat. Maude, installed behind the wheel, started the engine.

As they headed off out of the car park – accompanied, as had been their arrival, by the clouds of blue smoke – they drove past Matthew.

'What the fuck are you doing?' he shouted furiously. He caught sight of Isobel. 'And what's *she* doing here?'

'Oh, do you know my sister?' Maude called back. 'Don't yell, Matthew, someone'll hear. You don't want anyone seeing you, do you?'

Isobel was shaking with terrified, thrilled laughter. Winding down her window, she yelled, 'Great legs! Bye, Matthew!'

Maude was waving the trousers out of her window, clutching on to them firmly. 'I'll drop these off outside your consulting rooms,' she shouted. 'Draped on the railings.'

Accelerating out of the car park, they left him standing there.

Maude said as they shot off down the road, 'I don't know what it is, but there's something quite ludicrous about a man wearing a shirt, jacket and tie but no trousers. It's so – farcical.'

'Especially if he's only wearing one sock.'

Maude snorted with laughter. 'Don't. I've got to drive sensibly to his consulting rooms. Just hold it in a little longer, then we can let rip.'

Back in town, there were few people about and only light traffic, which was just as well as Maude's smoke-wreathed car was already attracting attention. Maude hovered on the double yellow line while Isobel hopped out and draped Matthew's trousers artistically on the iron railings.

As she did so, something hard in the right-hand pocket

clinked against the metal railing. Sliding in her hand, she found Matthew's keys; one, very obviously, was the key to the Daimler.

Hurrying back to Maude, she told her. 'Do we go back?' she asked, chewing her lip. Matthew would be left in the hotel car park, no trousers, unable to get into his car . . . 'God, Maude, it's even worse than we planned!'

But Maude was smiling, already setting off towards Richmond, the opposite direction from the hotel.

'Even *better*,' she corrected. 'No, my sweet Isobel, we're not going back.'

In the safety of Maude's flat, they toasted their success with a bottle of cold white wine.

'You were quite brilliant,' Isobel told her sister. 'I honestly thought he was going to see through you when you were being the helpless little woman. You were laying it on with a trowel.'

'Yes, I wondered if I was going too far.' Maude topped up their glasses – she had found a second bottle. It wasn't chilled, but neither of them cared. 'But he's such an arrogant man, and a total chauvinist. He'd quite expect a woman to know sod-all about engines.'

'Even a woman who's a university lecturer?'

'Even that.' A lovely smile spread across Maude's face. 'Wasn't it wonderful when he stood there in the car park, boxer shorts flapping in the breeze, only one sock?'

'It was superb,' Isobel agreed. 'Maude, thank you.'

'No problem. You can pay to have my engine steam-cleaned.'

They finished the wine, then Maude said she'd go and see if she could rustle them up something to eat.

Isobel sat, legs curled up beneath her, thinking about the day. About all that had happened since Lawrence dropped her off at the station this morning. Goodness, it seemed *weeks* ago! She'd done so much, experienced so many strong emotions, that she felt worn out.

She leaned her head back against the generous cushions in Maude's armchair, trying to empty her mind, trying to relax.

She felt so tired. So sleepy.

But one image kept recurring. Despite the fatigue, despite the happiness, one image wouldn't go away.

Lawrence. And the expression in his eyes when she'd said she'd be back tonight, promise.

What was the time? *Half-past eight!*

She leapt up. 'Maude, can I use the phone?'

'Help yourself,' Maude called from the kitchen.

She dialled the number. Dory said, 'Hello?'

'Darling, it's Mum.'

'Mum, where are you? Dad did us supper, and he burnt the potatoes, and he *said* you'd be home, and –'

Isobel interrupted gently. 'Dory, I've been held up, but everything's fine. May I speak to Dad, please?'

She heard Dory yell, 'Dad, it's Mum. She's fine.'

Lawrence came on the line. His voice sounding slightly wary, he said, 'Izzy?'

'Hello.' She found she was smiling.

'Are you okay?'

'I'm wonderful.'

There was a pause. Then: 'Izzy, have you been drinking?'

'Yes. Maude and I have been celebrating.'

'Celebrating?' He still sounded wary.

Emboldened by the effects of almost a bottle of wine on a near-empty stomach, she said, 'I had to see, darling Lawrence. I had to come back, to see if I still wanted to be here.'

He said, 'And do you?'

'No, no, *no!*'

273

'Can we take that as a negative?' He sounded amused now. Relieved?

'Lawrence, honestly, it didn't seem like I remembered it. All the things I used to love, they – well, it was great, shopping, being in the buzz of town again, but I don't want it always, not any more. I want what we're doing.' She realised she wasn't being totally lucid. 'I mean, I'm happy with the new life.'

He said quickly, 'I was thinking this morning, after you'd gone, you could often go up to town for the day. Even stay, if that's what you want. Just as long as –' He broke off.

'As long as I come back?' she said softly. 'I said I would, didn't I? I absolutely promised.'

He said, as well he might, 'But you haven't come back. Izzy, where *are* you?'

She realised she hadn't told him. 'I'm at Maude's. We had – there was something we had to do together.' She was on the point of telling him. But Maude, who had been standing in the kitchen doorway listening, shook her head violently and mouthed, '*NO.*'

'What?'

'It's not important.' It wasn't, not any more. 'Just one of our things.'

'Oh.'

'It's all right,' she said.

'Right.' He cleared his throat. 'Do I take it from your obviously inebriated state that you're not in fact coming home tonight?'

'I think I'd better stay here.' Her legs, she noticed, felt wobbly. 'But will you meet me from the train tomorrow morning?'

'Of course.' He sounded pleased to be asked. 'Let me know when, I'll be there.'

'Thanks. Bye, then – sleep well.'

'You too. Hope the room doesn't spin too much. Give my love to Maude.'

'I will.' She was about to ring off. Then suddenly she said, 'Lawrence?'

'Yes?'

She tried to remember his exact words. Weeks ago – the night he'd told her and Maude about Oxleat Place.

Yes.

She drew in a breath.

'Lawrence, I do love you.'

CHAPTER TWENTY-TWO

The August sun was shining down brilliantly on the village green, bleaching the musty greyish-beige of old tents and awnings to dazzling white.

The summer fête was in full swing, and the hot day had attracted a capacity crowd. Jacob and Brian won seven coconuts. The man on the coconut shy, grudgingly handing out the seventh to Jacob, had muttered out of the corner of his mouth, 'Now bugger orf, else I won't have any left.' They had three turns each on the go-karts, had their fortunes told – Brian was going to travel a lot and Jacob could expect something to his advantage in next week's post – and ate enough candyfloss and hot dogs to make them feel slightly sick. Jacob was doing his best to work up an appetite for a '99'.

They were dividing their time between the fête and the limited-overs cricket match which was going on up the road, on the village pitch. Jacob liked watching his dad batting: Dad's technique varied between the sort of tentativeness that kept him in for about an hour, with a score of something like twelve, and a wild flamboyance that would get him a six with the first ball and out with the second. At the moment, Dad's side – he was playing for the village – were fielding, and Dad was going to be first change bowler. He'd told Jacob to come back in about an hour.

The opposition was a team of local celebrities, so Brian

had brought his autograph book. Apparently some bloke from *The Bill* was in the side, but as yet the boys hadn't managed to identify him. There was also someone who'd once played bass guitar with David Bowie – whoever *he* was – and a man whose wife wrote novels; she was going to present the prize to the winning team. The prize was a barrel of beer, so Jacob hoped she was a big strong novelist or she wouldn't manage to lift it. He'd never heard of her, but his mum said she'd read one of her books and it was quite good.

They ran up the road to the cricket pitch. Lawrence, who was standing just inside the boundary, gave them a cheerful wave and called out, 'I'm bowling in a minute.'

'How are they doing, Dad?' Jacob called back.

'Forty-eight for three.'

'Let's go and suss out the batsmen, see if there's anyone for my autograph book,' Brian suggested.

'Okay.'

They trotted round the outside of the boundary to the little pavilion, where several men in a variety of shapes and sizes were sitting in small chairs or lounging on the grass. Some had very smart pads and their own bats, which impressed Jacob very much. They stared at the faces, trying hard not to *look* as if they were, and Jacob whispered, 'Is *that* the man from *The Bill*?'

Brian looked. 'Nah!' he said dismissively. 'That's some bloke from the Council. Vice Mayor, or something.'

Jacob didn't think you had a vice mayor. Even if you did, Brian probably wouldn't want his autograph.

He went up the steps into the pavilion, where Mum's nice friend Nan Black was putting out little cakes. 'Hello, Mrs Black,' he said winningly. 'Is there anything I can do to help?'

Nan eyed him. 'Now you, Jacob, are the very picture of a boy hoping to be given a cake. You can have one, and one for your friend, if you put out some of those folding chairs for me.'

'Right,' he said. 'C'mon, Brian.'

They put out thirteen chairs in a very rough semi-circle beside the pavilion, claimed their cakes, then went to watch Lawrence bowling.

Jacob was so happy he didn't even feel embarrassed when Mrs Bellyflop shouted out to him to get out of her way. He sat down hastily, pulling Brian down beside him, and bit into his cake.

Then Dad came pelting down towards the crease – someone sitting near the scoreboard shouted out, 'Don't take such a long run, Lawrence, you'll be knackered by the time you throw the ball!' – and a viciously fast ball shot out of his hand. It pitched about two yards from the wicket, and the batsman made a rather timid swing at it. He missed, and the ball hit the offstump. The bails flew, there was a great shout from the village team, and Lawrence was jumping up and down like a lunatic, waving his arms in the air. The umpire pointed a firm finger, and the batsman left the crease.

As the applause died down, Brian said laconically, 'Your dad's not bad.'

Dory was trying not to admit that her new shoes were pinching. It was very hard, walking with shoes that hurt and not showing it. Especially when you were walking with Sam, who had long legs and took correspondingly big strides. Sam had won a plastic bangle on the shooting range. He'd been brilliant, knocking down masses of the tin ducks, and the man on the stall had said he could have either a fluffy bear or the bangle. He'd chosen the bangle, and put it on Dory's wrist. Then, to make things even better, he said, 'You have a go, you're getting to be a good shot.'

She'd wanted to refuse, afraid she'd make a fool of herself. But the man on the stall had given her a look that seemed to say shooting wasn't for girls, which had put her back up.

'Okay.'

She nestled the stock in between her neck and her shoulder, tried to calm her breathing, and, with the air rifle aimed, watched the parade of absurd little ducks go by for a few moments. Then she squeezed the trigger and hit one. Reloaded and squeezed again, again, then twice more. And hit four out of five.

'Bloody hell,' the man said. 'Well done, miss. D'you want another bangle?'

Dory chose a penknife instead. Returning the favour, she gave it to Sam.

They went on to the second-hand bookstall, which was being run by Emma Hardcastle's mother and Emma's sister. Emma's mum said Emma was coming over later, with her dad. Then she said Dory had been a very good Ferdinand. Dory said self-deprecatingly that it had been nothing, they'd had a very good teacher, and Mrs Hardcastle said Dory was modest as well as pretty, which made a change nowadays.

Dory didn't quite know how to reply, so she just smiled. Sam took her hand – she loved it when he did that when there were heaps of people around – and they went to buy ice creams. Sitting under a shady oak, she decided she didn't need new shoes that hurt, so she took them off. And Sam – lovely Sam! – said gallantly that he'd carry them for her.

Isobel was waiting for Maude and Bill, who were coming down from Richmond after lunch. To pass the time, she went to see if Judith needed any help with the donkeys. Judith had recruited a posse of preteenage girls who, being universally pony-mad, were more than happy to do the donkey rides, so Judith was sitting in a deckchair issuing the occasional command from a distance.

'May I join you?' Isobel asked.

'Of course. There's another chair there.' She pointed, and Isobel pulled it up beside Judith's.

'I don't know if it's just the heat,' Isobel said, fanning herself with a copy of *Dune* she'd just bought for fifteen pence at the Hardcastles' stall; it was actually too thick to make a good fan, 'but I feel whacked.'

'It *is* hot,' Judith agreed. 'You look a bit peaky. Feeling okay?'

Isobel shrugged. 'Not too bad.'

'Sit here in the shade for a while,' Judith suggested. 'Caroline! *Caroline!* Get him to shorten his reins! You may as well get them into good habits,' she added to Isobel, 'even when it's only a donkey ride.'

'Absolutely,' Isobel agreed. 'Who knows, maybe Willie Carson and Lucinda Prior-Palmer began with donkey rides.'

Judith grinned. '*He* might have done. Shouldn't think *she* did.'

'No, I expect you're right.'

They sat in a companionable silence for some time. Isobel felt better out of the hot sun. Then, after a few moments of wondering if she knew Judith well enough now to ask, and deciding she did, she said, 'How did Mike's second interview go?'

Mike had, at long last, got the prospect of a job. Nothing like the one he'd lost two years ago – he'd been a sales manager for a toiletries company, and the new job was in the shop run by a nearby stately home which had its own garden centre – but, as Mike had reputedly (and not very originally) said, beggars couldn't be choosers.

'It went well,' Judith said. Almost a year of friendship had taught Isobel that, just because Judith didn't *seem* to be excited by something, it didn't mean she wasn't.

'Do you think he'll get it?'

Judith said quietly, 'He's got it. Well, he'll do a month's trial, see if he suits.'

'And if they suit him,' Isobel added.

'Right. Anyway, there you are.'

'Judith, I'm so glad,' Isobel said. Judith gave her a quick look – her eyes were suddenly bright with tears – then, by mutual unspoken agreement, both women turned their attention back to the donkeys.

Walking over to the road to look out for Maude, Isobel saw Douglas coming up from the station. He was dressed in his best, even wearing a Panama hat, and on his arm was a handsome woman in a floaty, chiffony outfit and a huge straw hat that swept low over her right eye; she looked even smarter than Douglas.

Isobel went forward to greet them; Douglas had said he might 'pop in', but he hadn't mentioned bringing a dashing companion.

'Isobel my love,' he said when they'd kissed hello, 'this is Mrs Achieson.'

'Evadne,' said the woman, holding out a hand encased in smooth cream kid. *Gloves*, Isobel thought, impressed. 'How lovely to meet you, Isobel, Douglas has told me all about you.'

'Goodness,' Isobel said.

'What shouldn't we miss?' Douglas asked, tucking Isobel's hand under his free arm. 'Tombola? Dodgems? Bearded lady?'

'None of those here, I'm afraid.' Isobel squeezed his arm affectionately. 'The teas are good, though. You can have a Sussex cream tea for £2.75, which buys you a scone with strawberry jam and cream, a pot of tea for one and a slice of cake of your choice.'

'Tea, then, for me,' Douglas said. 'Evadne?'

'For me, too,' she said. 'Although really I shouldn't.' Isobel didn't think she need worry, since she was enviably slim. 'But today, I don't care!' She looked lovingly up at Douglas.

'We're going to Egypt,' Douglas confided to Isobel.

'Egypt? Good grief!'

'Douglas has never seen the Pyramids,' Evadne said, making it sound as if Douglas was the only person in the south of England who hadn't, and was guilty of slacking. 'And I've told him that sunset over the Nile at Luxor is about the most romantic thing in the world, so that's where we're going.'

'How wonderful,' Isobel said, genuinely pleased for them – for both of them. Although she'd only known Evadne Achieson for about four minutes, the first impression had been very favourable. And Douglas, bless him, looked as if his dearest wish had just been granted. 'Send us a postcard.'

'We will,' Evadne said. She gave Isobel a suddenly shy smile. 'I'll look after him,' she whispered, although even a whisper must have been perfectly audible to Douglas, who was walking between them.

'I'm quite sure you will,' Isobel whispered back. 'And I'm sure he'll do the same for you.'

'Oh!' Her face lit, as if that hadn't occurred to her. 'How nice. Will you join us for tea, Isobel? Do!'

'It's sweet of you, but no thank you.' Isobel thought that a rich cream tea in a hot marquee would probably finish her off. 'Actually I'm looking out for Maude – that's my sister – and her friend Bill. He's an architect, he's designing our new house.'

'How's it going?' Douglas asked.

'Very well, according to Bill, although to me it still looks like a building site.'

'It *is* a building site,' Evadne said logically, 'although I know what you mean. Don't worry, dear, there will soon be a magical moment when you go to see how it's coming on and it suddenly looks like a house. Your house, what's more.' She smiled encouragingly.

'Evadne speaks as one who knows,' Douglas supplied. 'Has her own little place on the Downs, outside Eastbourne. Picture-book cottage, built it herself.'

Isobel hid a smile; the idea of Evadne, in her chiffon and her huge straw hat, carrying hods and displaying a builder's bum was uniquely incongruous. 'How lovely,' she said.

'Come and see us, dear,' Evadne said. 'Bring the family. You'll all be welcome.'

'Thank you, we will,' Isobel said. Then, as Douglas led Evadne into the tea tent, 'See you later.'

She wondered, walking away, if 'us' was significant. If it was, she thought, adjusting to the slight shock, then how wonderful for dear old Douglas.

She'd better drop a gentle hint to Lawrence, in case his reaction to the news that his father was living with a woman was less controlled than her own.

Maude and Bill didn't arrive till quite late; Maude said Bill had wanted to go up to Oxleat Place first to check on something, and she'd gone too. 'I couldn't wait to have a look. It's going to be superb, isn't it?'

'I hope so,' Isobel said. Then, in case that sounded as if she doubted Bill, 'Yes, of course. I'm thrilled.'

'Where's Lawrence?' Bill asked. 'I want to ask you both about having a big window on the stairs.'

'He's playing cricket,' Isobel said. 'But won't you stay to supper? We can talk about it then.'

'Fine.' Bill was looking around. 'Is there a beer tent?'

'In the corner.' She pointed.

'Would you like a drink, Isobel? Maude?'

'Half of lager,' Maude said. Isobel shook her head.

'How are you?' Maude asked her as they found seats by the show ring, currently occupied by people trying to display how obedient their dogs were. 'Aren't you entering for this?'

Isobel laughed. 'Next year, perhaps. Millie and Rosie are very young still. I'm fine.' She glanced at her sister, who was looking radiant. 'No need to ask you how *you* are. Going well, is it, you and Bill?'

'Oh yes.' Maude smiled dreamily. 'He's accepted a commission to build a house for a rich Mancunian down on the Riviera. He'll be starting on it as soon as your place is finished.'

'Won't you miss him?'

Maude looked down at her hands. 'I'm going with him.'

'Maude! What about your lecturing?'

'I'm having a sabbatical. I've always wanted to write my book on Queen Matilda, remember?'

'Matilda, known as Maude. Your namesake. Yes, of course I remember.'

'Now's my chance. I'll pack my Canon Starwriter, and, while Bill's busy with his house, I shall sit on some shady balcony overlooking the Med and immerse myself in early-twelfth-century England.'

'I'm delighted for you.' Isobel gave Maude's hand a quick touch. 'It's serious, with Bill?'

Maude said only, 'It's serious.' But her face, Isobel thought, spoke volumes.

After a moment Maude said, 'I saw Matthew Fairburn the other evening.'

Isobel waited to see if there was going to be any reaction in her. There wasn't. Nothing at all. 'Really? Where?'

'Dinner party. I introduced him to Bill, told Bill he was one of our valued local medical practitioners, and a keen Rotarian as well.' She snorted with laughter. 'I said he was also a skilled car mechanic, and wasn't that useful?'

284

'*Maude!* What did he say?'

'He muttered something, and good old Bill, who didn't suspect a thing, said that was great, and he admired anyone who had a way with engines since his knowledge ran out with topping up the *oil.*'

'Oh, Maude! Matthew must have thought Bill knew everything!'

'Probably. Matthew made a point of not sitting anywhere near us for the rest of the evening.'

'I've sometimes been afraid there'd be some backlash,' Isobel said.

'Hard to see how there could be, since he has no idea where either of us lives.'

'True.'

Bill emerged from the beer tent, stopping to take a sip out of both his own bitter and Maude's lager. 'Before Bill comes back,' Maude said, 'there's something I want to say.'

'Yes?'

'Seriously, Isobel, although you now seem so happy here, I don't think you should cut yourself off entirely from town life.'

'But –'

'Hear me out. I was just going to say that my flat will be standing empty all the time Bill and I are in the South of France. You'd be doing me a favour if you'd go up some-times and air it. Pick up the post, check for leaks, that sort of thing. You could stay the night. Give yourself a real break, go to a concert, see a film, that sort of thing. Keep some smart clothes there, if you like. What do you think?'

'I think,' Isobel said after a moment, 'that's a brilliant idea.' Then, watching Maude's I-knew-she'd-like-it smile, 'If, say, I couldn't for any reason use it much over the *next* year, could I still come to stay when you're back again?'

Maude looked at her enquiringly. 'You – oh, I suppose you'll be busy with the new house. Yes, of course. Whether

I'm – we are – there or not, of course you'll always be welcome.'

It was, Isobel thought, recognising the perception behind her sister's offer, a luxury to be offered a lifeline even before you'd asked for one.

The fête wound to its close. The cricket finished quite late: the villagers, determined to win, had finally overtaken the celebrities' eleven, with a few overs to spare. Brian still hadn't discovered which was the bloke from *The Bill*, and Lawrence had been in for ages and almost made a half-century; what with that and his bowling – *and* a dramatic catch he'd taken when he was in the outfield – there was talk of his being made Man of the Match.

Isobel stood with her whole family, watching the novelist wife present the prize to the village team. Jacob was relieved to see she didn't try to lift the beer barrel – she contented herself with pointing at it, then she kissed the team captain on the cheek. Everyone had cheered. Then she'd given Dad his Man of the Match prize – it was three bottles of wine – and kissed him too. He came back with a big lipstick mark on his cheek, and Jacob wondered if the lady novelist wore that much lipstick when she was doing her writing.

Isobel leaned against Lawrence on the way home; her feet were swollen, and she was longing to sit down and put them up. She had told him about Maude and Bill coming to supper, and he'd seemed pleased. 'Your father and Mrs Achieson said they wouldn't, though,' she'd added. She had received the distinct impression that Evadne had planned a cosy and romantic supper for two back in her little house on the Downs, but didn't say so to Lawrence.

'I'll do supper,' Lawrence offered as they got home. 'It's cold stuff, isn't it?'

'Yes. You're a love.' She hugged him.

'I know. *And* I'm Man of the Match.'

She hugged him again. 'Don't let it go to your head.'

Dory had gone to have supper at the Hearsts', Jacob and Brian were earning additional pocket money helping to clear up after the fête, so the four of them, Lawrence, Isobel, Bill and Maude, had supper together.

Isobel had found it virtually impossible to keep her eyes open over the fruit salad dessert, and in the end had given up and gone up to bed.

Lying in the warm gentle breeze coming in through the open window, listening to the distant voices of the three downstairs, she thought back over the year since they'd become downshifters and embarked on their new life.

In the end, it had been, she decided, a good move. A *very* good move. Since she'd taken steps – unexpectedly dramatic ones, as it had turned out – to get Matthew Fairburn out of her system, it seemed to her that at last she'd felt able to enter unreservedly into enjoying the new life. Of course, this wonderful sense of wellbeing could just be temporary, a combination of all that had happened recently, and she must, she knew, prepare for it not always being this way. There would be days when it was raining and the new roof leaked, or when Lawrence failed to get the price he wanted for his wood, or Dory split up with some adored boyfriend and Jacob failed to make the first team.

But all families faced the possibility of problems like that, constantly. Uncertainty was part of life. And, in this sort of venture, she knew she could not have a better partner than Lawrence. He was sound, he didn't take silly risks, and the business was going well. The chestnuts he had cut in the spring were showing no ill effects – quite the opposite. He had proudly showed her how sturdy new growth was already shooting out from the stools. The course at the agricultural college had given him the expertise to turn all sorts of other ideas into actuality. He and Badger were talking about ideas for the trout fishing, and there was the possibility of keeping hens when the house was finished . . .

She was feeling drowsy, dream images starting to flow alongside her conscious thoughts.

The future, she thought, yawning, looked bright. Very bright. She prayed a small prayer that nothing unexpected would leap out of the woodwork and confound them. Reminded that she *must* talk to Lawrence, really, she couldn't continue putting it off, she drifted into sleep.

Lawrence had been down to Brighton to collect an obscure part for his tractor. As he drove along the foot of the South Downs, he thought about the new house. It was so exciting, watching it grow; Bill's plans were just perfect, resulting in a house which, while modern and easy to run, contrived to look something like the original Oxleat Place. They were keeping the name, too. Lawrence had suggested calling the house The Winds of Change, but the rest of the family, not understanding why it was appropriate, just accused him of being vulgar and voted the proposal out.

He realised he was approaching the spot where he'd stopped all those months ago – nearly a year ago, hell, didn't time fly? – and he drove the van into a gateway and got out. Trotting over the springy turf of the hillside – he was, he reflected, a lot fitter than he'd been a year ago – he got to the top of the Down and stood looking around him.

There, over in that direction, was Eastbourne. And Evadne Achieson's cottage, where his father appeared to have taken up residence. Lawrence grinned; good for Dad. Evadne Achieson was a strong-minded woman, Lawrence thought, but she was kind. And she certainly seemed exceedingly fond of Douglas. The pair of them were off to Egypt in a fortnight. Egypt! Lawrence wondered how his father – who had to date been no further afield than Torremolinos, and even that he'd found too hot and foreign – would react to Egypt.

And there, inland, was home. Where his precious woodlands lay, and where, with any luck, he would make a good living for his family. The first year hadn't been bad: they'd made a bit – and a bit more than the ''bout fourpence' Badger claimed it to be. And, Lawrence reassured himself, at least they hadn't *lost* money, which must be an achievement.

It was going to be all right.

And home meant Izzy. Lovely Izzy, who had miraculously turned back into the woman she'd been when they'd met, although of course she wasn't an air stewardess any more. But she was funny, easy-going, *close*, the way she'd been in the early days.

He'd never discovered what had happened in Ewell. Some wise part of him said it was best that way; whatever it was, it was over. He knew that without being told.

They were lovers again, and, knowing each other so well, it was even better than it had been in the early days. Sometimes they went to bed together like friends, sometimes with a passion that took his breath away. And sometimes – quite often – they'd finish up laughing. Well, he reflected ruefully, you couldn't expect all that much passion really, not after all those years.

Izzy. He pictured her in her SCATS dungarees, frowning earnestly as Judith Hearst taught her the rudiments of keeping chickens. Dear old Izzy.

He looked at his watch. It was time to go. If he didn't get back soon, Izzy would start peeling the potatoes for supper, and he'd said he'd do it for her as her ankles swelled in the evenings.

He *wanted* to peel the spuds; wanted to help out.

Because Izzy was a bit vulnerable at the moment; she'd just told him she was pregnant.

And that, on top of everything else, made Lawrence feel like singing.

Quality Time

Norma Curtis

Love means never having to say you're busy . . .

This is the caring, sharing nineties. So when Larry loses his job in advertising and takes over the nanny's role, Megan is happy to be the breadwinner - for a while, at least. In a marriage of equals, should it matter who is left holding the baby?

It matters to four-year-old Bill - why is his mother doing his father's job and his father the nanny's? And it matters to Megan - she might be a successful headhunter, but she is only a part-time mother. Meanwhile, Larry is discovering that being a househusband is not as simple as he thought it would be.

As Larry adapts to full-time fatherhood, its challenges, surprises and rewards, he begins to suspect that losing his job was the best thing that ever happened, to him and his family.

0 00 649025 5

Big Girls Don't Cry

Connie Briscoe

'Briscoe's pacing is brisk, and the plot touches on a range of key social issues . . . An empathetic portrait of a modern woman wrestling with issues of love, work and family obligations'

Publishers Weekly

Growing up in Washington DC in the 1960s, Naomi Jefferson, sheltered by her solid, middle-class black community, is only occasionally touched by racism. But when her adored older brother, Joshua, is involved in a tragic accident on his way to a civil rights demonstration, the rift between black and white America suddenly becomes personal.

At college, Naomi immerses herself in campus politics, and men, only to become disillusioned and facing some harsh re-alities. Then she makes a decision: politics are useless, romance is hopeless, what she really needs is a career. Despite her success at work, the promotions keep going to the white guys. But Naomi is determined to win where other black women have failed, and just when she thinks that the only person she can depend on is herself, two people walk into her life who make her believe once again that anything worth having is worth fighting for . . .

0 00 649974 0

Finding Maggie

Ann Stevens

It's never too late to start again . . .

Why should Margaret Fairbrother, recently widowed and in her early fifties, want to abandon her comfortable home, her two daughters, her friends and neighbours, for a remote villa in northern Spain?

Amidst bemusement and objection, Margaret casts off convention and responsibility and heads for a Spanish village where she meets a handful of ex-pats and some colourful local characters. Thus emerges Maggie, a new woman looking for adventure, fulfilment and freedom, which she finds in the most unexpected - and delightful - places.

Drawn by the vibrant, seductive atmosphere, yet pulled by the claims of her family, can she really escape the ties of the past? Exactly who, and what, is she running from? Maggie's odyssey is one of laughter, excitement, tragedy and even danger, showing her that life is always full of surprises, whoever or wherever you are . . .

0 00 649899 X

The Longing

Jane Asher

'Topical, emotion-charged . . . grips from the very first page'
Daily Mail

Michael and Juliet Evans are thirty-something, happily married and successful. Just one thing casts a shadow over their comfortable existence: the baby they long for has not, so far, materialised. So instead of decorating the nursery and visiting Mothercare, they resort to a world of private clinics and medical jargon, their hopes and fears rekindled by a young doctor with the power to transform their lives.

The waiting game has begun. But as the pressure builds, Juliet begins to lose her grip on reality. A different, more powerful longing takes hold, and her family and friends watch with agonising suspense while she struggles on the edge of darkness - until something happens that will twist all their lives again . . .

'A writer who does convey real emotional power . . . Like all really good novels, (*The Longing*) is true . . . in the way that its characters seem real and the world in which they move is one we recognise. Even better, its power increases as it goes on, drawing you further into its plot, gripping more tightly with every page . . . if Jane Asher were not already famous, this book would make her so'
Daily Express

0 00 649050 6

Sisters & Lovers

Connie Briscoe

'A frank and funny tale about the everyday lives of three black women' *Essence*

Beverly, Charmaine and Evelyn are three sisters living in the same Maryland town outside Washington D.C., each wishing her life were just a little different.

Beverly is twenty-nine and single, a successful magazine editor who would love to be in love. The problem is, no man can meet her high standards. Charmaine longs to finish her degree, but meanwhile she has to juggle a thankless job, a beautiful child, and an irresponsible husband she doesn't quite have the nerve to leave. Evelyn has her own psychology practice and her husband is a partner in a prestigious law firm. She seems to have it made - but there's trouble in paradise, and Evelyn is refusing to face the facts.

Warm and bittersweet, believable and real, *Sisters & Lovers* is a novel of families and love, heartache and hope, and above all, the triumph of sisterhood.

'In *Sisters & Lovers*, Connie Briscoe has drawn a vivid and dramatic portrait that will make readers laugh out loud and nod their heads in recognition' *Los Angeles Bay News Observer*

0 00 649804 3

The Deep End
of the Ocean

Jacquelyn Mitchard

The international number one bestseller.

'Watch your brother,' says Beth Cappadora to her seven-year-old son Vincent. Only minutes later she turns again and asks, 'Where's Ben?' It's the moment that every mother fears: for three-year-old Ben is gone. And no one can find him. Despite a police search that becomes a nationwide obsession, Ben has vanished, leaving behind a family that will be torn apart with anguish. Until, nine years later, a twelve-year-old boy knocks on their door - a boy who does not know them, but who will irrevocably twist their lives a second time . . .

'A blockbuster read . . . a rich, moving and altogether stunning first novel. Readers will find this compelling and heartbreaking story - sure to be compared to *The Good Mother* - impossible to put down'   *Publishers Weekly*

'So well observed and perceptive it's hard to shy away from . . . masterfully paced . . . A story of one family's slow tumble back into light'   *Los Angeles Times*

'*The Deep End of the Ocean* burns itself into the memory line by line. It is by turns lyrical and startling, brilliant. I wish I had written it. Ms Mitchard is blessed with a surplus of raw, vigorous talent'

KAYE GIBBONS, author of *Charms for the Easy Life*

0 00 649909 0